indivisible

RANDI T. SACHS

VIRGINIA BEACH
CAPE CHARLES

PRAISE FOR

indivisible

"You will not be able to put *Indivisible* down. It brought me to tears—tears of concern and sorrow to tears of joy and happiness. This will be the one you talk about with your friends."

— DAVID FLOYD
Former Vice President of
The Down Syndrome Association of Hampton Roads
Proud Father of 12-year-old Lauren,
who happens to have Down Syndrome

"There is a brevity and sincerity to Randi Sachs's prose that delivers an honest and poignant look at the human emotions that leave us the most vulnerable. Sachs deftly takes us through the stages of grief, but her story becomes so much more. You will fall in love with her characters; you will pull for them and you will care for them. You will remember what it means to love."

— DIANE LES BECQUETS
author of *Season of Ice: Love, Cajun Style,
The Stories of Morning Creek,* and *Breaking Wild*

Indivisible
by Randi T. Sachs

ISBN   978-1-63393-125-1

Published by

◤ köehlerbooks ™

210 60th Street
Virginia Beach, VA 23451
212-574-7939
www.koehlerbooks.com

dedication

This book is dedicated to my husband Danny, and to my sons and very special friends who have shown us both love and compassion.

Danny, we were just kids when we met. More than forty years later, I stick by my belief that when you hit gold on the first strike, you keep it and treasure it always. Recognizing that you are true gold will always be my greatest accomplishment.

...and to Cordelia and Bronwen, may you become indivisible sisters and friends for life.

This is also dedicated with great admiration to the Nassau AHRC parents and siblings who inspired me with their love and devotion to their children and to each other and who so graciously welcomed me into their world.

A special thank you to Carolyn and Sam Cukier, the hottest parents on the block.

In loving memory of a true mensch, Jack Ain, and his beautiful Pearl.

chapter one:
aaron

THE CHIRPY VOICE of a nursery school teacher singing, "Wake up, wake up, get out of bed, wake up, wake up, you sleepy head," jarred us out of our slumber.

"Aaron, you are not bringing that clock to our new place," Becca said.

We lay curled up together under the covers on my slightly lumpy double bed. In my off-campus apartment—no roommates—we had the privacy and space we craved. Technically, Becca still had a dorm room on campus, but she rarely slept there. We were planning to announce our engagement at tonight's post-graduation dinner with our families.

"Okay." I stretched out my arms and yawning like a bear brought them back in and around Becca, squeezing tightly. "Ahh, I love waking up next to you. That was a great party we held last night. I barely remember getting into bed."

"That's probably because you needed help getting there. Cal practically had to carry you. Do me a favor and don't get drunk before we announce our engagement tonight, okay?"

"Tonight, my fair Rebecca, I shall drink nothing stronger than tea, I promise."

I didn't tell Becca that I already bought the single-carat emerald-cut diamond engagement ring with the baguettes the saleslady said were absolute necessities. It was secreted in my treasure box painted with Donatello, my all-time favorite Teenage Mutant Ninja Turtle, but if all went well, I'd be giving it to her tonight at dinner with the parents.

After wriggling out of my embrace, she wiped the sleep from her eyes, then leaned over, and did the same for me. "Are you ready to take on the honor of becoming a member of Franklin & Marshall's Class of 2004?" she asked.

I looked at those bright blue eyes gazing at me as if I were perfection and in my best booming voice spoke Lou Gehrig's famous words, "Today I consider myself the luckiest man on the face of this earth. I still can't believe my luck at winning you over, my beautiful blonde California girl." I had blonde hair, too, but it was as stubbornly curly as hers was sleek and smooth. She said our kids would be model-gorgeous.

Becca grinned. "Shush, don't jinx my fairy tale come true. And you didn't 'win' me. We simply found each other, silly-face." She offered her lips to me for more kisses.

Just yesterday, I had received offers from four of the eight companies I had interviewed with on campus for an entry-level management job, and we were flying high. Two were in Manhattan; one was in Lancaster—in fact, I was leaning toward that one because we could keep my apartment; the fourth was in Santa Cruz, California. Fortunately, each of the companies had given me some time before they needed an answer. I had explained at the interviews that I wasn't sure exactly where my fiancée and I wanted to live next and that I would like to plan on starting my new job in July. Turned out it was no problem, as they all had new-employee training programs I would need to take, and they didn't even begin until the first week of August. I had a few weeks before they required any answer.

"I'm still amazed I got more than one offer—and we actually have time for a vacation before I start! Chasing those A's really paid off. My Dad is going to bust a gut!"

"You know my first choice is Santa Cruz—you'd love living in California, too," Becca said. "I honestly think you should consider it very seriously—no pressure. I'll admit that freshman year I found the Pennsylvania winter snowstorms enchanting, but after four years of it, I'm more than ready to go back to year-round sunshine. Still, location is secondary.

You need to pick the job you think you'll like the most. Money counts too, by the way. And I have no problem waiting to apply to schools for January admission."

I wasn't completely against living in California, but my moving across the country from my family would be hard on them, especially my twin brother, David. He has Down syndrome, and he had always looked to me to lead the way in life. My parents seemed to take it for granted I'd be living at home on Long Island and working in the city after school. They didn't even know I'd interviewed elsewhere. I wondered if there was any way I could convince them to move, too. *If only they were a little closer to retirement age,* I thought.

We made our way into the kitchen, collecting empty beer bottles along the way, and sat down to a late breakfast of muffins and tea when the doorbell rang.

A massive police officer filled the doorway. "Are you Aaron LeShay?" he asked.

I zeroed in on the steel gun in his holster and gulped. His expressionless face along with his imposing figure reminded me of a Tron robot.

"Yes. Can I help you?"

"My name is Police Chief Ken Carson. I have something to tell you."

"Yes?" I immediately thought about last night's party. *Will I be trading my blue cap and gown for an orange jumpsuit?*

"Your family has been in an accident on the Pennsylvania Turnpike. There were some serious injuries," he said. He may have been trying to appear compassionate, but in reality he remained stone-faced.

"What? Where are they now?"

"They're at Lehigh Valley Hospital in Allentown. It's about an hour-and-half drive from here. Would you like me to provide transportation?"

I could barely breathe, let alone answer him. I didn't want to go anywhere with this guy.

"Who's at the hospital? What? What happened?" Becca asked.

"My family was in a car accident," I said.

"I can drive you both there," the cop repeated.

"No, thank you, officer," I said, clearing my throat and breathing deeply. "Would you please get word to my family that I'm on the way? Where is that hospital?"

"It's right off Route 78. Please try to remain calm; they're in an excellent trauma facility."

As soon as he left, Becca and I got dressed in whatever we could find on the floor.

"Give me the car keys," she said. "Here's a map, you navigate and I'll drive. You know I can't stand maps."

"Okay, but drive fast."

As I raced to the door, I ran right into our caps and gowns hanging from the top of the hall closet door so they wouldn't get wrinkled. I fought my way out of the dry cleaner plastic that stuck to my body.

"We might not make it back in time; maybe you should stay here."

Becca just shook her head and ran to the car. "I'm going with you, no arguments."

The weather was beautiful. It was a perfect sunny seventy-five degrees, just right for graduation. We made it to the hospital in just under an hour. Becca clutched the steering wheel until her knuckles turned white and she had to shake her hands to get the circulation going. I barked out driving commands, keeping my eyes on the map held rigid in my hands. We parked in the closest spot, not checking to see if it was legal, and went right to the emergency room. The family resemblance must have shown because the triage nurse immediately asked me if I was Aaron LeShay.

"Yes, I am. Where is my family?"

The nurse brought us inside her office and sat us down. It was too quiet in that room. I felt numb. Years passed before a doctor in surgical scrubs joined us about five minutes later. I had never felt terror like this before. Everyone was acting too nice.

"Mr. LeShay, I'm Dr. Greenberg. I just operated on your brother. Most of his trauma was orthopedic in nature. He has some minor internal injuries, a few badly bruised ribs, and a compound fracture of his left leg. He's got contusions and abrasions on his face and arms, but he's going to be fine. Fortunately, he had no hemorrhaging or injuries to any organs.

You can see him in the ICU recovery in about half an hour."

"What about my parents and my sister, where are they?"

"Aaron, what have you been told about the accident?" asked Dr. Greenberg.

"Nothing. I wasn't told anything other than that they are here." Now he had switched to my first name; that couldn't be good.

He took a noticeably deep breath. "Their car was hit head-on by a truck going the wrong way on the turnpike. I'm very sorry. We worked on your family for a long time, but their injuries were too severe for us to save them. We gave them CPR for over an hour, we tried to stop the bleeding, but they had multiple internal injuries and the blood we transfused came out as fast as we could get it in. Your sister made it into surgery, but we were unable to complete it. Again, you have our sincere sympathies. Your brother is the only survivor."

The next thing I remember is waking up in a hospital bed with Becca holding my hand. I opened my eyes, shading them with my arm against bright lights, looked up at her, and asked, "Is it true?"

"Oh Aaron, I'm so sorry. You fainted when the doctor told you."

Again, I blinked back tears. "It's true? My parents and sister are *dead*? All of them?"

Becca covered my chest with her body and hugged me. My emotions burst into grief and fear as the tears from both of our eyes mingled. Soon my chest was wracked with sobs.

"Aaron, I'm so sorry. I'll try to be your family now."

I started to get control over myself and slowed my crying and hyperventilating. I sat up on the bed, hugged my knees to my chest, and started to rock a little. I had to hold myself together, or I thought I would literally fall apart.

"David. I've got to see David."

• • •

Becca gently persuaded me to lie back down. I was shivering, and the nurse brought in a warmed blanket, which Becca tucked in around me. I lay there in that hospital bed for a small eternity, shutting my eyes to everything around me. I lost sense of time passing. Eventually, I looked around and realized that I was in an ER bed. The only solid wall was behind me. A curtain on an oval track was all that gave us privacy. I had been transformed from the visitor to the patient. I didn't like that, but Becca held my hand and stroked my hair and I wanted to stay snuggled under the warmth of the blanket forever. I prayed I was dreaming, and when I woke up, I'd be in my own bed. Unfortunately, Becca's touch was so delicate, it soon began to creep me out. It felt as if a tiny insect was walking across my forehead, and I shook my head to make her stop. A nurse offered me some juice.

"Do you have some kind of a sedative you could give him?" Becca asked.

"No, I don't want that. I'll have the juice, thanks. My mouth is really dry."

Becca helped me sit up and sip the orange juice through a bent straw. I felt like a little child then, sipping slowly and concentrating intently, as if it could make everything all better. I thought of the time David and I had the chicken pox when we were nine. We sat together on the living room couch, wearing our matching cowboy pajamas, surrounded by pillows and blankets and watched cartoons. Mom served us juice in cups with built-in bendy straws. She made us wear mittens in the house so we wouldn't scratch ourselves and leave scars. That was so long ago. More than half our lives ago.

The cold drink helped clear my mind and fully wake me from my faint. I told Becca and the nurse, who was watching from several feet away, "I want to see David now."

"Are you sure you're ready for that? What are you going to tell him?" Becca asked.

"The truth. I don't have any other choice."

"Do you want me to come with you?"

Although we had been nearly inseparable for the past two years, I could not fathom taking her with me for this. The pain and fear in her eyes mirrored what I felt. We had bought into the delusion that the degrees we'd earned had prepared us for whatever curves life would throw us. Ha. Even before the ink was dry on our diplomas, we'd learned the truth. I felt Becca starting to get shaky, and I pulled her into the narrow bed with me, hugged her tenderly, and then rolled myself out of it on the other side. I pulled the still-warm blanket over her and told her to rest. The nurse waited for me to ready myself.

"You stay here. Take slow, deep breaths and try to calm down," I said to her.

"I want to call my parents," she said.

"That's a good idea." I looked at my watch, an early graduation gift from my parents. "They should be checking into the hotel about now."

Becca just nodded wordlessly. She took her cell phone from her pocket and looked at it. I sensed she wanted me to leave before she made the call. I steadied myself on the bed rail, my legs a bit wobbly. Following my own advice, I took some deep breaths and asked the nurse where my brother was.

"I'll take you there," she said. Gently holding my arm, she led me down the hall and through the doors marked ICU. We paused for a moment as the automatic doors opened and then closed behind us, and I surveyed our surroundings. I had never spent time in hospitals; it was like entering another world. The large open area was cool to kill bacteria, and it smelled of disinfectant. Small sections were separated by beige curtains with a print of purple and green geometric shapes, much like the ER. In the center, where the staff congregated, were a cluster of desks, cabinets, and a huge set of computer monitors that followed the status of every patient. It reminded me of the bridge of the Starship Enterprise. Bursts of incongruous laughter among the co-workers punctured their low murmurs. All of the patients were hooked up to smaller monitors that displayed blood pressure, temperature, respiration, and who knows what else. Beeps emanated from every machine as medications slipped silently through plastic tubing one drop at a time, sustaining life, holding death at bay. As we passed the first row of patients, I noticed that most of them had white hair and lay quietly. The nurse said that David was at the end of the row, and I saw that he was by a window. He always liked to sit next to the window. I used to fight him for the window seat on the train into the city. Usually I let him have it, but not every time.

His left leg was in a cast, held in traction with a canvas sling, and both his arms were bandaged. He had been cut by glass in the crash and had stitched up gashes on both his arms and a bandage on his forehead. I wonder if he's got a Harry Potter scar. *He'd probably like that,* I thought. Some blood was showing through the gauze, and my knees started to buckle as I felt my head spin, but I resisted fainting again and leaned against a pole, clutching it until I steadied myself. Blood out of the body and I don't do well. I refocused my eyes and tried to look beyond the bandages to see my brother as I knew him—happy, accepting, and always expecting me to know what to do, to lead the way. His chest was taped up to protect his bruised ribs. His head was turned toward the window. I followed his gaze and saw that he was watching a bird family nesting on a tree branch close to the window. He didn't see or hear me at first. He has a mild hearing deficit, but he refuses to wear a hearing aid.

"David," I said in hardly more than a husky whisper. I had lost my voice. It was like when you're dreaming and you wake up actually trying to yell for help, but no words come out. I couldn't protect him now despite the many times I had shielded my ever-sunny twin brother from the darker side of life. I had cheered him on through every accomplishment, large and small. I had even helped coach his Special Olympics basketball team. Outside of the chicken pox, a fair share of sidewalk-scraped knees, and a few bad colds, David had never been sick or hurt. He had not been in a hospital since his birth. We both still had our tonsils.

My parents, Carolyn; I wished I had seen them first before talking to David. I knew they were gone, but I wanted to see them for myself. Too late, David slowly turned his head toward me.

"Ari," he said in a soft, hoarse voice. "We had a accident."

I tried to find a place to touch him that wasn't covered with bandages. I rested my hand on his right shoulder. "Yes, David," I said, "Your car was hit by a very big truck."

David tried to sit up, but the sharp pain made him fall back into the bed. The only position he could take that did not make it worse was flat on his back. His leg sling stopped him from turning on his side. "Oww," he cried. "Oh, Ari, everything hurts." His eyes welled with tears that soon began to streak down his cheeks. "Where's Mom?"

I took a tissue from the box perched on the heart monitor and wiped his eyes, then helped him to blow his nose a little. He was very weak.

"David, I have something very hard to tell you. I wish I didn't have to."

"What, Ari? Where's Mom and Dad?"

Tears streaked my own face as I choked out the terrible words, trying to put it the way the doctor had told me. "Mom, Dad, and Carolyn were hurt very badly in the accident, David. The doctors weren't able to save them."

"What do you mean, save them? Where are they? I want Mom!" David started to get very anxious and loud, which brought the nurse over to his side. She had a hypodermic ready to sedate him. I held a hand up to her, signaling I wasn't ready for her yet. He was crying harder now as every movement brought him more pain. I think he understood what I was saying, but, as always, he needed me to say it directly.

I gently held his face still with my hands and made him look into my eyes as I had seen my parents do so many times.

"They died," I told him. His eyes squeezed shut tight, as if I had just slapped him across the face. "They were hurt too badly in the crash. But the doctor told me they didn't feel anything; it happened very fast. We can't see them anymore. They're in heaven now with Grandma Bea and Grandpa Fred."

"No, no, no, no," he cried, shaking his head back and forth violently. It was too much for him to take in all at once. He stared at me in disbelief. There were so many things David couldn't do for himself, but with his family he had always been safe. Spared by his disability of many of the worries that adults with "normal" IQs face, until now he always had a soft place to fall when bad things happened. He understood more quickly than I expected.

I stood close, afraid to sit on the bed and jostle him. I found his hand tightly gripping the bed rail under the sheet and closed my own hand over it. That hand I had taken so many times—crossing the street, trick or treating, climbing the stairs to our bedroom, and whenever we were in a crowd, holding on to him tightly so he couldn't get lost. He looked to me now to take care of him the way he had always been cared for. I was the only one left to do it.

The nurse with the hypodermic interrupted my thoughts, saying that David needed to rest, and she wanted to give him something to help him sleep.

"He's been through a very traumatic experience," she said. "I think he needs to rest quietly now." She used the hypodermic to add a sedative to his IV line. "This will let him get the sleep he needs and give him some relief from his discomfort."

Nurses always like to call pain discomfort. It doesn't make it hurt any less, I thought.

"Thanks, I think that would be good for him, too. David, you rest now."

His only answer was a slow shaking of his head as tears rolled down his cheeks.

I watched David drift off to sleep, and I bent down and kissed him on his head before turning my back. "I want to see the rest of my family now," I said. "Can I?"

How could anyone bear to have a job like this? I wondered. *How do these nurses handle seeing people in such emotional agony without feeling it themselves?* She simply nodded, took my arm, and led me out of the ICU. Becca was pacing in the corridor. When she saw me, she hugged me and stood on her toes to kiss my neck.

"I reached my parents. They were in Lancaster, but they're on their way here," she said. "How is David?"

"Pretty banged up with a broken leg and some bruised ribs, but he's sleeping now."

"Did you tell him?"

"Yes. I want to see my parents and my sister now."

"We do need you to make the official identification," the nurse said.

"I'll come with you," Becca said.

"No, you don't have to."

"I'm going with you," she insisted for the second time that day. She held me tighter, and I couldn't help leaning on her and letting her bear some of my weight. I walked forward without feeling the steps I took, as if walking on the moon at zero gravity. My head was spinning, and I felt both dizzy and numb, but I was determined to stay conscious. I held onto Becca and took small steps. I felt like I was a condemned man walking to the electric chair. The nurse led us to a room tucked away in the back of the Emergency Department, where my family lay on gurneys under stark white sheets. I was relieved they were not yet in the morgue; seeing them in refrigerated lockers would have been worse.

It was a surreal experience. Three people that had been my whole life, now dead, under white sheets as if they were already ghosts who might fly off the tables without warning. I was scared, but I told myself that they would never want to hurt me, and there was nothing that could hurt Mom, Dad, or Carolyn anymore.

The nurse looked at me for a signal, and I nodded.

She uncovered their faces one at a time, gently moving each sheet down as if she was taking care not to awaken a sleeping child. First, I approached my mother. She had been so proud of my graduation from college. I saw that she had dressed up for the occasion, and now her new clothes were stained with blood.

How could I take her place for David? Impossible, but I had no choice. I laid my hand on her arm under the sheet. "No more worrying, Mom. I'll take care of David, I promise."

Dad was next. Everyone always said we looked alike. His face had been crushed in the accident. His clothes also were covered with dried blood. All that was left of my father was a broken body. I bit my lip thinking about the fact that I hadn't told him about getting those job offers on the phone. I had wanted to see his enormous grin when I told him the news.

"Dad, I got four job offers. I did okay. They're all decent offers, too. You would be proud. I love you, Dad," I said.

Finally, I went over to see Carolyn. She had been in the back seat with David and looked more asleep than dead; her face looked normal. She was still pretty. Her small upturned nose was untouched, and her mouth had been set in a closed smile.

The nurse explained. "Your parents arrived here without any signs of life, but the Emergency Medicine team did everything they could before they conceded they were unable to reverse the outcome. Your sister was severely injured, but she made it up to surgery alive. The internal bleeding from multiple organs and extensive damage to her aorta were too much to repair. She expired on the operating table."

"She didn't know about your parents," the nurse said. "She asked for them, and we told her that we were taking care of them. As we were taking David and Carolyn up to surgery, she told your brother to listen to the doctors and to hang on. Those were her last words."

I looked at my sister; she had just turned thirty. She was the only one in the family I had told about my plans to marry Becca. I had detected a little envy that she had not yet been as lucky in love as I. Now it would never happen. It was so unfair.

I kissed her cheek and said, "Thanks for everything, Sis. You'll have to keep watching over us, Carrie. I can't believe I won't have you as my ally anymore. I can't believe your life has been cut so short. I'm so, so sorry."

chapter two:
aaron

IN MY JUNIOR year of high school it was time for me to start planning my next journey—to college. David could stay in the public education system until he was twenty-one, so there was still time to make decisions on his transition into the world beyond public school.

There was no question in my mind about going away to school. I knew it would be very hard on David, but the time had come to find out who I was apart from my brother. I think most twins would agree that separating for college is a hard decision. I've known twin friends who go away together, apart, or stay home and either go to the same or to different local colleges. Whatever decision a pair of twins does make, trust me, there is more involved than with other siblings, best friends, or high school couples who believe they will never break up. In our case the decision was only mine to make. Would I leave home instead of staying local, and how far should I go?

As much as I wanted to leave home, I didn't want to go too far, and I know my parents were relieved that Franklin & Marshall was within a few hours' drive. I had first seen it when I stayed there for a high school debate weekend, and they offered me some nice merit scholarship money. I also had a college fund from an unexpected source. Grandma Felice passed away two years after Grandpa Clayton when I was thirteen, and she had left a college trust fund for me. Later, I discovered there was also a trust fund in David's name, so I guess they weren't really as uncaring as my Mom had thought them to be.

My entire family decided to visit Franklin & Marshall College before we sent in the deposit to make it official. Even Carolyn, who was living on her own in New York City and teaching Special Ed (a profession siblings are often drawn to), came along for the trip.

Lancaster is home to a large Pennsylvania Dutch Amish population. The Amish don't use technological advances, and their deep commitment is to keep everything "plain and separate." David got very excited seeing them ride through town in horse-drawn buggies with "slow caution" signs on the back to warn those of us non-Amish in cars. We also saw a number of the Amish farms along the way.

We suspected it might be one of the last trips the LeShays would take together for a long time, and we made the most of it. I guess I wanted to be a kid one last time before moving away. We declared there were no calories in Lancaster, and our first stop was a famous tourist attraction, The Good & Plenty Restaurant, with the emphasis on plenty, but just as good as they claimed. The home-style food was served on a huge buffet in the center of the room, and we piled our plates high with mashed potatoes, yams, roast beef, ham, homemade sausage, and buttered noodles. Somehow we never bothered to make any room for green vegetables; even Mom left them off. Of course, David got a little too enthusiastic and wanted to try everything. David loved eating, and he was a good twenty pounds heavier than me—and about six inches shorter. As he would take a serving spoon of food and put it on his plate, Mom or Carolyn would be right behind him cleaning up whatever had spilled and trying to surreptitiously put it back on the serving platters.

Dessert choices were an endless display of cakes and pies, including their famous shoofly pie, which we all opted to have with vanilla ice cream and whipped cream. I grabbed the whipped cream canister before David could and gave him a healthy portion so he wouldn't get it onto any of the customers nearby. I noticed some of the diners were giving us a wide berth, but others were smiling at David and seemed to appreciate how much fun the buffet was for him.

It was a warm night, and we decided to play a round of mini-golf for old times' sake at one of the more than half dozen courses in town. It was a family joke that you can always tell just how dull the town is when the number of miniature golf courses outnumbers the bars. I think Lancaster set a record for most miniature golf courses in town.

"So, don't you think we should see the campus?" Carolyn asked, as we all pushed ourselves away from the breakfast table the next morning. This time we had stuffed ourselves with pancakes, sausages, bacon, hash browns, grits, and muffins. Dutifully, we had signed up for the campus tour beginning at ten-thirty. We met at the Administration Center and joined a group of about twenty other students, parents, and siblings. Most of the questions came from the parents, and in fact more than half must have come from my own mother, who broke away from us so that she could be right next to the student guide. She kept asking questions like: "Where are the laundry rooms?" "How do the meal plans work?" None of us would-be students cared about those things. We all knew that whatever it was, we'd get used to it. We were checking each other out, along with the current students who passed us by.

The siblings mostly just traipsed along looking glum and bored. Carolyn was one of the few older siblings there. And then there was David.

David had his own questions to ask, and as always, his own information to share. "This where my brother will live?" he asked Glenna, our tour guide, pushing ahead to climb the steps to the dorm with her. "My brother and I share a room at home. I gonna visit him, that okay?"

"I'm not sure if he will be in this exact building," Glenna said, smiling broadly at him. "But most freshmen are in this quad area." Glenna gestured around at the green lawn and shade trees surrounding us and added, "The dining hall is right over there."

"My name is David," said my brother, offering his hand to shake. "My brother Aaron is looking for college. I get to stay in school at home a few more years. The teacher says she needs me there."

Glenna shook David's hand and smiled. "I'm sure she does. It's nice to meet you, David. I'll bet you are doing a good job helping your brother choose where to go to college."

"Yes, I am. Thank you very much," said David with a huge grin on his face. Dad quietly maneuvered forward to steer him toward a statue of Benjamin Franklin.

The small family groups looked like clones of one another. The fathers wore polo shirts and khakis, and the mothers were in their mom jeans with matching sweater sets, most of their sweaters tied around their shoulders in an attempt to look jaunty. The prospective students, like me, were almost all boys, I noticed with disappointment. The guidebook had assured me that the male–female ratio was about fifty-fifty, so I figured that I had just gotten stuck in a crummy tour group and shouldn't worry about it. The other prospective students had either been coerced into dressing like their dads or were more comfortable in their regular jeans and T-shirts, as I was. I saw them exchange looks of amusement when David introduced himself to Glenna.

"Yeah, somehow I didn't think he was applying here," said one kid who looked about fourteen.

I gave him my sharpest look of disdain—it was a well-practiced one. No matter how many times I heard a thoughtless or cruel remark from a stranger, it never failed to land like a stomach punch. Did people think Down syndrome kids couldn't recognize an insult? Would they make a snide comment about a kid in a wheelchair, too? I made sure the brat had gotten my message.

David was sometimes hard to understand, but we had no trouble, and my mother had long ago given up trying to correct his grammar. He didn't have perfect hearing, but he knew when people were being cruel. The snotty kid ducked away from me and then hung back until he was at the end of the group. I thought to myself that September could not come soon enough for me. I needed a break from this. I needed to be on my own.

The last stop was the bookstore, just like most museums and tourist traps make sure you pass through the gift shop on your way out.

"Well, Aaron, what do you think? Are you sure? Should I buy a Franklin & Marshall Mom sweatshirt?" Mom asked.

"I doubt there's any way I could stop you," I said.

About one hunded and fifty dollars later, we had bought T-shirts, sweatshirts, car decals, hats, and a Benjamin Franklin doll for David, along with a college calendar for him that had all the dates I would be home for holidays. David wanted to wear his T-shirt right away, so we went into the men's room and changed together.

"Oh, no," I laughed. "We're dressing like twins again."

David laughed, too, and put his arm around my shoulder. "Yeah, now no one can tell us apart."

I saw a number of people turn their heads to look at us in the bookstore. I tried to ignore that, but the truth is, unlike that jerky kid, they usually had looks on their faces that said "how sweet." I also suspect they said a silent prayer of thanks that their own children had been born with the correct number of chromosomes. David, Carolyn, Dad, and I all had the same blonde curly hair, and Mom still had her long straight hair, unlike so many other mothers who felt some odd obligation to keep their hair short when they got older than thirty. I think that all the years of parenting a *special* child had taught my parents not to sweat the small stuff, and despite my mother asking a multitude of questions of the guide, I thought we were a pretty cool family.

David looked so proud in his F&M T-shirt and clutched the mascot doll under his arm. I was glad he looked happy and tried not to think about how he would feel when I really did leave for college. He'd been so much younger when Carolyn left; it hadn't hit him as hard. He always had me. I knew it was going to be a tough adjustment, and I didn't envy Mom and Dad trying to fill the void in his life that I would leave.

It would have been an altogether fine trip, but when we opened the door to leave the bookstore, it was raining. Hard. David doesn't do rain. He's scared of it. I don't get it. He takes a shower on his own at home, but anything more than a fine drizzle and he has a fit.

Dad ran back into the bookstore and bought a giant golf umbrella with Franklin & Marshall emblazoned on it and tried to coax David to stay under it and walk to the car. I don't know why he thought it would work; it never had before. It wasn't possible to drive the car to the bookstore; it's on a part of the campus accessible only on foot. So David did his rain freak dance, as I called it. He started spinning around in circles, pulled his shirt up over his nose and mouth and just kept saying "No rain, no rain, no rain, no rain."

At that point I lost it.

"What are you going to do now?" I challenged Mom and Dad. "I'm supposed to be having the guys over for poker tonight at eight. If we leave now, we'll make it home in time. But we can't wait here for two hours because he doesn't want to get wet."

"Aaron, we're sorry. You know how he is. We can't drag him out in this weather. He'll just make a bigger scene. Let's go back to the food court and have some ice cream. This could be a passing downpour."

So, as usual, David got his way, plus the reward of ice cream. *Was he playing us?* He swims, he showers, he's gone on rowboats on a lake, but a little rain falling from the sky and he just shuts down.

It wasn't a passing storm. We had three hours to kill. The bookstore made some more money from us, since we bought books to pass the time, and David was happy watching a huge flat screen TV. He didn't care what was on; I think they were watching sports, baseball maybe. I called my friend Max and told him the game would have to move to Jeff's house. I'd try to come by late, but I couldn't say when.

I took a seat on a comfortable chair across the room from the rest of my family. My mood had changed from excited to self-pitying. I opened the newest Dan Brown book and tried to lose myself in his mystery. Eventually I dozed off, and when the rain stopped, Mom gently woke me.

"All clear," she said. "Come on, we're going home."

I looked at my watch and shook my head. No poker for me that night. Chalk up another one for David.

chapter three:
aaron

"BECCA." HER MOTHER shouted from across the hospital cafeteria where we were sipping tea, waiting for David to wake up. I was trying to come to grips with how my grand plan for life was now circling the drain. Becca's parents ran over to us while her twelve-year-old sister, Brittany, stood flipping through her cell phone, all brain cells focused on herself.

"How is everyone?" her mother, Fran, asked. "Will they be able to make it to the graduation?" She looked at us and realized it was much worse than she had thought. "Oh, no, it's very bad then, isn't it?"

I suddenly pushed back my chair and stood up.

"My parents and sister are gone—dead," I said. "Only my twin brother survived the crash. They were hit head-on by a truck going the wrong way on the turnpike."

"Oh, my God! That's unbelievable," Fran said.

"That really sucks," Brittany mumbled.

"Excuse me," I said and headed toward the men's room, making it just in time to vomit into the toilet. Becca's father, Howard, followed me and helped me clean myself up. I splashed water on my face and gargled with water from the sink I cupped in my hand.

"So does this mean no graduation?" Brittany asked.

Becca kicked her under the table. Brittany yelled and rubbed her shin, but didn't ask any more questions. I was just returning to the table.

"Honey, what do you want to do? We still have time to make the ceremony, and then we can come right back here afterwards," Fran said.

"Mom, I'm not going anywhere without Aaron. I'm sure there are all sorts of arrangements that have to be made. Can you help us with that?"

"But what about the rest of his family? Does he, umm, Aaron, do you have aunts, uncles, grandparents?" Fran automatically assumed there was an older generation of my family who would be the ones to take charge of that.

"No," I said. "There's no one. My parents were both only children, and my grandparents all passed away within the last ten years."

"Family friends?" she asked.

"Sure, they had friends, but I wouldn't put this on any of them. I've got to do this myself, but I'm not sure what to do."

"Of course we'll help you Aaron. I just wanted to make sure we weren't stepping in where we shouldn't."

"Excuse me, are you Aaron LeShay?" The woman's braids distracted me from what she was saying. There must have been about one hundred of them tied behind her head, some of the braids tying up the others. Blue and pink beads were strung on each braid. They flowed down her back about six inches shy of her waist.

I looked at her and stood up, nodding my head.

"I'm Destinee Muller. I'm a social worker with the hospital, and I'm here to help you and your brother. Please accept my deepest sympathies on your losses. I can only imagine how hard and confusing this is for you. I hope you will let me take care of whatever I can. I have experience with situations like this. Please, sit down"

For the first time, I felt I was in good hands. Here was someone who would help us. Becca's parents seemed pretty useless in this situation.

"Thank you for coming to find us," said Fran. "We're completely overwhelmed. We're not sure what to do first or how to help Aaron."

"Please, call me Destinee." Seeing me with my arm around Becca, she asked her, "Will you be helping Aaron throughout this, or is there someone else I should call?"

Becca sat up straight now. "I'm his girlfriend, Becca; we're sort of unofficially engaged." She shot a look at her mother that said, *Don't ask any questions about that now.* "We were going to tell our families about our plans at dinner tonight. I'm Aaron's whole family now, except for David, and he's, you know, he's mentally challenged."

I cringed at how Becca said that, but kept quiet; it didn't really matter.

"Yes, I looked in on David before I came here," Destinee said. "He's sleeping at the moment. I see he has Down syndrome. His ID indicates he lived at home with his parents, is that right?"

I nodded. "He's supposed to graduate next month from public school."

"He should be able to do that. The doctors believe he'll have a full recovery. The leg fracture was a clean one. There should be no permanent physical damage. In fact, he will probably be able to be discharged by Thursday or Friday."

"I want to take my family home," I said. "I want to bring David home and let him finish school if he's up to it. My father is—was—a lawyer, and all the papers we'll need are probably with one of the partners at the firm. I don't know whom exactly, but I'll be able to find out at home. I was planning on going back with them anyway. I need to go home. Can you help with that?"

"Do you know if your parents had pre-arranged for burial or other options?" Destinee asked.

I took a deep breath. "Well, I know there are plots for them next to my father's parents. I'm not sure about Carolyn, but from what I remember from my grandfather's service, there was room for her there, too." My voice shook despite my efforts to control it.

She wrote down the names and dates that I could remember. "I'm going to do a little investigating and find out what I can. I'm going to help you to arrange for your family's transportation. Do you know if your parents had legal guardianship of your brother? At twenty-one now, he's an adult."

"That much I know. They took legal guardianship of him when we turned eighteen. I'm designated to be his guardian if my parents and sister are unable. I'm sure they didn't ever expect it to come to this, but that's irrelevant now. We discussed it again when we turned twenty-one, just as a formality. My parents said repeatedly that they did not want him separated from his family and put in one of those group homes with a bunch of strangers. I'm all that David has now. I'm going to take him home. We both need to go home."

I turned from the social worker and said, "I'm sorry, Becca, if you still want to marry me, David and I are now a package deal."

Becca took my arm and pulled me over to a table out of hearing distance from her parents, whose mouths had fallen agape. Her sister wandered off to look at the desserts.

"Aaron, of course I still want to marry you. But don't you think considering what's happened it might be better for all of us to be near *my* family now? You have no one left in New York, right? Really, you should think about this."

"I have thought it through. I've thought about it since we got here. David has enough trouble with change. I'm not going to move him across the country now. It will be some comfort being in his own home, and I want him to have that. And it's not just him. I need to go home, too."

"What about me? Us?"

"I think you should go back with your parents for now, then—"

"No way. I'm staying with you, Aaron. I love you. Don't you love me? Don't you want me with you?"

I took her in my arms and held her close, just as I had done so many times over the past two years. But never before had we embraced in sorrow and fear. "Of course I want you with me. But I can't put you through this. It's too much. Go home with your parents, and take that trip to Jamaica with Shari like you planned."

Becca pushed away from me, and gave me an angry stare. "That's not happening. You wouldn't abandon me if this were the other way around. We'll get through this together. Just please do me a favor."

"What?"

"Don't turn down any of the job offers you got just yet. They all said you could have a few weeks to make that choice."

I nodded okay and said I would wait on that. I couldn't think about that now anyway.

We looked over to where Becca's parents were talking quietly to one another. I started back, and Becca held my arm. "Let's give them a little time to absorb this. They are probably freaking out about our engagement plans. And I'm sure they would have been fine with it if this horrible accident had never happened. But don't let it upset you. I'm staying with you. No one knows the future. But I want to spend mine with you . . . and David," she said.

Desiree interrupted us to tell me that the hospital had received a call for me from attorney Mitchell Gerwin.

"Would you like them to transfer the call to the house phone over there?" she asked, pointing to the cafeteria wall.

"Yes. That's my father's colleague, please transfer the call."

Mitchell had heard about the accident on the news and had tracked us to this hospital.

"Aaron, I am so sorry. The whole firm is in shock. I wanted to get to you quickly to do whatever I can to help. I have your parents' wills, and I also know that they had cemetery plots. Would you like me to call and make the arrangements for your family to be taken to the same funeral home your father used for his parents?" Mitchell asked. "Is there anyone there at the hospital helping you?"

"Yes, there's a social worker here, Destinee Muller."

"May I speak to her?"

I was tremendously relieved to hand the phone over to Destinee. She and Mitchell seemed to know just what to do. After Destinee spoke with Mitchell on the phone, she told me what they would do now.

"My father's colleague is going to be able to help with all the legal stuff," I told Becca and her parents. "Becca, you should all go back to F&M now, spend some time together. My parents' car was totaled, so I'll have whatever stuff we can't fit in my car shipped to us, but I'm sure Cal will help with that. He's staying here this summer to finish up his last three credits. I'm going to stay with David tonight. With luck, we'll be able to drive home on Thursday."

"I'm going to pack what I'll need for at least the summer, and the rest of my things will be shipped home. I'm not sure when

I'm coming home; we'll talk about it next week," Becca told Fran and Howard.

"If you're sure you're okay, Aaron, I'm going back to the hotel with my parents now. Please, please call me if there are any changes. Are you sure you don't need me here?"

"No, go spend some time with your parents. This hasn't been the happy occasion they came across the country for."

chapter four:
david

I CAN'T BELIEVE it. Yesterday Mom said this was our last trip to Lancaster. I tried to hold my ears so I wouldn't hear my own thinking. I might talk slow, but not when I talked inside my head.

I remember Mom told Dad she can't get used to the idea of my brother graduating college. "Weren't they just six?" she said.

I was so excited I could hardly sit still. Since I'm twenty-one, it's my graduation from school next month. Now I can hardly move.

We were driving to Lancaster for the graduation ceremony. We were supposed to have dinner with Aaron and Becca and her family. Aaron brang Becca home with him for Christmas. He went to California with her the next vacation.

Mom says that things looked serious, especially since they were getting the four parents together. She sounded worried. She told Dad that Aaron could do better; something about Becca bothered her. She didn't want Aaron to move far away after graduation. Aaron hadn't told us his plans. He promised to tell them over dinner. He didn't want to talk about it on the phone.

Mom set two coffee cups on the kitchen table and put four chocolate chip cookies on a plate for Dad to share. "Come, sit down, Honey," she said.

I stayed out of sight in the family room, but I could hear

them. Mom always said I was a fly on the wall. That was her way of saying I was a snoop. I did know how to spy on them.

"We have that meeting about David coming up," Dad said.

Mom sighed. "Let's just concentrate on Aaron this weekend, Jonathan. It's his time. David's not going anywhere, just changing routines. We still don't know what Aaron is doing. We're not even sure if he's coming home. You're not keeping secrets for him, are you?" she asked, sipping her coffee.

"I wish. I'd tell you if I was. I have a feeling he has some news to tell us, but he's waiting until he sees us."

"Well, do you think it is about Becca or about a job?"

"Laur, I swear I don't know. We'll find out his plans at the same time, I'm sure. Try not to worry too much."

Carolyn came home a little bit later and said she'd sleep in Aaron's bed to keep me company. She just turned thirty and asked me if I thought she would ever have a great love like her parents. What did I know? "Sure you will," I said.

"I have a new girlfriend at school," I told Carolyn when we were getting under the blue and orange NY Mets comforters in my room.

"Really, David? What's her name?"

"Isabella. Isn't that pretty?"

"Yes, it's one of my favorites."

"She's pretty, too. She has dark hair that's long and twisty, green eyes, and a great smile."

"So, have you and Isabella gone out on a date yet?"

"We did!" I sat up in bed and raised my fist in victory. "We went to McDonald's and had French fries. We both like to dip them in ketchup, but just a little, not too goopy."

"Well, it sounds like you have some things in common there going for you."

"You'll never guess what else!"

Carolyn looked a little afraid, but she asked, "Well, what else happened?"

"She asked me to prom with her! And I said yes!"

Carolyn's eyes started to get teary. "Oh, David, that's so exciting. Did you tell Mom and Dad yet?"

"Yes, but I want to tell you and Aaron myself. I can't wait to tell him tomorrow."

"Oh, he's going to be very happy for you."

"Yep, all of us in our class are going together. Mom even hired a big white stretch limo to take us. It's June 25th at a Country Club with all the seniors. It's a whole month away, and I don't know how I wait that long. Mom's making us a party before the party!"

"You're going to look great in a tux," Carolyn said. "You have to take plenty of pictures, Davy. Can I come to the send-off?"

"You better! I'm so happy. Ari going to be proud of me, don't you think?"

"Definitely! Now let's try to get some sleep; we've got a big weekend ahead of us."

In the morning, playing snoop again, I heard Carolyn and Mom talking about Isabella.

Mom told Carolyn it was a sad story. Her parents, Carmella and Louie, had told her about it at one of the parent nights.

"What happened?" Carolyn asked.

Isabella was born perfectly healthy. When she was eighteen months old she got a very high fever in the middle of the night. She had a seizure. They rushed her to the hospital, but she got brain damaged anyway.

"It's another of the many stories we've heard over the years, Mom," said Carolyn.

"Yes, and each one of them heartbreaking. But I'm going to allow myself to enjoy David's big date for the prom. I'm sure they'll have a great time."

I can't really remember the accident. All I felt was a big, big bump with a loud crash. Now I don't even know if I'll be able to go to the prom, and even if I do, they won't be there to see me. It makes me so sad and so scared.

chapter five:
aaron

THE HOSPITAL SOCIAL worker knew her stuff, and so did Mr. Gerwin. The next day I spoke to him, and arrangements were set to transport my family from the hospital to the funeral home in our town. They would stay there until the funeral.

I slept on the chair in David's room that first night; it folded out to a bed. For the next few days I drove back and forth, getting my things in order in Lancaster, talking to doctors at the hospital, and mostly just holding David's hand and commiserating with him about our loss.

Two hearses arrived on Monday. Destinee had been hovering over me since Saturday, and when one of the drivers called her cell phone, she was with me in David's room.

She put her hand on my shoulder and said softly, "Aaron, the funeral home is here for your family. Do you want to go down and see them off?"

I did. She came with me to the morgue, and the men were bringing in the caskets. I'd had to pick them out from their website on-line. Creepy.

Destinee and I stood a few yards down the hall from the morgue and just stared at the men doing their jobs. They were unaware we were there. They took Mom out first.

"Now, you know they will be taken to Dulton's, and they are

calling the wake for Sunday from noon to four and then six to nine. The funeral home has put the notice in *Newsday*."

I nodded to Destinee, but was riveted to the process of the coffins being loaded into the hearses. Mom and Dad were in one hearse and Carolyn in the other. Just as they were getting ready to pull out, I ran up and stopped them and said I wanted to say goodbye to my parents and sister. The men immediately stepped aside and let me come forward.

"Don't worry about David and me. David's healing well. We'll be home Thursday; I'll come see you then. I miss you all. I love you and so does David." Then I whispered, "God bless you, rest in peace."

I stopped at the cafeteria for some coffee to settle my nerves, and then I went back to David's room. I told him that Mom, Dad, and Carolyn were on their way back to Westbury.

"I just don't unnerstand, Ari. How could God let this happen?" David said for the hundredth time. Still, I tried to answer him again.

"I don't know, David. When things like this happen, people like to say it's God's will, but I find it hard to accept. We're taught that God is good and all knowing, all forgiving. What possible plan could God have with this? I just don't have an answer for you, David, but I promise I will get us through this."

The doctors had predicted he would be discharged in a few days, and they were true to their word. Thursday morning I was given pages of instructions, bottles of pain medication, and Xanax for anxiety—also prescribed for me—and instructions on how and where to take him to an orthopedist, and later on, physical therapy.

"Xanax is a narcotic, Aaron," the doctor said. "You want to be very careful how you take it. Follow the prescription, no more than two per day. It can be addicting, but for now, I think you need the pills to get through the next month or so."

I shipped almost all my stuff by UPS so there would be room in the car. David needed the whole back seat to put his leg up. The hospital had given him crutches, which he had not yet mastered, and we bought a wheelchair to take home with us. He would have to keep the cast on for six more weeks. He asked me if he would be able to go to his prom. I had to laugh; that was a new one to me. It seemed he had a girlfriend that nobody told me about. Well, he may have the mind of a child, but he's got the hormones of a man. This should be interesting.

chapter six:
aaron

I KNEW DAVID was different from as far back as I remember, but for some reason my parents tried to keep the truth from me as long as they could. It must have been some kind of state of denial—like it was okay if they knew it, but if they admitted it to me, then it was reality. It all came out when we got our first two-wheelers, the summer before first grade.

They were a present from my Dad's parents, Grandma Bea and Grandpa Fred. As soon as I saw them, I grabbed the red bike and pedaled as fast as I could. When I stopped at the corner, I looked back to see David far behind on the blue bike.

For the rest of July, we pedaled up and down the sidewalk in front of the house. I would lead and David would follow at a distance, our mother's eyes following us intently. By the end of the month I told her I was ready to take off the training wheels. I remember a worried look flashed into her eyes, and she tried to talk me out of it, telling me I was too young, it wasn't time, I needed to practice more, but I was adamant. I was anxious to take this monumental step forward, to be a big kid. I knew she was stalling for some reason. I figured it had to do with David, and I guess at that point I decided in my little six-year-old head that I was going to get it out in the open already.

"Mom, look at me, my training wheels don't even touch the ground. I'm ready, right?"

My demonstration of my riding abilities was so good, Mom couldn't argue with me.

"Yes, that's great, Sweetie," she said, yet I saw no smile of pride on her lips. Anyway, Mom started twisting her hands together, and I saw her look at David pedaling slowly down the street toward us, his bike wobbling back and forth on the training wheels, before finally saying that she'd ask Dad to help me on the weekend. I saw her fading into that zone again.

As far back as I can remember, Mom would get this hollow sadness about her, which I was sensitive to even as a toddler. One of my earliest memories is of a time when I felt her retreating into her worry place, so I went into my room and brought out my latest Duplo masterpiece to cheer her up. I was only about four and a half, but I remember it very clearly. I had tried to copy the Leaning Tower of Pisa from a book Mom had shown me about great architecture.

"Look, Mom," I told her, "I made the Leaning Tower of Pizza, I used all my round Duplos." I set the green building board carefully on the kitchen table. The Tower was about a foot high.

"Oh, Ari, that's wonderful," she said.

We admired it together until David came into the room wanting juice.

"Wow, you do that, Ari?" he asked, reaching for it with his stubby hands.

I tried to stop him, but it was too late. David brought my tower crashing down. I started to yell, and he started to cry. Then I looked at Mom and saw she was frozen, trying to figure out how she should react, who she should comfort first. I had to save her.

"No, David," I said. "King Kong destroys the Empire State Building. That was the Tower of Pizza." I made myself laugh instead of getting angry, so he laughed, too.

I looked up to see her swipe away a tear and smile brightly at the two of us. I had successfully averted what could have been a tantrum from David and heartache for Mom, sublimating my own disappointment at the tower wreckage. I didn't like it when that melancholy of hers surfaced.

The next Saturday, Dad got out his giant wrench to take off my training wheels. He was wearing his weekend work clothes, a faded purple NYU sweatshirt and his jeans with the holes in the knees.

"Are you sure you're ready for this?" he asked. "It's not as easy as it looks. I don't think I rode without training wheels until I was at least seven. Carolyn wasn't riding on two wheels at your age, either."

But he couldn't change my mind. I pointed out that the bikes when he was a kid were probably not as good. Dad stopped fiddling with the wrench and smiled at me. He flipped the bike upside down and started turning one of the nuts with the wrench. I still remember hesitating, but deciding to go ahead and force the issue.

"What about David?" I asked. "Are you going to take his off, too?"

Dad stopped working the wrench and looked at me. We both knew that I already knew the answer to this one, and I suspect he knew the big question was coming up. His unease showed clearly on his face. It worried me the same way that Mom's sad face made me feel. Sometimes I wish they weren't so damned expressive. Neither one hid their feelings well.

"Aaron, I don't think David is ready yet. He needs more time before we can take off his training wheels."

"Why, Daddy?' I persisted. "David is exactly the same age as me."

I guess I had heard enough excuses for David. There were so many of them—he's tired, he doesn't like that, you do it for him, Aaron. And there were always special appointments for him—physical therapy, occupational therapy, and speech. But they never explained why. Why was he treated like that, and why did he act so different if we were twins?

Then Dad said it. "Yes, but even though you're twins, David's not as strong or as fast as you, right?" I shrugged my shoulders to say that didn't matter, just as he and Mom had always insisted.

"Now that you're getting older you'll start to see more differences between the two of you. He's never going to catch up to you." He got up from crouching over the bike and sat down on the stoop. He patted his knees, and I climbed into his lap. He quickly rubbed his eyes.

"Why never?" I asked, a little sorry I'd pushed him to tell me.

"It's not David's fault, you know, he tries. It's because of a condition he was born with. Things are harder for him; it's called Down syndrome." I had heard that term a lot before, but no one had ever said it directly to me. Now I finally understood.

All I could say then was, "Oh."

"It's why he takes a longer time to learn new things. He's always going to need our understanding and patience, and we're all going to have to help him to do his best, especially you, my man, because you're so close with each other."

"Is that why people can't understand when he talks? Won't he outgrow it? Is he sick? Can't the doctor make him better?"

Dad shook his head. I tried not to let him know I could see that he was blinking back tears. I was relieved he wasn't telling me that David was dying or something like that.

"No, he's not sick, and he'll never outgrow it. He was born with this condition. His speech is hard to understand because his tongue is actually thicker than most people's, and it makes it tough for him to say certain letters, like *r* and *l* and some others. Down syndrome doesn't make you sick, but like I said, it makes things harder for him. It's why his hearing is not as sharp as yours; that's common for people with Down syndrome. That's why he goes for his therapies. They can help him improve, but he will always have trouble keeping up with you and the other kids his age. Ari, Mom and I are worried that David will feel bad when he sees you riding without the training wheels. Can you be grown-up and not tease him?"

"I won't tease him, Dad." I stood up and gave him a solemn handshake. I felt bad for David, but I had wondered about this for a long time and was glad I finally knew the truth. "I promise. Now can we take off the training wheels?"

When the training wheels were off, Dad put my bicycle in his car and drove us to the high school parking lot to practice. He held the back of my bicycle seat and ran while I rode around the lot. Once I could balance, I was riding fast with confidence. I remember now the words he said to me; it's so pitifully ironic. "Now you watch it, Aaron; always be aware of what else is around you. Always watch the road ahead."

David eventually noticed my missing training wheels, but Mom swooped in to smooth it out. As soon as David started to cry, she whisked him away to the toy store, and an hour later they came home with the one toy they had always said was too expensive to buy for us—a motorized police car. We shared it, of course, but I knew it was really for David. It was a great solution, though. On his police car, David could follow me, then sound his siren, and I would have to pull over to the side so that he could give me a ticket.

From then on I was even more aware of David's disabilities. But when we were young, we had fun together most of the time. Just like any other twins, we were a team. For preschool, my parents found an integrated class that we could go to together from age three through kindergarten, and we stuck close to one another. I could always understand what he was saying, even if other people had trouble, and I remember the teacher, Miss Wendy, asking for my help sometimes. I guess it was a twin thing. But it was only a few more years before I began to want to distance myself from him a little.

To his credit, David didn't give up on the bicycle though; he practiced all he could, and when he was about eight, Dad took his big wrench out again, and the kid was bursting with pride at his accomplishment.

I was about seven, in second grade, when I started to resent always having David following me. Sometimes I just wanted to play with the other boys from school. It wasn't really fun always being the leader, always winning the game, or letting him win on occasion. By the first grade we were no longer in class together. He was still in the same school, but with the *special* students.

One day, a kid named Stephen asked me over to his house after school, and Mom did what she always did, she invited the other mother to bring my friend to our house so that David would not be left out. But this time I was prepared to counterattack.

I interrupted her before she could finish, saying that Stephen just got the new Nintendo system and we were going to play with his older brother. "David can't do that; he would just be bored," I said, loud enough so Stephen's mother could hear. The next time, I told her we were playing basketball with some other kids on his block that we wanted to play with. After a while, she reconciled herself to the fact that she couldn't force David on us all the time. It would just frustrate David and embarrass me.

But I didn't abandon David all the time—maybe two or three times a week I pushed for some freedom of my own. David was fun, but there was no more denying that he couldn't keep up with my other friends, and I was afraid they would tease both of us. I'd seen the kids pointing at him in recess. Still, on Saturday mornings when we woke up at least two hours before the rest of the house, we were again Batman and Robin, the Dynamic Duo. We had our own way of playing and doing things together in which we became two halves of a whole—maybe not equal halves, but we were stronger as a team.

My parents told me that when we were first born, they were able to treat us pretty much the same. All infants are naturally helpless, well or disabled, and twins are always a challenge. We both needed to be fed, changed, dressed, and held equally. David was easy for a baby with Down syndrome. His heart was normal, and he was not that far behind me physically at first. It really wasn't until those training wheels came off that my parents were forced to talk honestly about the difference between my twin and me.

• • •

I often heard my mother talking on the phone to my grandmother Felice, who lived in Florida. We didn't see them much, but they sent us toys in the mail. She seemed to take David's Down syndrome very seriously, and I felt that for some reason she blamed my mother for it. It didn't make sense to me.

There was one time I remember when I was about eight years old, I was hiding in the hall closet listening to Mom's side of the conversation. Her voice always went up in pitch when she spoke to my Florida grandparents, as if her vocal cords were guitar strings and the tuning knobs were being tightened each time they talked. At first it sounded as if they were getting along fine. I remember Mom saying she would love to see some sunshine right about now, as it was mid-January and that we were all looking forward to visiting them the next month. But then Mom's words started to get heated.

"Well, I'm sorry you feel you wasted your money on my education, Mother. I think it served me very well," Mom said.

Oh no, Mom was having one of her phone fights with Grandma Felice again. She was standing over a pot of brisket balancing the phone receiver on her shoulder, and the countertop was dotted with spice bottles. I decided to stay put in the closet where I could monitor the situation without being noticed.

Then Grandma must have brought up the money issue again, because Mom sounded very angry when she answered her, saying, "We're managing just fine on Jonathan's salary. I'm not asking you for anything, am I?"

Her lips tightened into a straight line as she allowed her mother to speak again. "Aaron is quite happy going to the summer recreation program in the park. Believe me, children can have plenty of fun without going to expensive camps."

Spying from my hiding place while trying to get comfortable straddling the canister vacuum, I saw Mom vigorously shake garlic into the pot. Mom was a good cook, but sometimes when she was distracted things could come out with too many spices that I'd have to cover up with a dunking of ketchup on the side. Now Mom had switched back to her calm voice, and I could tell she was so upset that she had internally exploded.

"Look, I'm tired of repeating this to you," she said. Then she gave one of her long explanations about Dad's job and why it was okay he wasn't going to be a partner. Mom stabbed the brisket with a giant serving fork and flipped it over to the other side. She then added a few bay leaves, ground in some black pepper from her oversized wooden mill, and poured a lot of water from the teakettle into the pot. Next, she took a bowl of chopped onions and tossed them in, mixing it up with the big spoon. A few shakes of the ketchup bottle and a measured half-cup of white wine, and she covered the pot and left the brisket to cook on a low heat setting. I knew that soon the whole house would smell of the sweet and sour aroma as she let the brisket simmer for hours until dinnertime.

Raising her voice again, she answered, "Well, this is not a normal situation, now, is it?" Then, back to the voice she used when she was completely tired of arguing, she said quietly, "Mother, can we please change the subject now? How is Aunt Florence doing? Did she have her surgery yet?"

Mom moved from the stove and sat at the kitchen table,

skimming through the catalogs that had come in the mail. Her shoulders looked more relaxed, and I guessed that Grandma Felice had stopped her criticizing and had started reporting on more innocuous news, like Aunt Florence's gall bladder and her latest ranking in the golfing league.

I think, though, just before the call ended, Grandma took another shot at Mom because her hand was shaking when she tried to hang up the receiver, and it took her a few times before she was able to fit the pieces together. When that tin-voice recording came on "If you'd like to make a call, please hang up..." Mom slammed the phone down and shouted, "Oh, shut the hell up." Mom hardly every cursed. Waiting until I heard her footsteps going down the basement stairs, I crept out of the closet, grabbed some cookies to take up to our room for David and me. I was quite an accomplished snack sneaker by seven and stayed there until Mom called us for dinner. As I expected, the brisket was a little too garlicky, but with a smidge of ketchup it was delicious.

Later, when David and I were supposed to be asleep, I heard her retelling the conversation with Grandma Felice to my father when they were in the living room, which was just below our bedroom. "I don't know why she persists in giving me such a hard time. I think we should cancel our visit," Mom said. It sounded like she was crying.

David heard it, too. "Is Mommy crying?"

"Shh, let me listen to this, David, then I'll explain it to you, okay?"

David nodded; he knew my hearing was better than his and that I would help him understand what our parents were talking about.

From what I could hear, Mom was thinking of canceling our trip to Florida, and Dad was arguing against that.

"You swear we'll leave if things get bad with them?" Mom asked.

"I promise," he said. "If things get bad, we'll just leave and go to Disney World."

I liked the sound of that. It seemed like a win-win situation to me. I jumped onto David's bed and whispered, "David, don't worry. Mom is just a little nervous about our trip to Florida next month. She gets all cranky sometimes, you know?"

David looked at me and grinned, "Yeah, she was really upset when I painted on the wall instead of paper."

"Yeah, but it looks like we have a good chance of going to Disney World after we see Grandma and Grandpa. In fact, you can help make that happen."

"Really? What'd I do?"

"Don't worry about that now; I'll think of some things we can do to make sure we get to Disney World." I started formulating *Operation Get to Disney* in my mind. I thought about letting Carolyn in on my plans, but decided against it. She was eighteen, and I never knew when she'd decide to act like a grown-up or side with us kids. Then I stopped listening to my parents and fell asleep dreaming of Mickey Mouse and Fantasy Land. I wouldn't be surprised if David had the same dreams. The twin stuff between us could get kind of mysterious like that.

After three days in Miami Marvel Villas, where David and I had a great time playing in the pool and making a fort with the lounge chairs (several times accidentally running over an octogenarian's foot with the chairs), Grandma Felice started coming down with migraines. When David's sauce-covered meatball managed to slip off his plate and onto her white cotton dining room chair cushion, that pretty much sealed the deal, and the next day we were off to Disney World, where kids of all ages are free to have fun and make messes and plenty of noise. As a matter of fact, Disney is one of those places that if they see a family with a child with a disability, they sometimes let them ahead in line. It was one of the rare times that having a twin with Down syndrome got me special privileges.

chapter seven:
aaron

BY NOON ON Thursday, David, Becca, and I were ready to drive home. Becca had insisted that her parents go home on Tuesday; she told them they did not have to go to the funeral. Brittany practically turned cartwheels at hearing that.

The Jersey Turnpike was jammed with people making long weekend getaways, and the traffic in Brooklyn was even worse. We didn't pull into the driveway until seven for a trip that should have taken us just four hours.

Finally, we arrived home. Becca and I left David sleeping in the backseat and went into the house. Since they were only going away for the weekend, the house had been left in its usual lived-in state. Mom and Dad's current books were on the living room coffee table, Carolyn's driving gloves and keys had been left on the hall table, and there were some scraps of wrapping paper I guessed were from a gift they had gotten me for graduation. I wondered if they had left it here or taken it with them. I didn't remember seeing any gifts in what remained of their car when I had removed their belongings.

Our cats, Stan and Ollie, sprang at us with accusation in their angry eyes. I'm sure their high-pitched meows meant, "You only left us food for three days, what the hell took you so long?" Before even taking in the mail and the newspapers that had piled up on the porch, I filled their bowls with cat food, added some treats and changed their water. Fortunately, my parents had filled the cat's water fountain before they left. The litter box, ugh, overflowed. I wondered if the neighbors knew what had happened. Was it in *Newsday*?

I sorted through the papers and found Monday's edition. There was a box on the front page that said *Westbury Parents and Daughter Killed in Auto Accident. See story, page 8.* I turned to the page, and there was a picture of my whole family taken at a Special Olympics tournament last year. A banner, two-line head read: *MOM, DAD, AND SISTER PERISH IN ACCIDENT DRIVING TO SON'S GRADUATION: DOWN SYNDROME TWIN BROTHER ONLY SURVIVOR.*

I tried to read the article. I could see the words, but they looked like just a jumble of letters. When tears plopped onto the picture blurring my own face, I realized I was crying. Becca had gone ahead to the kitchen to check out the refrigerator, but I must have let out a moan, because she came running back to me.

"What is it?" she asked. She knelt beside me and took the newspaper from my hands.

"It has all the details here," she said. "It even says that the wake will be Sunday and the funeral is planned for Monday. They are now at Dulton's Funeral Home. It says they are together in the home's largest room, and it has been filling up with flowers all week."

Then I noticed the answering machine on the front hall desk. The message light was blinking messages. *Yeah, everyone knew.*

The neighbors must have been watching our house from their windows. When I went to get David out of the car and into his wheelchair, doors began to open on both sides of the block. Women carrying casseroles, husbands with bent heads, and children trying to look sad, even though they sensed excitement in the air, came from all directions to descend on the house. It kind of reminded me of a scene from *The Stepford Wives*. Our block had become a small battalion armed with home-cooked meals. The first ones to reach me were my next-door neighbors, the whole Stillman family, parents Jim and Elaine and teens Charlie and Evan. Jim immediately took the wheelchair from me and set it up with surprising expertise.

"I worked in a veteran's hospital when I was younger," he said. "Now, I'll go around the other side and carry him under his arms, you try to keep his leg from bumping on the driveway or the car door."

David was still asleep, but he was in his wheelchair in no time at all, starting to stir. I looked up at the three steps leading to our porch and the two other steps after the landing. Now what?

"Let's take him in through the garage," said Jim.

Brilliant, would I have ever figured that out?

There were two cars in the garage, Mom's Taurus and Carolyn's little Civic. Mom and Dad had been pretty upset when Carolyn bought the Civic.

"That is just too small," Mom had said. "You have no protection in an accident."

But Carolyn assured her that small cars were the only reasonable purchase when you park on city streets. "I've never had an accident yet, Mom. Please, I'm twenty-seven years old. I get to choose my own car."

It was easy to maneuver past the runt of a Civic. Becca opened the garage door from inside. Then we noticed the banner hanging across the den ceiling. "Welcome Home College Graduate!"

It was set up for a typical LeShay family celebration. "Would you mind getting rid of that, Jim?" I asked, and started moving David into the guest room on the main floor.

"Why here?" he asked, now fully awake, "I want *my* room."

"David, remember we discussed this already. It's going to be too hard for you to go up and down the stairs with the cast on. We'll bring your clothes and things you need here. Look, you've even got a television."

"Mom and Dad say no TV in our room." His voice began to quiver.

"It's okay, you get special dispensation from the Pope for a broken leg," I assured him.

"Special what?"

"Special permission, David, you'll be more comfortable here. You have your own bathroom, and you're close to the kitchen for food."

David shrugged. "If you say so, I don't want to make Mom and Dad mad."

"They won't be mad, David, I promise."

"Are you going to sleep here with me, too?"

It wasn't an unreasonable question; it was a queen-sized bed. But I intended to sleep with Becca.

"No, I'd jiggle around and hurt your leg. Becca and I will sleep upstairs. I'll stay in our room, and she can have Carolyn's," I lied. "Carolyn's furniture is a bit more feminine," I said to Becca. She just looked at me and remained silent. I wasn't ready to start talking to David about sex. I wondered if our parents had, and prayed that they did.

"Oh, that's good," said David.

"And look what Becca found, David, a kazoo," I said. "If you need help getting out of bed or going to the bathroom, just give a few loud toots on the kazoo, and we'll be right down."

"Gee, thanks," David said, turning the kazoo over in his hands. "My favorite color, too, blue."

He put it in his mouth and gave a very loud blast. He laughed at the funny noise and said, "Well, you can hear that upstairs, right?"

I nodded. "Any time you need something, all you have to do is kazoo."

Despite the nap he had in the car, David was tired and wanted to go to sleep. I helped him get into pajama tops and after helping him in the bathroom and leaving a water bottle within reach on the night table, I asked once again if there was anything else he needed.

"I need Mom and Dad," he said, starting to cry.

I sat down carefully on the edge of his bed.

"I need them, too, David, but somehow God needed them and Carolyn more. We'll be okay, you'll see. Hey, aren't we the Dynamic Duo?"

"Right, Batman," he said, and gave me a weak smile.

"Well, go to sleep now, Robin," I said. "The next few days are going to be very strange, so just try to stay calm. You give me the bat signal whenever you feel you need me."

We had come up with the bat signal when we were little kids. Nothing very imaginative, David would just flap both hands at the wrist to catch my eye, and I would do my best to get him away from whatever was making him nervous or scared or uncomfortable.

While I was tending to David, Becca had been phenomenal with the neighbors. She had put away all the casseroles, after making sure that each dish had a name on it so that we could thank them properly and return the dishes to their rightful owners. She had explained that we really needed to get some things done before we went to bed, and all but Jim and Elaine Stillman had left; their kids had gone back home. Elaine, a petite, delicate-looking woman with a strong Irish fight in her, had been one of my mother's closest friends, and Jim and Dad were also good buddies. Jim was a former college football player—you could see that in a glance, but he was a kind-hearted softie who had been through traumas of his own.

"Do you want us to stay here with you?" Elaine asked.

I smiled and gave her a hug. "Thanks, Elaine, but we really can manage here on our own."

"Becca is a lovely girl," she said. "I hope you know she's a keeper."

"Oh, believe me, I know it. But thank you, she'll be glad to know that you approve."

"I still feel there's something else we should be doing," Elaine fretted.

"E, I think we should give these people some privacy now." Jim came up and rested his hands on Elaine's shoulders. "Aaron, we're just next door. You can call or come over any time day or night if you need something. Oh, and please apologize to Stan and Ollie for us; we forgot all about feeding them when you were gone."

I almost smiled. "That's okay, they survived the week."

"We're just so sorry, so very sorry. We loved your parents and sister, too."

"I know." I gulped, choking back more tears. "Everyone did. They were amazing people. Hopefully, some of their strength rubbed off on me."

"Oh, I'm sure of that," Jim said and gave me a bear hug. "You've always been a great source of pride for them. But this is very hard. Please, let Elaine and me help you, will you?"

"Thanks, Jim. That makes me feel a bit better. Good night now. I'm sure we'll see you tomorrow."

Becca and I looked in on David and were relieved he was

fast asleep. In the recesses of my mind I supposed I had always known the possibility existed that one day I would be solely responsible for David. But not this soon. Just like a baby, he looked so peaceful in his sleep. He didn't look like he could be too much trouble. My parents had done a great job with him, and he looked up to me with trust and loyalty. I felt very good about bringing my brother back to the home he loved, and I vowed to myself to follow my parents' wishes and not put him in a group home with strangers. They had entrusted my brother to me, and I would not let anyone separate us.

The answering machine was still blinking the number at us. I hit the button, and it said "You have fourteen new messages."

"What do you think, should we leave it until tomorrow?" I asked Becca.

"I think the best thing would be to listen to them now, write down whoever we need to return calls to and then make those calls in the morning," she said. "Do you have the energy to do it now?"

"Okay, but will you do the writing down? I can't always read my own writing."

Becca smiled and went into the kitchen for a pad and pen and some cold drinks. She made sure we were both comfortably settled before starting.

"Ready," she said, "push the button."

The messages were a mixture of sales calls, people calling with condolences and breaking down and crying. We needed to return some first thing in the morning, such as the messages from the lawyer, Father Charles, and David's school counselor. The next to last call was for Becca from her friend Shari. She told Becca she had found someone to buy her tickets for the vacation they had planned to take.

Becca shrugged. "Well, I guess I'm easily replaced."

"Not for me, you're not," I said, pulling her close to me on the couch and kissing her on the head. "Why don't you go up to my parents' room and settle in? Would you mind changing the sheets? They're in the hall linen closet. Thank you, Becca." Shit, I never thought I'd be sharing my parents' bed like this.

I pushed the button to hear the last message: Aaron, this is Colin. I'm so sorry I didn't see you at school before you left. I was out of town during grad week. Please call me when you get this message, any time day or night.

I had kind of wondered why he never called me. I decided to return that call tonight.

I yelled upstairs to tell Becca I was making one phone call, and then I dialed Colin's number.

I had stopped seeing him for therapy when I finished my sophomore year, but we'd see each other on campus and sometimes have lunch or coffee together. Eventually, we developed a friendship. Technically, that's not allowed, but since we weren't professionally involved anymore, we ignored that. He was never one to carry a rulebook around; we genuinely enjoyed spending time together on a casual basis. Sometimes we would even shoot some hoops.

"Colin, this is Aaron," I said. "I hope I'm not calling too late."

"No, no, not at all. Aaron, how are you? Stupid question, it's just an automatic reflex. I am so sorry about this accident. How are you holding up?"

"Honestly, I think I'm still in a state of shock. We just got home."

"*We* . . . being?"

"My girlfriend Becca and David and I. David's sleeping in the guest room downstairs. He has a broken leg and bruised ribs, but he's going to be okay, according to the doctors."

"How is he taking the loss emotionally? Do you think he understands?"

"Yes and no. He understands what death is, and he knows that they are gone, but I have a feeling he doesn't really understand that the situation is permanent. He asks for Mom and Dad, but he has me and Becca, and as for me, well, for now, I think just having him to take care of is stopping me from collapsing."

"It always has, Aaron. But this would bring anybody to his knees. When is the funeral service? I want to be there for you."

"Oh Colin, it's such a long drive, you don't have to come."

"I didn't ask if I had to, I said I want to. Please Aaron, I want to be there."

"It's at ten Monday morning at St. Brigid's Catholic Church in Westbury. I can email you the details."

"Fine. What are your plans until then?"

"Always with the questions, huh, Doc?" I said.

"Can't help it, it's an ingrained habit."

"We have to meet with the lawyer and the priest before the service. People have been coming over and bringing us enough food to feed an army. I think other than those meetings we'll try to stay home and just get some rest before tackling the rest of the issues, like David's school and getting him to an orthopedist here."

"You sound like you have a good plan there. I'm sure you are still in shock over this. You've been busy handling things, but this is a tremendous blow. You'll have to allow yourself to mourn for your own losses, not just David's. And Aaron, please, remember the answer is not in the bottom of a bottle."

I sighed heavily. Colin and I had spent two years discussing my family dynamics and the bond between David and me. He knew I felt responsible for him before this happened, so I was sure he was freaking out for me, even more than I probably was.

"Thanks, Colin. The truth is you are the only call I returned tonight. I'm going to go to bed now. I guess I'll see you Monday."

• • •

I hung up the phone, looked in on David snoring peacefully, and then steeled myself to go upstairs to the bedrooms. Stan and Ollie followed me, softly mewing. We'd been in the house for about three hours, and I had yet to go upstairs. The guest room, the den, the kitchen—they were bad enough, but seeing their bedrooms . . .

Becca was in my parents' room getting settled. I noticed immediately that the comforter was not the one my parents had slept under for the last six years. I remembered Mom telling me about buying it last month. I'd only half listened to her at the time. It was a kind of modern design of splashes of red, blue, purple, and green and haphazard black squiggly lines. Sort of like a Jackson Pollock painting, she described it. My father told me on the phone he was a little surprised that Mom went to this style from the pastel flower designs she favored. She said felt like a new look this time, according to Dad. She'd asked him, "Do you like it?"

Married for more than thirty years, Dad knew it was a moot point. But he probably really did like it. I can picture him saying, "Yeah, this is cool, Laur, it really makes the room brighter."

The rest of the room was pretty much the same. Mom's jewelry box was on the dresser. I reached into my pocket and pulled out the baggie the hospital gave me with my family's valuables. I took out the heart-shaped birthstone necklace Dad had made for her after David and I were born. All the birthstones representing the members of our family were set in a gold heart. For Carolyn, born the last day of February on a leap year, there was a purple amethyst. For David and me there were two rubies to represent our July birthday; Dad's birthday is in May, so he had a green emerald. Mom was a September baby so she had sapphire, a blue that was always her favorite color. In the center was a small diamond, because as Mom said, "Why not, who doesn't want a diamond around her heart?" I would give it to the funeral director for her to wear.

I opened the jewelry box and placed the necklace on the hook she always kept it on at night, for now. Her wedding and engagement rings I placed side by side in the ring section, and her watch went into the drawer underneath. I fleetingly thought that maybe David could give her engagement ring to a woman someday, then laughed to myself—yeah, as if. Dad didn't have a place for his wedding ring. He never took it off. I thought about burying it with him, but decided I really wanted to wear it when Becca and I got married. Becca would want a new ring. For now, I left it in his sock drawer, and I put his watch on the dresser, as if he were coming home later. Then I remembered my Donatello box with Becca's ring inside.

"Just a sec," I told Becca. I ran back down the stairs to get it and stash it in the bureau in mine and David's room. I'd need to find a new right moment to give it to her. This time, she might have to think about her answer when I formally popped the question.

The rest of the jewelry was Carolyn's: a necklace, a watch, and a pair of earrings. She didn't wear rings much. She hadn't received the right kind yet, she'd say. "At my age, only one kind of ring counts." We'll have to go to her apartment, too, I thought.

On the matching nightstands on either side of my parents'

queen-sized bed were a variety of items I'd never taken notice of before. On Mom's side were, as always, the Tiffany shade lamp, clip-on book light, the water bottle on a coaster, alarm clock, tissues, phone, and a personal phone book that said "Friends, Family, and More" stuffed with business cards, long-outdated class lists going as far back as Carolyn's kindergarten list, and some favorite family photos.

Dad's side was less cluttered. He had a lamp to match Mom's, reading glasses, an alarm clock, and a box of tissues. There was also a little pile of change, which he took out of his pocket every night and put in his pocket each morning. I wondered why he had left this pile home. He never did that. There was also a framed photo of Mom taken when they were at NYU together. She was laughing at something. Her head was tilted back letting her hair flow behind her, and her mouth was open. Carolyn had made the frame out of Popsicle sticks, glitter, and glue in the second grade before David and I were even born.

The big Monet reproduction of Water Lilies over their bed looked a little out of place above the new Pollack-like blanket. Maybe she had planned to replace that, too. The triple dresser was covered with family photos, and a thin coat of dust marked each one's place if I picked it up. It started on the far left with their wedding photo, moving on to photos of Carolyn at various ages, and then there was a picture of the five of us crowded into Mom's hospital bed just after David and I were born. Mom held David, Dad held me, and Carolyn was in the middle. The photos chronicled our family up to my high school graduation and years at F&M.

Becca was looking intently at the photos and picked up one when we were about four.

"I think this is the first picture that you don't look like twins anymore," she said. "Your eyes are bigger now, and David's are smaller now that his face has grown. You can really see the Down syndrome eyes here, and also, you can see from this picture that you're quite a bit taller. You still have the same blonde curly hair, and your eye color is the same. You even have similar noses, but the mouths are very different."

"Okay, that's enough, you're examining ancient history." I took the photo from her hand and placed it back in the dusty space that matched its size.

The door to their huge walk-in closet was open, and the closet was over-crammed with clothing. Shoes were Mom's weakness, and they were piled high in every corner. About two-thirds of the clothes belonged to my Mom; Dad made do with the rest. As I was taking it all in, as if for the first time, Becca quietly joined me and placed her hand in mine.

"Oh, Aaron, you were such an adorable baby, um, David, too," she said, lifting some of the photos for a closer look.

"Yeah, thanks," I said, still looking at the closet. "Umm, Becca, I'm going to need you to help pick out clothes for them. I just remembered I have to bring them to the funeral director."

"Of course, no problem. We can do it in the morning, okay?" She gently closed the closet door.

It was a little weird for us to be in that room together, but everything felt odd now. We moved to Carolyn's room, and I put her jewelry in her bureau drawer. She no longer had a jewelry box here. Then we went into the room that I had shared with David.

I saw the F&M doll on David's bed and decided to take it to him, more for my sake than for his.

"I'll be right back." Ollie followed me downstairs to see if I was adding to his food. Just like their namesakes, Ollie had a white face with a black mustache and was tremendously overweight, and Stan was thin and beige colored; we thought he was part Siamese.

I tiptoed into the guest room and put the doll on the pillow next to David. I thought it might make him smile when he woke up. He hadn't been smiling since the accident, and his smile was something that had almost always been there. I understood, but it added to my anxieties, which were growing each day as the funeral approached.

I felt jittery and popped one of the Xanax that the doctor prescribed "just in case you need something when things get too stressful." Becca's suitcase was on the wicker chest my mother kept her pocketbooks in, and her nightgown and toiletries were on top.

"I'm going to use the bathroom for a few minutes," she said.

In about fifteen minutes Becca came out wearing a thin

pink F&M nightshirt. I was already under the covers, on Mom's side—I don't know why—just wearing my briefs. My mind raced despite the tranquilizer. I waited for her to get under the covers with me before turning off the lamp. We reached for one another in the dark, and she snuggled into my arms. I smelled the kiwi shampoo she had used that morning. I brushed her hair off her face and found that her cheek was wet with tears. Immediately, my own eyes filled up again. Occasionally, we'd wipe our faces with the Jackson Pollack quilt. We held each other close and let the tears fall until out of sheer exhaustion she fell asleep. Stan curled up at Becca's feet, and Ollie slept at mine.

After about an hour of trying to sleep, I still couldn't turn off all my worries, and so very slowly I rolled over and out from under the covers and grabbed Mom's book light. I'd been in this room a million times, but I'd never seen the things they kept inside their furniture. I figured I might as well check it out. Moving as quietly as I could so as not to disturb Becca, first I brought the book light over to Dad's chest of drawers. In the bottom drawer he had some mementos beneath his sweats: a NYSSMA medal he'd won in the sixth grade for the French horn, a law review article with his byline, and the box from the wedding band he had never removed in thirty-one years. I retrieved the ring from the top drawer and put it in the box in the bottom, covering it with his NYU sweatshirt.

Mom's nightstand was pretty messy. Mom kept the surface of the home as neat as she could, and hid most of the clutter on the main floors. Bedrooms were harder for her to keep neat.

I started with the bottom drawer and saw that pushed against the side, away from two boxes with her elite collections of her very favorites of the trinkets and things we kids had made, was a large manila envelope. I took the envelope and the book light and went next door to my room. Ollie followed me. He was making sure he would not be forgotten again.

Inside the envelope was one of those blank books—a journal. Light blue lined pages between a burgundy leather cover. I began to read and saw that the first entry she had written was about when she found out she was pregnant with us. There was an inscription on the inside cover:

Dearest Laurel, Use this journal to report on your new adventure carrying and raising twins. We wish all of you the best of health and happiness, and hope you will have lots of fun stories to fill these pages.

Love, Bea and Fred.

I scanned the entries until I came to the one that told the story of when we were born. It was evidently written with a shaky hand. I read:

I was so determined to get those kids out of me the first baby emerged with only two powerful pushes, and just as we had hoped for, we heard, It's a boy! Four minutes later, our second son was born. Wow, I thought, we are set, a girl and two boys. I was ecstatic. The nurse handed me my firstborn twin, and he latched on to nurse immediately. I cradled him in my arms and ordered Jonathan to go make sure our second son was okay. I was worried that he was too quiet. Jonathan kissed the baby and me and gently shoved his way into what had become a huddle of medical people surrounding our tiny baby.

How is he? What's the matter? Jonathan asked.

Our doctor stepped out of the huddle and put her arm around his shoulder. I couldn't hear them. Then I heard Jonathan; he sounded upset.

However what? What are you not saying about him? Jonathan had taken a quick inventory of the baby; he looked a bit lethargic but he had ten fingers and toes, a penis, and arms and legs that seemed to be in working condition. He even had the same blonde curly hair as his brother and sister. There was no bleeding, no cleft palate or clubfoot. But the doctors were all scrutinizing him. Jonathan told me later it was like they were treating him as if he was made of glass and he was about to shatter.

Very quietly, the doctor answered him. All I heard her say was, I'm sorry. Do you want me to tell your wife?

Jonathan shook his head. I was nursing the baby, feeling joy and terror simultaneously.

Then she picked up the tiny baby and put him in Jonathan's arms.

Here's our little guy, Jonathan said as he brought him to me. Laurel, the doctor says he's doing fine, but, but...

But what? I was starting to panic. I tried to sit up but I couldn't without disturbing the first baby's nursing.

Then Jonathan just broke down, still holding onto the baby. I was shocked as I saw Jonathan cry for the first time, heard his voice tremble, and then was completely stunned when he said the next words, He has Down syndrome. He's retarded.

That can't be! Doctor Winiker, why is he saying that? I asked.

She said she was sorry, but it was true. They were going to do a genetic test, but he has the telltale characteristics. See his palm here. She gently unfolded his tiny fingers to reveal his hand to us. Nothing is more heart grabbing than a newborn's hand. Jonathan held him a little tighter. We felt so inadequate and powerless.

Look at how he has one line that goes across his hand horizontally, and just one curved line underneath it, she said. Then she took hold of the first twin's little hand, which was grasping my hospital gown as he continued to suckle.

This baby's palm has three creases in it, just as yours and mine do, she said. We both unclenched the fists we had made instinctively in self-defense and stared at our own palms. How could a wrinkle in your hand make such a tremendous difference? We couldn't deny it though; this child's palms were different than his twin's and different than our own. We stared and stared at the baby's palm, but wishing as hard as we could, we could not make another crease appear. We looked to see if his eyes had a different shape, but they were closed.

Dr. Winiker gave us some time and then asked if I still wanted to have my tubes tied.

I looked at the baby and asked, Are you sure he is healthy?

She assured us he was, that he had a high Apgar score for a Down's baby. She even predicted he would be at the higher-functioning range.

Then yes. I looked at Jonathan who nodded his agreement.

Three is our lucky number, Doctor. I still want you to tie my tubes. I had not yet cried.

As I held him in my arms, I made a decision. This one is David, I said, and his brother is Aaron. This baby was ours, disabled or not, and I loved him already.

We'd chosen David and Aaron for two boys. I wanted our smaller, more fragile son to have the name that meant "beloved." Jonathan just nodded again.

Gently, I removed Aaron from my breast and handed him to Jonathan, who placed David in my arms. With a little struggle, I got him to latch on. I held him close to me, and then I allowed my tears to fall.

Staring at the pages that were now damp from my own tears, my mother's words confirmed what I had known all along. Down syndrome hadn't made my parents love David any less; it had made them love him more. My parents had ten years with Carolyn before fertility treatments helped them conceive us. How the hell was I going to replace them?

I then went downstairs to Dad's computer. Why Aaron? What did my name mean? I looked it up on the Internet and saw that it came from the Hebrew translation. Mountain of strength. Yeah, that was me. A small ironic laugh escaped me. Just to be sure I was up to it all, I popped another Xanax.

• • •

I started asking my parents more questions when I was about ten. I found some advertising awards Mom had won under a pile of books in the basement and took them to show her. Both of them had been successful with their careers, Dad had told me. Mom had a great job as an advertising account manager at Goren and Shafer, and he was then a junior partner at a corporate law firm, just two years from being considered for full partner when we were born. Her firm had generously doubled her paid eight weeks of maternity leave because she was having twins, and so she could stay home for four months on her full salary.

Dad told me that after we were born, Mom put all the energy she had previously used on getting ahead in her career to helping David reach his potential. She joined a local chapter of the Association for Children with Down Syndrome (ACDS) and learned everything she could about how the one extra chromosome would affect David's life.

Although we were fraternal twins, we looked very much alike, with our curly blonde hair and pudgy cheeks. Bundled up in our double stroller, we stopped pedestrian traffic as unknown admirers strained to see the twins, smiling at the pretty mom proudly parading her sons through the streets and parks. Long before her maternity leave was over, Mom decided she was not going back to work.

Dad admitted to me when I was in high school that when we first came home from the hospital, he often heard Mom crying or moaning in the few hours of sleep she got at night. He stayed home for the first two weeks, cuddling us, changing us, feeding us, and doing everything he could to try and ease his wife's pain. He tried to put his own pain about David's future aside.

When I was seventeen, I was reading the Ann Landers advice column in the paper, and I came across an essay written by the mother of a son with Down syndrome. Ann had thought it was worth reprinting it in its entirety. I showed it to my Mom, and she cried when she read it, and then she hugged me. The author was Emily Perl Kingsley, whose son Jason was born with Down syndrome. It was called "Welcome to Holland." Jason later became an actor.

She compared having a child like her son Jason to planning a trip to Italy, but somehow there is a mix-up and you arrive in Holland. Everyone who plans a baby expects to land in Italy, she says, the most beautiful country you could imagine with incredible sights to see. But suddenly your child is born with a condition that will limit him for his whole life. You selected Italy, but instead you got Holland. This just can't be right, you think. I wanted Italy, I bought my tickets to Italy, why am I here now? However, Kingsley ends on a positive note, all the while acknowledging the loss you feel when you land in Holland.

"But, if you spend your life mourning the fact that you didn't get to Italy, you may never be free to enjoy the very special, the very lovely things about Holland."

Mom had made the most of her trip to Holland.

• • •

Grandma Bea and Grandpa Fred both died when we were sixteen, so our family had significantly shrunk in the past six years. After years of traveling, helping to care for David and me, and loving one another with abandon, they had moved to a retirement community. It was that ubiquitous golfing at their new condo townhouse on the green that took them from us. Out on the course, Grandma Bea was struck in the head by an errant golf ball that burst a long-silent aneurysm in her brain. Grandpa Fred, rushing to get the cart back to Grandma, skidded along one of the many hills on the course in the golf cart, rolling over several times. His panic triggered a massive heart attack, and by the time the ambulance arrived, both had gone together. It was such a ridiculous set of circumstances that mourning their loss was hard to do without cracking a smile as we pictured the event. We missed them terribly. I wished they could have been here to see their great grandchildren.

chapter eight:
david

I WOKE UP in the guest room, and at first I wasn't remembering it all. It hurt going home in the backseat of the car, even with my leg wrapped in blankets. Ari is a good driver, but I didn't feel safe anymore. Now I'm in the guest room. I can't go upstairs. I feel like I'm still dreaming. *Is this real?* We were so happy on our way to see Ari graduate.

Looking out the window, unable to get out of bed, I played my secret game with myself. It's just something retarded people do. Mom hates that word. She says I have dee-velop-metal disability. But most people say retarded when teachers or mothers aren't around. Once when we were younger, I stepped on a project that Ari was making for school, and he got so mad he called me a retard! Mom slapped him across the mouth. It was loud. I don't know who cried the most, Mom, Ari, or me.

Anyway, it was all clouds that I could make into different shapes in my head. It probably sounds *stupid*—that's a word my Mom hates, too—but the clouds had some great shapes. I saw a giant sea turtle that looked like a T-Rex dinosaur was chasing. Then I saw a polar bear swimming to reach for an iceberg. It's just silly stuff I do, but it helped keep me from thinking about the accident for a little while.

No sounds were from upstairs, so I waited to blow the kazoo. I can't help thinking about going to the prom with Isabella. She is so nice and pretty, and she makes me feel all tingly when we hold hands. But now I won't be able to dance with her. Maybe she won't want to go with me. Mom said we had four more weeks of school and then the prom and graduation. Now someone else will have to hold the prom send-off party. Maybe Isabella's parents.

Mom and Dad always said I was brave not to let other people upset me if they talked different to me, or when people would look at me and decide things for me without asking, as if I wasn't even there or I couldn't answer their questions. I just didn't want to be trouble. Well, I know there are a lot of things I can do. But I don't know if I can do this. Aaron said there would be a wake and then a funeral. I'm scared. I wouldn't go to Grandma Bea's and Grandpa Fred's funeral. But Ari says I have to go. He said, "You don't want to be disrespectable." He said it's okay to cry. I'll just have to trust Ari and do what he does. He'll take care of everything. He's so smart. Not like me. Then I crossed my fingers for luck and blew on my kazoo, and it all started. It hurt worse than my leg.

chapter nine:
aaron

AFTER GETTING DAVID breakfast and helping him get washed and dressed, we delivered the clothing to Dulton's. Fortunately, there were still some clothes for Carolyn in her closet. We also had an appointment with Mitchell Gerwin to go over my parents' estate. I thought that could have waited, but Mitchell kind of insisted. That meant going into the city. We had to take the Long Island Railroad (LIRR) from Westbury to get to New York's Penn Station on time for our eleven-thirty meeting. Elaine Stillman came over and stayed with David. We even had the horror of changing at Jamaica—something no one from Long Island ever wants to do—but we made it in time. The secretary hurried over to make sure we were comfortable.

"Can I get you some tea or coffee?"

Becca and I shook our heads. "No, thank you," I said.

"I'll just let Mr. Gerwin know you are here; it'll just be a minute," she said, hurrying away as if tragedy was contagious.

We sat in two of ten upholstered chairs that circled the gigantic conference table and couldn't help but sway a bit in the chairs that both swiveled and were on wheels.

Mitch Gerwin briskly entered wearing a blue suit with the standard white shirt and striped tie. I used to tease my Dad about that. I think it's all just to make you think the lawyers are smarter than you. We stood up and made awkward introductions, even though I had met Mr. Gerwin several times before. He was carrying a brown oak-tag expanding folder labeled *LeShay*. I stared at the label. I was still hoping to wake up from this nightmare.

"First, let me say, Becca, it is nice to meet you, although the circumstances are certainly sad. I take it you two are quite close?" he asked, looking at me as if he could see through me.

"We were going to announce our engagement at the graduation dinner we had planned with our families," I said.

Becca ducked her hands under the table at that. She still didn't have the ring.

"Oh, I'm sorry that didn't occur." He paused in an effort to show his humanity. But with the exception of my father, I didn't really believe lawyers cared too much about the grief of their clients; grief was an everyday part of their job, although since he worked with Dad, he might have been sincere.

"These wills of your parents are pretty standard." He handed me a copy, which I shared with Becca. "In each of your parent's cases, their estate goes to their spouse. If the spouse predeceases him or her or dies at the same time, the money is split between their remaining children, with David's portion placed in a trust in your sister's hands, and should that not be possible, David's trust, and, as you are aware, his guardianship, is passed on to you, Aaron. I want you to understand that they had taken out the very highest insurance policies they could, and that along with a very good investment portfolio, plus mortgage insurance, you and David have quite an inheritance coming to you. Your parents were each insured for a million dollars and Carolyn for a half million; with that doubled because of the accident, that's five million for your brother and you."

I nodded. "That doesn't surprise me, I'm sure they wanted to make sure we had no financial burdens. I'll have to figure out something special someday to honor them with part of that insurance money."

I looked sideways at Becca, who appeared to be quite surprised by the large numbers Mr. Gerwin had just shared.

"Your parents also left a letter addressed to Carolyn, but under the circumstances, I believe we should consider it addressed to you, Aaron. Is that okay? Do you want Becca to remain here while I read it to you?"

I took Becca's hand in mine. "Yes, of course."

"This is what they wrote:

> *Our Dear Carolyn,*
>
> *If you are reading this, then we are both gone. We hope our passings weren't too much of a shock for you, and that you are not seeing this until you are older and married with a family of your own.*

Becca began to sniffle, and Mr. Gerwin handed her the box of tissues he kept handy. Lawyers were used to having people cry in their office.

> *We have thought long and hard about this, and as you know, we have discussed it with you many times since the time you turned 21 and you agreed with us each time. If we, Laurel and Jonathan LeShay, should both die, we appoint you legal guardian of your brother David. In the event that Aaron has turned 21 and he has agreed to be the secondary guardian, he will take your place if you cannot carry out this responsibility.*
>
> *It is our express wish that David is allowed to remain living at home with a relative and that he is not placed in a group home for adults with developmental disabilities. You have both agreed to this.*
>
> *We deeply appreciate your taking care of your brother and know that Aaron will also help in caring for David. We hope you will continue to cherish one another and be loving siblings to one another, in addition to the romantic loves we also hope each of you will find.*
>
> *All our love, Mom and Dad*

We let the words sink in.

"So now what happens?" Becca spoke first.

"Well, it is clear the LeShays did not foresee this particular scenario. No one ever does," said Gerwin. "Legally, the house and estate belong equally to Aaron and to David, with David's share placed in Aaron's fiduciary care. I have the papers to ensure this. It is clear that your parents would be fine with your living together in the house, but they understood the real possibility that you may choose to sell it. They expressed their wish for David to remain with a relative, which as far as I can tell would most likely be you, Aaron. Am I correct?"

"Yes, our grandparents are gone, and our parents were both only children. There is no one I would even consider. David is staying with me."

"Is that true, Mr. Gerwin? Does David have to stay with Aaron? Would we be in breach of the will if we found an appropriate group home for him?" Becca said.

"Well, it was their wish, but Aaron doesn't . . ." he started to say.

I jumped up and cut him off. I could feel my face turning red.

"I don't care about that, Becca," I admonished. "I care about David. I wish you wouldn't try thinking of ways to get rid of him!"

Becca started to cry harder. "Aaron, I'm so sorry. I didn't mean to—I just wanted to know." She stopped without finishing the sentence. "You're right, we'll be okay. I'm sorry."

I took a long drink of the cold water before me on the conference table.

"Are there any papers to sign now, Mr. Gerwin?"

"No, it's not necessary. We have to get the death certificates and take care of all insurance policies and bank accounts, and I believe your father kept a listing of all his assets with me. He may have updated it; I'll check on that, too." All the time he answered me, he kept his eyes on Becca.

"By next week I'll have this sent to probate, where you will officially be named by the court as guardian. I don't even think you have to appear in person, if you want to sign this document now." He slid a paper that was marked with an X where I should sign it. "Now, this is your chance to opt out if you feel you can't handle it. Aaron, are you sure you want to assume guardianship?"

"Yes, I am. David and I are the only family we have. I know I'm young, but I honestly wouldn't have it any other way. David is not as impaired as other people see him. Everything will be fine with us." I signed the document quickly and gave it right back to him.

"I'm sure you're right, Aaron, you're very capable. Your father was always so proud of you. He always told us stories about what a good brother you are to David."

"We're twins; we have a special bond. I remember when we learned the pledge of allegiance," I said, beginning to get choked up but forcing myself to finish what I had started to say, "and we learned the last line 'indivisible with liberty and justice for all,' someone in the class asked what that long word meant and the teacher said that it means it cannot be broken apart. David turned to me and said, 'Aaron, that's what we are, in-di-vis-ible,' and he was right. I am very grateful that he was able to survive that accident. If I had lost him too, I don't know what I would have done."

Mr. Gerwin looked at me with the kind of admiration usually reserved for heroes.

"Is there anything else? Is everything here okay?" I looked around and gestured with my hands to signify the office as a whole, not that I could do anything about it.

"Don't even think about us. Your father's work at the firm is all in order, and we have access to all the cases he was working on. He had planned to take vacation after . . ." he trailed off realizing what he was about to say. "You can go through his personal things next week or the week after, whenever."

"In that case, we'll get going. My neighbor is staying with David while we're here, and I don't want to be gone too long."

"I will see you at the service Monday."

I took Becca's hand once again as we left the office.

chapter ten:
aaron

SATURDAY WAS THE only time we had to try to relax and prepare ourselves for the next two days, the wake and then the funeral. My best friends from high school, Max and Shelby, came over that night with their six-month-old daughter, Zoey. David was already asleep. I was giving him a generous amount of painkillers for his leg, and they made him drowsy. We opened a bottle of wine and sat around the kitchen table. Shelby tried to amuse us with baby stories to cut the silence, but we couldn't listen to them. They left at about eleven, promising to see us the next day at Dulton's.

We slept late Sunday morning, none of us wanting to get up and face the business of the day. But eventually, I rolled myself out of bed, showered, dressed in a suit, and got David into his suit, too. We got to the funeral home at eleven-thirty. We snuck in the back door, but people were already lining up outside for the noon wake. Father Charles talked to us soothingly before we had to move into the room. I thanked God that we could not have open caskets; my family had been too badly hurt in the accident. I was keenly aware of David's every move, every twitch, afraid he would make a scene that would make us both have a complete meltdown.

At the doctor's suggestion, I gave David two Xanax before we got there, and Becca and I each took one, too. It looked like it was keeping David calm at first, but I don't think it did me any good. Everyone who approached us was crying, and each new burst of tears set my own deep grief in motion all over again. I didn't bother trying not to cry, but I tried to remain composed as much as possible. At first, I think David was too confused to react strongly. But when the men in black suits said it was time, we moved into the chapel, and he saw the three coffins, each with a picture of Mom, Dad or Carolyn, he finally truly understood.

"No, no, Ari, no!" Forgetting about his physical injuries, he tried to get up out of the wheelchair, but the pain in his leg and ribs made him fall back with a hard thud. I quickly wheeled him into the funeral director's office, and together Father Charles and I worked to calm him. Becca stayed behind, and she and the black suits were left to keep things going forward, steering mourners to take their seats, answering questions, and making excuses when people asked where David and I were.

"Listen, David," I said, as Father Charles caressed his arms and shoulders lightly, wary of causing him any pain. I knelt down to talk to him face to face. "This is the hardest thing we will ever go through in our lives. But it's you and me, Batman and Robin, and we have to be the bravest we've ever been. If you can't do this, you can stay here and take a nap. But I have to be in there to say goodbye to Mom and Dad and Carolyn. I know they would be so proud of you if you came with me. It's okay to cry. Try not to look at the caskets. But please don't yell, David, because it won't bring them back to us and will just make it worse. Do you want to come with me and let all those people know how brave you are and how much we both loved them? It's your choice, but please, please, you can't make a scene." I was shaking, but I looked David directly in the eyes.

David wiped his face with his sleeve, and the Father handed him a new box of tissues. "Here, David, you hold these for you and Aaron and Becca. It really is okay to cry. Crying doesn't mean you aren't being brave. Losing your parents and sister is very, very sad, and everyone understands."

David nodded, "Take me with you, Batman," he said.

For the rest of that long, torturous day, David stayed in his wheelchair with his back to the caskets. He shook hands weakly with everyone in the never-ending line and kept saying, "Thanks for coming." He seemed to have placed himself somewhere very far off.

• • •

The next day was the funeral Mass. I barely recognized the church we'd been to almost every Sunday all our lives. The church service and the burial that followed were packed with people both out of sympathy, and I had to face it, curiosity. There were so many flowers, we couldn't fit them all in the church. I asked Father Charles to have most of them sent to Winthrop Hospital after the service. For about an hour we waited inside as hoards of people kept arriving by the carful and others walked from all corners of the neighborhood. This was the biggest show in town, and no one was missing it.

After the cemetery we went back to the church where they held a potluck dinner for us, and everyone brought even more casseroles. Isabella and her parents were there. For some reason I had assumed she had Down syndrome, but she didn't. She had suffered brain damage as a toddler, but at first sight she looked like a pretty girl, no different than the typical twenty-one year old. Like David, she was high functioning, and from talking to her I got the impression she had about the same intelligence level as David, which was comparable to a nine-year-old child, and an IQ of approximately sixty-five.

Inevitably, the gathering took on the feel of a social occasion as the combination of people who hadn't seen one another in a long time, good home-cooked food, and wine was a powerful one that resulted in sharing family news, gossip, and even the telling of a joke or two between hugging David and me and saying how sorry they were. "A tremendous loss" was probably the most-used platitude. They also shared memories of my family.

"Your parents were absolute saints," said fat Mrs. Merkel, whose hair I had never seen without curlers before, and whose skin always had these big pink blotches. She lived two doors down, and the only thing I had ever seen her wear was what Mom called a housedress. Today she was dressed in her funeral best. "I never once heard them complain that things were too difficult at home," she said.

Fearing she would say something to upset David, I cut her off quickly. "Now Mrs. Merkel, I'm sure we were just as much trouble as any set of twins, but my parents were very easygoing. They rolled with the punches and taught us how to do the same."

"Oh, bless your heart," she whispered. "But what will become of your brother?"

"Mrs. Merkel, thanks for your concern, but David and I are going to be okay. We're going to take care of each other; we'll be fine."

Becca tried to cut off the next blubbering woman who looked as if she would start on the same theme, but it wasn't that easy. After deflecting several well-meaning questions about what to do about David, I grabbed hold of his wheelchair and guided Becca away from the crowd. David, for his part, was sitting in a near zombie-like state. He didn't even want to eat.

"Becca, I hope you're not letting these people get you upset," I said.

"Me? It's you I'm worried about."

"I mean all this talk about the David problem, I'll handle it, I've been doing it all my life, and with you helping . . ."

"Well, you have me, you can count on that," Becca said. "Now I think we can start easing our way out of here; it's been a long day."

chapter eleven:
david

I NEVER SAW so many dressed up people crying. I didn't know everyone, but Ari warned me. He said a lot of people would come to the funeral because it was for three people. My leg was hurting, so I sat in the wheelchair and Becca helped me. Isabella was there, and her parents stayed with her, looking very sad and worried. She said it was ok if we didn't dance at the prom if I would still go with her. I cheered up a little and said, "sure I would," and her mom promised we'd have a good time. I think she does like me a lot.

That funeral was terrible. Even the music was sad. I hated seeing the boxes again with Mom, Dad, and Carolyn. They had their pictures on top with them smiling and happy, and I didn't want to look, but Ari and Father Charles calmed me down, and I sat through the service.

After Mass a bunch of people besides Father Charles talked about Mom, Dad, and Carolyn. Mom's friend said how much she loved her family and never complained about life being unfair. Mr. Stillman said what a good friend Dad was and how much he loved his family. Carolyn's college roommate said she never would have passed half her classes without her, and that all the girls came to Carolyn for her to solve their problems. Aaron got up too, and he said thank you to everyone for coming and that he and I would take care of each other, with Becca's help. He was crying and that was all he could say, then Becca came up to the altar and held his hand and walked him back.

I saw Ari and Becca crying, and it made me cry more. I knew Ari will take good care of me, but would Becca really take care of him? Can she do that? Mom and Dad did so much, even I knew that. Suddenly, I had to talk, too.

"Father Charles," I called out. "I want to say something."

He rushed over to me and wheeled me up to the platform. "Here's the microphone, David, say whatever you feel."

"I just want to say my Mom and Dad and sister Carolyn was the best. They loved me, and I loved them. I'm lucky to still have my brother. We will stay together always. Thanks to everyone for being here. That's it, Father."

"If anyone hadn't shed a tear before, they certainly did at that," Ari said to me.

Ari told me that we was almost done, we just had to get through the burial and then go back to the church for lunch.

"You're doing great," he told me. "Now just pay attention and act respectful." He was already taking Dad's place and watching how I behave. But this was different. I tried to make him proud of me. Ari explained earlier that people would be watching us to see if we are ready to take care of ourselves, and that it's up to us to show them that we are.

At the cemetery we helped a little by tossing some dirt on the boxes. I tried hard not to think about my family inside them. Just before we left the cemetery, Becca and Ari had given me another little pill, and I think it maybe helped me get through the day.

chapter twelve:
aaron

JUST AS WE turned to leave the potluck the churchwomen had made, I saw Colin. I had forgotten he was coming.

"Aaron, I've been looking for you," Colin said, taking me in his arms for a big hug. "I'm so glad I found you. Hello, Becca, I believe we met at school a few times," he said.

Becca said hello, shook his hand, and gave Colin her sweetest smile.

"David, how are you? I'm Colin. I'm so sorry for your loss. I met you once when you were visiting your brother at school. How are you feeling? You got pretty smashed up, I see." Colin knelt down to talk to David.

"Oh yeah, I remember you," said David. "Thanks for coming."

"Aaron, I'm at the Marriott. I'm there for the week to help you however I can."

I was a bit overwhelmed. "Are you sure that's okay with your family?"

"Absolutely, I'm on break for the summer, and my kids are still in school until the end of June. It was Abbey's idea. She wanted me to be here for you. What do you think?"

"I think you're amazing, Colin. Becca and I were just trying to make an exit. Why don't you meet us at the house in about an hour and a half? We've got plenty of food at the house, so don't feel you have to bring anything."

"That's fine. Is there anything I can do now?"

"Actually, you can grab our coats from Father Charles's office and let him know that we're very touched by all the sympathy, but we're exhausted and need to get home."

He soon returned with our coats, and we left by the side door. I got David settled in the backseat, and I think we were out of the parking lot before anyone noticed we were gone.

We rode in silence for about ten minutes, and then Becca said in a whisper, "Why him?"

"Why him, who?"

"Shh, lower your voice. Why did you ask Colin back to the house? Why didn't you ask that friend of yours from high school, Max, or why not Cal? Why Colin?" she said.

I hadn't planned on Colin's visit, but I tried to be honest. "Colin makes me feel safe. He helps me sort things out. Just seeing him helps, I guess."

"Oh, and you wouldn't say those things about me?"

"No, no, of course I would. It's just different. He's older, more experienced than we are, more like a father figure. Please, Becca, he's already coming. I didn't know you would object. Let's just get through today. I'm trying to appear so strong and mature so people think I can handle all this, but I feel like I'm drowning in quicksand. I would never have survived this far without you. I just think he'll help, too. Please don't be mad."

"I'm not mad," she said. "I'm sorry, Aaron, it's been a hard day for me too. I just don't know this guy like you do. I'm sure I'll like him."

• • •

Back in college, I didn't like the idea of going to a therapist at first. They always say that the key to therapy is the relationship you build with your therapist, and I found that hard to swallow. First of all, you pay for him to listen to you. Sure, it was free for me, but my tuition helped pay his salary. He was getting paid to listen to me. How can that be a meaningful relationship? I just didn't buy it. Myself, I was a business major. I believed in numbers and facts.

My freshman year RA sent me to Colin because I was drinking alone every Sunday night and he said it was getting out of control. I guess it was when you consider what happened the day he sent me.

That morning, about six weeks into my freshman fall semester, my clock radio went off so loud it almost blew me out of bed. I had about an hour to get to my nine o'clock class. Sitting up to shut off the radio gave me such a pounding headache, I shut my eyes and tried not to move at all. This was definitely my worst hangover yet. I considered skipping my first class, when my stomach growled and started to lurch. I had to get out of there fast. Tripping over a pile of dirty clothes on the floor, I made it to the bathroom just in time to get to the bowl and hurl. I could hear two guys talking about me. They obviously wanted me to hear them.

"Looks like LeShay partied a little too much," said Greg, one of the older students brushing his teeth at the sink.

"Some kids just can't hold their booze," Eric answered. "LeShay sure can't. It seems every Monday morning he looks like shit. I suppose it's my job to deal with him."

Emerging from the stall and wiping my face with a fistful of toilet paper, I spit a few more times and rinsed my mouth with water from the sink cupped in one hand, while I balanced precariously on shaky legs. I looked into the mirror. "Ugh, I look worse than I feel," I said.

"That's probably not saying much," said Greg.

That's when my RA Eric spoke up. He asked me to see him between classes this morning.

Eric and Greg left, and I managed to crawl into a shower and sober up. My T-shirt and pajama bottoms were on the floor, soaking up the shower run-off. I pulled on the soggy pants and slogged down the hall to my room. The door was locked.

Dreading how he'd react, I banged on the door and woke up my roommate, Mike.

"What the fuck, LeShay?" Mike said as he opened the door. "Next time I'm leaving you out there. I was asleep! I don't have class until noon!"

"Sorry, I ran out without my key."

Mike looked at me and saw that I was wet and shivering.

"You're a loser, LeShay," he said. "Get your act together already." Mike picked up one of my towels from the floor and threw it at me.

I knew better than to mess with Mike; he's a big guy with a quick temper, so I just dressed quietly. The small dorm room had no space for privacy: two beds, two dressers, two desks, each lined up against opposite beige plaster walls. Mike had some NASCAR posters on his side and a red carpet for his bare morning feet, but my wall was still blank. I just had a picture of my family on my desk. My head ached, but my embarrassment hurt more. I slunk off to class, very slowly pulling the door closed, glad that Mike had gone back to sleep.

The result of my meeting with Eric was an appointment with Colin that afternoon.

"Why do you think you've made it a habit to drink too much for the past several Sunday nights?" Colin asked me right off the bat.

"I don't know," I said. "I guess I get a little lonely on Sunday nights."

"Are you homesick? Miss your girlfriend at home? Having roommate problems?"

"Nah, I'm not going with anyone. I just feel like, um, I don't know. Yeah, I guess you could say I have some homesick issues."

"Do you mind telling me a little about your family?" he asked.

Grateful to get away from the drinking issue, I settled back and began to relax a little. My family was a topic I could talk about easily.

"Okay, what do you want to know?"

"Let's start with the basics. Parents married or divorced? Siblings? Where do you fit in the pecking order?"

I smiled at the last question, but answered them each in turn.

"My parents are very married, legitimately happy as far as I know. They met in college and got married right after graduation. My sister Carolyn was conceived on their honeymoon, or so the story goes. We didn't come along until ten years after her."

"We?"

"Yeah, I have a twin brother, David."

"Aha, the plot thickens," he said, trying to lighten the session with a detective impersonation, curling an imaginary mustache end. "Where is David now, is he here at F&M with you, or is he at another college?"

"My brother has Down syndrome." I waited a few seconds for that to sink in. "The politically correct way to describe him is a young man with developmental disabilities."

I could almost see the wheels spinning around in his head, probably searching his mind for all the psychological ramifications in such a situation, but he just nodded and went kind of classic Freudian for a moment there.

"I see," he said. All he lacked was the pipe.

But to be completely honest, Colin was cool. I couldn't help liking him. He had a good sense of humor, and it was his job to be encouraging, nonjudgmental, and reflective—all things good for the ego. He'd often just repeat what I was saying so that I could think about it more deeply. Sometimes just saying something out loud makes you realize it is a bad idea, or maybe a good one. He pointed out the obvious problems I was having, and that they weren't especially original. I was like many freshmen: On top of the game at home and then going off to college with high expectations and finding out I was just another face in the crowd.

Fortunately, F&M is a small school, so it wasn't a very big crowd. No, he wanted me to see that my family has left its legacy of always expecting the most from me, including my acceptance of sharing responsibility for David, even though we were technically the same age. Colin's plan was to examine it with therapy, like the degree on the wall said.

So I kept going to Colin every Monday for the next two years and did a lot of talking about feelings I had never voiced before. He usually kept the conversation focused on my family. His primary goal was to help me talk through how my childhood had been atypical because of my brother David.

I protested at first. "Honestly, Colin, I never felt abnormal. If anything, David's disability probably gave me a little too much self-confidence. Well, put it this way, when we played, I was always Batman and he was always Robin."

"And Batman was always kind to Robin. I don't remember him ever raising his voice in anger to the Boy Wonder, do you?"

"No, he was patient with him. I see what you're saying, that I was also patient with David. But Robin helped Batman, too."

When I visited Colin for the last time freshman year, he

was again encouraging to me. "You've grown so much this year, Aaron. I hope you have a great summer with your family. Do you think you'll want to continue our sessions in September?"

I thought about it for a moment. "Sure, Colin, let's go for it. I do always feel better after meeting with you, and hey, it's free. You have a good summer, too, and I'll see you in September."

As I left, I heard Colin humming that old song, *See You in September*. I guess I have to admit that we had developed a relationship, even if it started falsely. I was definitely willing to keep him in my life. *Maybe even after I graduate,* I thought.

Now he wanted to help me, not as a patient but as a friend.

• • •

So Colin followed us back to the house after the funeral. David went right to sleep, and Becca soon complained of a headache and went upstairs to lie down for a while. When she came back downstairs about nine-thirty, Colin and I were deep in conversation. I saw her starting to clean up and grabbed her hand, pulling her over to sit next to me.

"Colin, I don't think I could be sitting here now if it wasn't for this beautiful woman. They would have probably had to put me in the hospital, too. Here's to my Becca, beauty, brains, class, and kindness all in one woman." I lifted my wineglass and drained what little remained.

Becca took the glasses and the bottle away. "You're done with the wine for tonight, right, Aaron? It's getting late."

Colin turned to her. "Don't worry Becca, he's just destressing right now. He's promised not to make this a habit, in fact, before I leave, I'm going to clear out some of this liquor that people brought. Aaron's not an alcoholic, but he does tend to take comfort in the bottle, and he's agreed this house has much too much temptation at the moment."

Colin got up and put some bottles in a box he found on the floor. "I'll call you tomorrow," he said.

Becca and I stood and started cleaning up the rest of the room. It almost looked as if we'd had a party there, when the truth was we'd just been leaving things wherever they were.

Once I sobered up, I went upstairs, changed out of my suit, and slipped my hand into my Ninja Turtle box. It might not have been the magic moment I was waiting for, but Becca and I both needed something to lift our moods. Then I heard the blast of the kazoo.

"Ari, Ari help me!"

"I'll be right there."

I tended to David's needs, bringing him a fresh bottle of water and some cookies after helping him to the guest bathroom.

"Now try to get some sleep," I said as I closed David's door. "I need to talk to Becca now; don't call for me unless you are really in trouble, okay? I'm not kidding."

With David taken care of for the night, we hoped, it was the first time that whole day we had been alone. Becca was rinsing out glasses in the kitchen, and I led her into the family room so that David couldn't hear us. We sunk down into the overstuffed burgundy leather love seat. Both of us immediately kicked off our shoes and put our feet up on the coffee table. She rested hers on top of mine.

"Did I thank you for everything you did for us today?" I said, wrapping my arm around Becca and helping her settle into a comfortable position with her head on my chest.

"I think you might have," she said.

"You were incredible. I kept thinking how lucky I was to have you with me and how you made even this possible for me to get through."

"I'm glad you feel that way, Aaron," she barely whispered. I felt her body tense up as if she was expecting something. I think she read my mind.

I pulled the ring box out of my pocket, but I felt if I kneeled, she'd have to pull me up. I hoped she would forgive me for that.

"Becca, I love you and I want to marry you and be with you for the rest of my life. Things aren't going to be quite what I thought. David will be a part of our family, but I hope that doesn't scare you off. It will take time, but you'll come to love him, too. I'm sure of it."

I placed the closed velvet box in her hand and squeezed her hand lovingly. I didn't open the box, like in the movies. "Don't open this until you give me your answer, think about this, it's not what we planned," I said. I didn't want her to be influenced by the diamond.

"Aaron, you're the man I want to spend my life with. We're a perfect fit. And it's impossible not to love David, too; he adores you, he needs us, and yes, all our lives have been radically, forever changed. But the way I love you hasn't changed. I want to wear this ring now and always and be your wife. Yes, of course I will marry you."

Slowly, she opened the box and gazed at the sparkling diamond. I knew it was just what she wanted, an emerald cut with tiny chips down the sides. Not too big, not too small, maybe altogether a carat and a half. I had taken her friend with me to pick it out, just to be sure.

I took the ring out of the box and placed it on her left ring finger. I pushed the ring to the end of her finger.

"Oh, Aaron, I'm so excited we're finally getting engaged. When I saw the box I was jumping up and down and screaming inside my head, 'the ring, he's giving me the ring.'"

"I lied," I said. "I don't think I could have gone on if you hadn't said yes."

chapter thirteen:
aaron

THE NEXT MORNING Becca politely requested the pleasure of our absence saying she wanted to do some things around the house—and no, she didn't want my help this time. She also wanted to get started on her grad school applications, since she knew we were going to stay in New York for now.

I called Colin and asked him if he wanted to come with David and me for breakfast and then help us pick out his tuxedo for his prom. I wanted to cheer David up and show him that our lives would go on. After that, we could go see a guy movie, one Becca would be very glad to miss. I'd pick him up at the hotel.

I chose Thomas's Diner because it is an awesome place that only the locals really know about, and they make the best breakfasts in the world. It's one of those railroad car diners that looked like an aluminum RV. It looks pretty dingy, but it's as efficient as Santa's workshop and produces food like you wished your mother could make. People are in and out constantly all day, but instead of complaining about the wait, people stand patiently outside on cement steps pitted with erosion, ignoring the traffic going by on Old Country Road and blithely inhaling the carbon monoxide. Sooner than you would expect, your name is called.

In a few minutes we were sharing side orders of bacon and fries and stuffing our faces, barely speaking to each other except for the occasional "pass the syrup." Colin was so absorbed in eating he didn't try to get me to unload on him. We left with our bellies filled to satisfaction.

Next we went to Mr. Formal to rent David a black tux with a pink tie and a gray and pink paisley vest to match Isabella's dress. Isabella had been very clear that he was to get the right color tie and vest for the prom, and he was so thrilled we all got a little overzealous. The tailor was professional, but I recognized the look on his face when he saw David, and his cast. He looked perturbed, but I honestly didn't care. Nothing could hold back our excitement. I only wished Mom could see David. If I let myself stay in the moment, the whole catastrophe of the past week seemed like a bad dream.

After the movie, I turned to Colin. "This was a great day. Thanks for coming"

"I was hoping we'd get more of a chance to talk. I think I've let you down."

"Not one bit. It was a good break from all we've been doing, an escape, really. We don't need to talk about everything. Nothing can change what has happened. And I promise, if I do need to talk, I'll call."

Wednesday, we had an appointment at David's school for his transition meeting, and I was beginning to feel like we were a trio, a family who could do this. Colin had called at the last minute, and he offered to meet us there. I was glad to have his input. But when I told Becca, she was not happy.

"Hasn't he spent enough time with us? When is he going back to Lancaster?"

Determined not to let it get to me, when I saw him walking towards us, I just walked up to greet him and left Becca to take care of David, pushing him in his wheelchair. I told Colin I had given Becca the ring, and he went running back to her, asking if he could kiss the bride. David still didn't know anything about it. Becca showed David the ring and told him I had proposed the night before.

I could see David was hurt that this was the first he was hearing of it. There really was no time for us to have a big heart to heart now, so we went into the meeting.

Miss Ferguson was not very professional. She broke into

tears when she saw us, even though she had come to the funeral and had done enough crying then. Then Colin came up with some therapeutic words of solace, and eventually we were able to carry on with the meeting. Bottom line, David was going to work as one of those grocery baggers at Waldbaum's Supermarket and his prom date, Isabella, was going to do that, too. He was thrilled when he heard that and wouldn't consider any other choice, so, meeting over. In fact, it was kind of cute. His eyes lit up, and he crossed his arms and said, "I want to work at Waldbaum's with Isabella. That's it. I am Done and Done. Decision made."

I remarked that we might be able to work out a carpool arrangement with Isabella's parents, the Romanos. David was also given permission to skip school, which ends in two and a half weeks. We would return for graduation.

Before we got to our cars, Becca pulled me close to her.

"Please," she whispered in my ear, "do not ask Colin to come back to the house. If he offers, tell him we have things we have to take care of."

"But he came all the way here from . . ."

"Aaron, please, it's enough already with him, just say goodbye and thanks."

A few minutes later, I shook Colin's hand. "Thanks for coming, we're going to head home now and have a little family meeting. Have a good night."

Colin got the message. "Well, I'll be leaving in the morning. I'll check in with you tomorrow, okay?"

"Sure," I said. "Talk to you then."

The ride home was a bit chilly, and I don't mean the temperature.

David wheeled over to the phone and called Isabella as soon as we got home. From his side of the conversation I could tell she was just as happy as he was that they would be working together. Becca and I had moved to the living room couch and called him in when we heard the phone call end.

"Hey, David, can you make it in here, or do you want me to come help you?" I called to him.

Holding on to furniture, David made it to the living room and sat down on the recliner. I jumped up and adjusted the chair for him so he could keep his leg up.

"Okay, guys, I think it's time for a family meeting," I started.

"Like we had with Mom and Dad."

"Exactly like that, David. Give me a few minutes to make sure we're all on the same page."

"What are we reading?"

I tried to stifle a laugh, and Becca tried not to crack a smile.

"Nothing, David, it's just an expression. It's time for you to listen."

"What about Becca, does she get to talk?"

Now David was just goading me in his pretend innocent way, so I did what worked best and ignored him.

"Today was a good day for you, David. You have a new job to look forward to when you are all healed."

"And you and Becca are getting married, don't forget that."

I hesitated a moment and then asked, "David, are you upset about that? We had planned to get married before the accident. Last night was really the first time we had alone together in all the time since then."

"Well," David said slowly, "I sorta feel in the way. You used to tell me your secrets."

"You're not in the way," Becca and I said at almost exactly the same time; then we looked at each other and had to laugh.

"David, I think there is one really important thing I forgot to tell you," I said.

"More important than you are getting married?"

"Yes, even that. I don't think I ever took the time to tell you how grateful I am that you lived through the accident. You're my twin brother, and I don't think I could have survived if you hadn't. I think I've been so busy taking care of all this horrible business of funerals and wills and hospitals that I didn't have time to tell you. I can see why you felt in the way. Becca and I were doing a lot of things without including you. But you've had a job to do, too, and that's to heal, do you understand that?"

David said nothing.

"And another thing, David," I said. "If you were in the way, then Becca and I might not be getting married. But we both love you, and together we'll be a family."

"But if you get married, you could have a baby. Then what about me?"

"David, Becca and I don't plan on having any babies for years. And when we do, guess what?"

"What?"

"You'll be an uncle. Uncle David."

"Uncle David. I like the sound of that. And if Isabella and I get married, you'll be Uncle Aaron."

"Whoa, pardner," I said. "You and Isabella just started dating. Becca and I have been a couple for a very long time."

"How long?"

"Um, at least two and a half years, right, Becca?"

"That's right, and we still have the wedding to plan, but when we do have it, guess what, we're all going on a plane to California."

"California? When did we decide that?" I asked.

"I talked to my mother this morning. It only makes sense. We don't have the time to do everything, and she does. She promised to find a place as soon as we pick a date. I figured you and I could have a party for our East Coast friends when we get back."

"Oh, I didn't know you had it all planned."

"Well, you're a guy. Girls start planning these things when we're twelve."

"Oh, yeah, right," I said. "I should have known. Anyway, David, getting engaged is very serious. You and Isabella will have a great time at the prom, but it's way too early to even think about marriage, okay?"

"Besides," Becca said. "You're not ready to settle down. Statistics show people hardly ever marry their prom date."

David looked up at us with an expression that was new even to me. "You know, people like Isabella and me can get married, too. I read it in one of Mom's magazines from the 'sociation. And Becca, I don't know about 'tistics, but Mom told me I have my own path to follow. I think that means I might do things different than you guys."

I sat back on the couch. I had to choose my next words carefully.

"You're right, David," I said. "Someday you may get married. But, as you just said, there are differences between even us twins. So Robin, don't try too hard to do everything Batman does. You will go at your pace and I'll go at mine, and we'll always have each other's backs. Now we have Becca, too, and I promise that's a good thing."

"Becca?" David asked, "Will you be our Batgirl?

"Is it okay if I'm Batwoman?" she asked.

"Absotively!" said David.

"I hereby swear you in as Batwoman!" I said.

I picked up my soda glass to raise a toast, and David and Becca followed suit. We clinked glasses, and I proclaimed, "Here's to the Bat Team! Now that concludes this family meeting. Who wants to eat some more casseroles?"

chapter fourteen:
aaron

AFTER WE'D ALL nuked our food for dinner, I couldn't wait any longer to talk to Becca. David was looking through a magazine, we went into the family room, and I kept my voice low, hoping he wasn't listening.

"A California wedding? That's what you really want?" I asked.

"Why are you so surprised? It's traditional for the wedding to be hosted by the bride's parents and held near her home. It's been done that way for centuries."

"I guess I'm lacking in my knowledge of wedding etiquette. Umm, did you and your mother pick a date by any chance?"

"No silly, I want to decide that with you." She found my leg under the table and rubbed her foot along it teasingly. "I did ask her to find out when the venues she likes best are available, but I said we hadn't decided anything. I told her not before the spring, maybe March or April. What were you thinking?"

Shit. I hadn't given any thought at all to a date for the wedding, not before the accident or since. I was just concentrating on getting the ring and becoming engaged. I wish I'd talked to my parents when I'd had the chance. It never occurred to me that Becca would expect to take the next step so soon. I was so naïve. I thought I was giving the woman I loved a ring to ensure the *future*. A vision of overly opulent weddings flashed through my mind at lightning speed. Becca was waiting for me to say something, and she would definitely not like a flippant answer.

"I can't say I had any date in mind, Becca. I kind of expected my parents to be helping us plan it, too." That was a good way to stall, good answer, Aaron, I told myself. I absolutely wanted to marry Becca, but I needed some time before our lives became all about the wedding. I'd heard from some older friends that's what always happens.

"I know, and it's horrible that your parents aren't here, but what can we do? We don't have to have it in the spring. Would you rather wait until the summer, maybe a June wedding? That's a whole year from now."

I had nothing. She had been planning a wedding that soon all along, and I had no good reason to object.

"Yeah, I think I'd like to wait at least until June. Out of respect for my family we should wait a full year until we make such a big celebration. I'm grieving, how can I plan a happy event now?" Yes, waiting a year was the answer.

Becca threw her arms around my neck and kissed me.

"You're right, summer of next year will be the right time. I'll tell my mother to look for summer dates. Do you have a special one that's important do you? Do you want it on or near your birthday, July 10th? We could see if that's a Saturday. I only want a Saturday night. That's the most fun. And don't worry about the planning, Mom and I will do most of it."

"The one date I don't want is July 10th. Let's have it at least two weeks away from *our* birthday," I said, nodding my head in David's direction. I wasn't going to take over David's birthday and make it my wedding anniversary.

"Oh, gotcha," Becca winked at me. "I'll tell Mom." Then she raised her voice back to normal volume and said, "Hey David, how's that lasagna Mrs. Romano made?"

David had gone into the kitchen and was busy polishing off his dinner. I don't know how much attention he'd been paying to Becca and me. You never do know with him just how much he is listening or what he understands. Sometimes he butts into your conversation, and other times I think he just eavesdrops with no comment.

"It's great! Isabella's mom is a really good cook. She's Italian, she cooks all the time."

"Well, save me some, brother," I said, and without waiting for an answer scooped some off his plate and shoved it in my mouth. "Oh, you're right. This is some good Italian cooking. I definitely approve of your girlfriend's mother."

In the morning, after getting dressed, I went in the guest room at 8:20 to get David ready. I sat down next to him and tapped him lightly on his shoulder.

"Wake up, David, time to get up."

"What? I sleeping. Go away, Ari." David struck out with his left arm to try to push me off the bed, just missing my right eye.

"Sorry, David, but you have to go to the doctor. He needs to see how your leg is healing. He might even be able to give you a different cast. C'mon, get up."

David pulled the blanket up over his head and tried to burrow into the mattress, but that hurt his ribs.

"Owww, Aaron, I hurt all over, leave me alone."

"We can stop at Dunkin Donuts on the way there if you don't take too long."

"Don't want a donut."

"Look, we have no choice. We have to go." I removed David's pillow and blanket.

"Hey, that's not fair. Leave me alone! Don't wanna go!"

I sighed. It used to be Mom or Dad doing the coaxing, and I had the luxury of pulling the covers over my own head, turning over, and ignoring what was going on with them across the room.

"I know you don't want to go. I'd love to get back in bed myself, but we're going. Now stop fighting me, and I'll help you get dressed."

I helped him dress, ignoring his odd choices of clothing, and took him to the bathroom, but David was pulling his silent anger thing and wouldn't talk or answer any of my questions with more than a grunt, pulling away whenever he could manage it.

I was sweating and cursing under my breath by the time I got David into the car. There was no time to eat if we were to make the morning appointment at the orthopedist. I got into the car and surreptitiously swallowed a Xanax.

"I don't know why you have to be so difficult, David. I thought you were more grown up than this."

"Oh, so you're all grown up and you tell me what to do? You're not Dad, you're still my brother!"

"Yes, David, I am still your brother. But Dad and Mom left me in charge since they can't be here for you. I'm your brother, but I'm also what's legally called your guardian."

"How can you be two people?" David asked.

"I'm just one person, but because you need help with a lot of things—you know that's true," I said loudly, cutting David off from protesting, "I'm the one who is going to take Mom and Dad's place in helping you. I'm not trying to be the boss of you, David, but there are some things that we have to do, like go to the doctor now whether we feel like it or not. If I have to push you, I will. But I wish you wouldn't fight me. I'm always looking out for you, aren't I?"

"Yeah, but I want Mom and Dad...and Carolyn, too."

"So do I, David, so do I."

We had made it to the doctor's office and had moved to the second waiting room for the orthopedist. I hated the amount of waiting you were forced into at every doctor's office. You always spend double or triple the time waiting than actually being examined. I wondered if this guy's name had influenced the specialty he had chosen, but he'd been highly recommended by our GP. Still, as big as he was, he looked more like an over-sized Willy Wonka than anyone who would tend to bones for both pleasure and profit. Standing six foot three inches and weighing about three hundred pounds, a good portion of it settling in his belly. Dr. Axe towered over David and me. His curly hair was dark brown sprinkled with gray, and a matching handlebar mustache curled at both sides reaching almost to his smiling eyes, below very thick, very expressive eyebrows. He was evidently someone who liked attention; he welcomed each new reaction he received with a knowing chuckle.

"Didn't expect to see the likes of me coming in here, did you?" he said to David, who made no attempt to hide his astonishment.

"Are you really the doctor?

"Sure, I'm Doctor Axe, and you must be David. I understand you have had quite a bad break in your leg. It's had almost three

weeks to heal in this concrete prison, how's about I take it off
and have a look?"

"You're going to take off my leg?" David gulped hard.

"Oh, that's a good one, Davey," he said. "No, I'm just going
to take off your cast."

"With a axe?"

"I should be able to, shouldn't I?" he said. "No, I've got this
special saw for that. It's going to sound very screechy, but I
promise it won't hurt you."

"Not now, I'm not ready."

"Well, what would make you ready?" the doctor asked.
"Would a cherry lollypop to suck on take your mind off it?"

David considered it. "Can my brother have one, too?"

Dr. Axe produced two red pops from a hidden candy jar,
and we unwrapped them and popped them in our mouths. He
directed me to stand at David's shoulders near the front of the
table, blocking him from seeing, and being prepared to hold him
down by the shoulders if necessary.

SCREEEEEEEEEEEEEEEEEEEEEeeeeeee. The drill went
straight up the cast the whole length of David's leg in one stroke.
David shut his eyes tight and put his fingers in his ears. The doctor
moved the drill over several inches, and without having David
move, he brought the drill SCREEEEEEEEEEEEEEEEEeeeeee
all the way back. With a quick pop of a tool he plucked off about
one third of the cast, leaving it open so that he could look inside
at the leg.

David tried to sit up so that he could see, too.

"Not so fast, Buddy, your leg is not looking its best. Are you
sure you want to see what's under that cast?" said Dr. Axe.

"Why?"

I was doing my own looking, and the next thing I remember
is Dr. Axe's nurse grabbing me and sitting me on a chair against
the wall. She had me put my head down between my knees and
handed me a napkin with some smelling salts. *This passing out
thing has got to stop,* I decided.

"Here, dear, we don't want to lose you. Just sit down and if
you feel faint, take a whiff of that napkin, okay?"

"Don't worry, either one of you. It looks much worse than it
is. It's definitely healing," said Dr. Axe. "Greta, would you help

with the X-ray?"

Wheeling the machine over to the table where David was flat on his back and not making a move, Dr. Axe put the X-ray above the leg and covered David's groin with a lead blanket. Then, the doctor told David to stay very still while they took some pictures of his leg and he and the nurse left the room.

When they ran quickly back into the room, David was beginning to get upset.

"Now what's happening? I saw that leg, it's all purple and wrinkly, and there's a big ugly line down the middle."

"Hey, Davey, no reason to get riled up. We're not done working on your leg. It's going to heal a lot more over time. I'll tell you what; I'm going to replace that big heavy cast with a smaller cast that goes from your foot only up to about three inches above your knee. We call that a walking cast, and with a cane, you may be able to do just that. Now what color would you like?"

"RED!" David declared.

"Um, David," I said, "maybe something a little more subtle would look better at the prom? Doctor, could you give him a black one?"

"Sure, sure, I didn't know you had a formal affair coming up," he said, going to the supply room to get the materials.

"But I like red best, Ari," David said.

"Ordinarily I would agree with you, but the prom is in just two weeks, and don't you think a black cast will blend in better with the tuxedo? Right? Isn't that important?"

"You're right! I didn't think of that! Thanks, Ari, I'm glad you said it. Isabella might not have liked the red one."

And another crisis averted.

David was fitted with a walking cast that had a rubber bumper on the bottom and left his toes sticking out, and a four-pronged cane. "Look, David, your cane has its own walker."David was almost able to walk out of the office without help. With practice, he would be able to put away the wheelchair except for long distances.

Before leaving the office, I took the doctor aside.

"Dr. Axe, could you give David a prescription for the tranquilizers they gave him at the hospital? He only has a few left, and it's hard to keep him calm with the leg and everything else."

"What is he taking?"

"Xanax .5, but I think he could use something stronger."

The doctor scribbled something quickly on his pad. "Here's a prescription for 1 mg Xanax. Don't let him take them regularly. Just give them to him when you feel he is really anxious and can't calm himself, and don't go over two a day. He could become dependent on them if you overdo it."

"Thanks Doctor, I'll be careful with them."

• • •

We got home around noon, and I was exhausted from dealing with a recalcitrant David all morning. Becca greeted us at the door, took one look at me, and insisted I take a nap. David quickly settled into his bed in the guest room to watch a video. I swallowed another Xanax and curled up on the living room couch. Ollie curled up beside my chest, and I gently stroked the cat, listening to his motorboat purr. All was right with Ollie's world. He had Stan and food and people to pet him. Soon, we were both snoring lightly.

This time it was Becca doing the waking up. "Aaron, it's two-fifteen, I think you had better wake up and have some lunch, or you'll be all off schedule and have trouble sleeping tonight."

I yawned ferociously, stretching my body so that my legs hung over the couch arm. I shook my head a few times to get the blood flowing there. "Okay, I'm up. Where is David?"

"Oh, he's already started eating lunch. I let him pick out what he wanted from our store of casseroles and just heated it up for him."

"Thanks so much. Becca. You didn't have to; I would have done it."

"Aaron, let's be realistic here. You are not going to do everything for David. I'm here, and I'm part of the family, too, right?"

"Of course."

"When it gets too hard for me, I'll let you know. Getting David lunch is not a problem. Now, you come have some lunch with me."

"Gee, I should sleep more often, good things can happen

while I'm asleep," I said.

We sat down and dug into some of the casseroles, taking turns using the microwave and enjoying the spoils that come with suffering such a great loss—the abundance of people bringing you good comfort food.

chapter fifteen: david

AARON AND BECCA helped me get ready for the prom. Becca even did my fingernails, making them look smooth and shiny, and she wrapped a pink ribbon all around my cane. She said it was "festive." They made my left pants leg fit on over my cast. Becca cut a black sock and sewed it to cover my toes. We had to be at Isabella's house at five-thirty, but I was ready by four. I didn't dare eat in that tux.

Aaron asked if I wanted to play some video games, and we played some of our old *Super Marios*. Then Becca took the controller from Aaron and was pretty good for a girl. Finally it was time to go.

We got to the send-off party first. Isabella looked beautiful. She said her pink dress was made of chiffon, and it floated around down to her ankles, puffing out in ripples like an angel's robe. The top had ruffles and no sleeves, just skinny little straps to show off her shoulders. I told her she looked like a real princess. In her high heels she was taller than me. Her mom kissed me, and her dad shook my hand and put his arm around me. They seemed glad to see me.

When all the parents and kids got there, I thought how my own parents should be there and started to feel shaky. My eyes were watering, so I told Isabella I had to go to the bathroom. Aaron was just coming out, and his eyes were red. Before he could say anything, I did start to cry, and he pulled me into the bathroom with him.

He held my arms and whispered.

"I know, David. This is hard, with all these parents here. Our parents should be here, too, and it sucks. But this is your big night. I know Mom and Dad and Carolyn are smiling down on you from heaven, so happy for you." Ari's voice broke, and he stopped to calm himself. "Did you see how bright the sun is now? That's gotta be them. But you have to put them out of your mind tonight for Isabella. You want to be a good date to her, right?"

I nodded and sniffled, and Ari handed me a tissue to blow my nose. "Yes. She looks like a princess, doesn't she?"

"Absotively. Tonight, she is a princess. So let's man up and smile. It's almost time to go off in the limo. How about we get a few more photos of the two of you?" Aaron said.

Once we got in the limo and waved goodbye, I felt better and started to have fun. Our group was at two tables, and even though most of us were paired up as dates, all the guys took turns dancing with all the girls. Most of us were together for all of school in the Special Ed class. Sometimes the other kids in normal classes picked on us, but we always stuck up for each other. The food at dinner was just okay, but we all kidded around and then told what we were planning to do next, after graduation.

After dessert, as we were beginning to yawn, there was an announcement.

"Grab your honey," the DJ said, "and hold her tight for the last dance of the prom. You are one great-looking class, so go out into the world and show them what you've got."

I pushed up off the table and held my hand out for Isabella. She did a little spin and landed flat up against me, and I did hold her close, not caring a bit about my ribs. We rocked back and forth to the music. I didn't need my cane with her, and my leg didn't hurt at all. Isabella put her arms up around my neck and rested her head on my chest and I felt like I had clouds circling my head. I think it's called *cloud nine*. I looked down at Isabella, and our eyes locked. I didn't plan it, and I don't think she did either, but our faces moved together and our lips touched. I never felt anything like that in my whole life.

Our lips moved and our tongues smooshed together, and we were kissing and kissing and I didn't want to stop. I was tingling all over, even down there. I think I forgot there was anyone else around, and that we were in the middle of a room full of people. When the music stopped, a teacher came over and held onto me while Isabella smiled up at me. I think she had that special feeling inside of her that I had. She kissed my cheek and said, "David, I'm so glad we're going to work together. I would miss you."

"Me, too," I said, and held her, wishing I would never have to let her go.

chapter sixteen:
aaron

DAVID'S GRADUATION WAS a week after his prom, and it was another event tough to get through without our parents.

The graduates were all on the stage, but I felt the stares and saw the fingers pointed at me by the other family members in the audience, and I was extremely self-conscious about being alone among all the parents and siblings gathered. Becca had stayed home with a headache. Our family was still a topic of community conversation.

David's class was the first graduates to walk across the stage and receive their diplomas. David still had his cast on and was using a cane. When he was called, there was an enormous response from the crowd, and he received a standing ovation. He grinned from ear to ear.

The principal stepped forward. I think it must have been impromptu.

"David, we are so happy to have you with us, and I am honored to present your diploma. As you can see, the whole school community is proud of you and wishes you well. Would you care to say anything?" He stuck the microphone in front of David.

"Thank you all, and thank you, Aaron."

As David made his way back to his seat, I felt many eyes upon me. My own were leaking tears. I was very proud and relieved that he had made it this far.

• • •

It was the first of July, my family had been wiped out eight weeks now, and it was time for David to get his cast removed.

Dr. Axe was ready for us with two red lollypops, and in one *screeeeeeeee* of the saw, the cast was off. The doctor wrapped his leg in a flexible Ace bandage to protect it. He prescribed five weeks of physical therapy so that David's leg would fully regain its strength. I counted in my head and realized that with my work's start date of August 1st, I'd have to ask Becca to take him to physical therapy for the last week. We walked out slowly, David still using his cane, once again bare of the pink ribbon, with a prescription to start the next day at a PT center about five miles away from home.

"Are you sure that doctor knew what he was doing? My leg still hurts," David said.

"That's what the physical therapy is going to fix; your leg is weak and they will help you strengthen it. They'll explain everything there, I'm sure. Just take it easy for the rest of the day, and I'll give you some Tylenol for the pain."

The next morning David got up and seemed like his old cheerful self.

"It felt better without the cast last night," he said. "Pretty soon I can move back into our room with you, right, Batman?"

Becca and I were comfortably settled into the master bedroom. I was very happy with David sleeping downstairs and did not want him next door to us. "Um, yeah, we'll see," I said, then quickly changed the topic.

I had passed the physical therapy center many times, but never really noticed it. Now I pulled into the parking lot and realized it was a booming business. We walked into the main room where patient-therapist teams were working on some intriguing looking equipment. A very large man was plunked behind a too-small desk. His badge read, "Tiny." David came up to the desk and handed him the prescription, David approaching Goliath.

Tiny stared at the prescription and then at the book. "Hmm,

four days a week for five weeks. It's best to stay with the same therapist."

I remained mute, no disagreements from me.

"Are you at all flexible with the time? Does it have to be the same time every day?" he asked.

"I guess not," David and I said at the same time.

"Okay, let me just talk to someone a minute. Why don't you men take a seat?"

Tiny was at least a head taller than my five-feet, eleven inches, and I'll bet he was heavier than David and me put together. His remarkable width was in the shoulders, not his stomach. He was built like a mafia bodyguard, and I wondered if this was just his day job.

"He's really big," David said, once Tiny had left the area. "I hope he's not my therapist; he'd snap my leg off."

Ha, David had made a good joke. "I see what you mean. He wouldn't be my first choice either."

Fortunately, when Tiny returned, he was with a petite young woman who was going to work with David.

She reached out her hand to David to shake. "G'day, David, I'm Jessie. I hope you're going to work hard to fix that leg of yours, mate."

David turned to me and whispered too loudly behind his hand, "She talks funny."

"I heard that, David. I do talk funny to you, I s'pose. I moved here from Australia to come to grad school about five years ago."

David loved maps, and he knew exactly how far away she had come from.

"And you're not going back? What about your parents? Don't they miss you? Both my parents and my sister died in the accident that hurt my leg. It's just my twin brother and me left."

"David, what did I tell you about asking people personal questions?" I said, giving him the look he knew well. "I'm sorry, Jessie, you have a charming accent."

"Hey, you go to my church, don't you?" David asked.

Jessie nodded her head and laughed. She had auburn hair in loose curls all over that came to her shoulders and bounced when she moved. "Yes, I believe I do, David. And yes, I do miss my folks, and they miss me, but we talk and email all the time.

I was planning to get married and stay here for years. I'm very sorry for your losses. I read about that in *Newsday*. That must have been so terrifying."

"My brother's getting married, probly next year."

"Oh, well, congratulations um..." she waited for me to fill in the blank.

"Aaron, and thank you for working with my brother. I will make sure he's a cooperative patient if he ever stops talking. Oh, and congratulations to you, too."

"Yes, well, my plans have changed a bit. The marriage isn't going to happen as it were, but I still plan to stay in the States for a time. I've got the work visa I need for now."

"I'm glad that David will benefit from your decision to stay. I guess, um, Tiny told you that David needs to work with you every Tuesday through Friday for the next five weeks. Do you want to work out a schedule?"

"Tell you what, Aaron. Let me get David here started on some beginning exercises, and at the end of the session we'll work it all out. Come back in about ninety minutes, okay?"

I left to do some errands, and when I returned, David looked exhausted, but happy.

"We worked really hard on my leg. But Jessie and I played games, too. We had fun, Ari."

"That's great David. Thanks," I said to Jessie, "you must be very good with him. He can get ornery when he's pushed too hard."

"Oh, David was a real trooper. I've got my calendar 'ere, shall we get ourselves in sync?"

Jessie was able to fit him in, but she would need to see him on different times each day.

"I know it's a might jumpy, but if you keep a careful eye on the dates, it should work out without too much stress."

"Thanks, Jessie, we'll see you tomorrow then at ten-thirty," I said, consulting the calendar. "Fortunately, I don't start my own job until August, so it's not an inconvenience."

When we got home, Becca was just hanging up the phone with her mother.

"Oh, Aaron, my mother found the most beautiful place for the wedding. It's available August 13, of next year. It's exactly the kind of place I wanted, and they have a room that's perfect for one hundred fifty."

"Sounds good," I said as I shuffled through the day's mail. I never knew my parents got so many bills just from living in a house.

"Aaron, are you listening to me?"

"Yes, August 13 sounds fine. In fact I'll be at my job a year, and I should be able to take vacation for our honeymoon. Yeah, that should work out well."

"She wants me to see it before she gives the rest of the deposit, and I want to see it, too. I was thinking I could go next week. You don't start work for a month, right?"

Now she had my attention. I hated the thought of her leaving, "How long do you plan on staying with your parents?"

"I think if I leave this Sunday, I can be back by the following Sunday."

"Why a whole week? You know your parents are going to try to talk you out of getting married."

"No they won't. Just stop it about that already!"

I held my tongue and didn't allow myself to go there. "Then why do you need a week? I'll...I'll miss you. I'm excited about the wedding, too, but don't we have time before we need to start all the planning?" She gave me a skeptical look. "I'm still so sad I can't get into it, I need more time, and I need you with me." I tried to look pathetic.

"I'm staying the week so we'll have time to shop for my dress, too. These flights are expensive. I want to make good use of my time."

I shook my head. "But the wedding is a year away. You're going to look for a dress now?"

"Of course, they make them to order. I'm not buying off the rack, you know. I'm going to go see if I can get flights for the next two Sundays. You'll be able to take me to and from the airport, right?"

"Madam," I said, snapping my heels together and giving a salute, "I am at your service." I was resigned this was happening, and I can be a wimp when it comes to Becca.

On Sunday, we drove Becca to Kennedy airport. We watched her check her bags in at curbside, and when she and I kissed goodbye, David moved up to the front passenger seat.

I kissed her as desperately as if she was shipping out with the Marines and I might never see her again. Actually, I was frightened. I'd be home alone with David for the first time since the accident. Maybe I could invite some of my old friends over, I thought.

"Aaron, take it easy." Becca sensed my fear. "Everything will be fine."

I squeezed her tightly and was just about to say goodbye when a taxi pulled up.

"Hey, either move your car or get a room; I've got a fare to unload," the cabbie shouted.

That broke the mood. Becca hoisted her carry-on bag on her shoulder and gave me a peck on the lips. The cab driver honked his horn again, and I got back in the car and sped away from the curb.

Not wanting to face the house without Becca just yet, I suggested to David that we treat ourselves to a movie. But David had another idea.

"It's Sunday, Ari. Maybe we should go to church."

Church. We hadn't been there since the funeral. My family had been steady attendees, but I hadn't gone when I was at school. Still, I couldn't see how I could say no to David on this one.

"I think Mom and Dad would want us to," he added, turning the figurative thumbscrew tighter. "Aren't we supposed to light a candle or something for them?"

He had me there again. We pulled into the parking lot about ten minutes before services started. Neighbors hesitatingly approached us and shook our hands. They acknowledged our loss, then rushed into the church as if seats were hard to get.

We went inside just as the organ started.

Father Charles nodded at us and began with, "Friends, before we start, let's all welcome Aaron and David LeShay who are here with us today." He raised his arms and made the sign of the cross as he said, "The peace of the Lord be with you."

And the congregation answered, "And also with you."

"Aaron and David," he continued, "we are so happy you are with us again. This is a time when you both need God's guidance more than ever. May he give you fortitude and grant you peace. Before we begin the service, let us all say a silent prayer for our courageous brethren."

My ears were red, and my eyes started to fill with tears that I quickly blinked back down. No more crying in public, I decided then and there. Crying didn't solve anything, and it gave me a headache. Stop it, I ordered myself. David, on the other hand, looked as if he liked getting the attention. We bent our heads and I tried earnestly to feel God's presence, but I couldn't. Out of habit and the far-fetched chance that God was actually there and listening, I prayed that my family was at peace and for the wisdom and strength to care for my brother, and I asked for his blessing of the wedding Becca was planning with such exuberance. Before long I was actually praying, or talking to God, as was always my way, even before the accident. The service continued, but I was holding my own conversation with God, and I suspected he might be listening at last. I wasn't going to stop to repeat some refrain in a book; that's why I quit going in the first place. David was participating eagerly in the service.

Ever since the accident I had a lot of trouble believing in a God that would let such a thing happen. I somewhat envied that David still had his faith to hold onto. There are two sides to developmental disability. The first is obvious; his IQ is well below normal, and the second is that David just doesn't hold onto his anger for long. He doesn't really worry about the future; he has always had people to take care of that for him. Now I was all the people he had, plus Becca. Maybe God would help us with that. I didn't know.

At the end of his sermon, Father Charles again encouraged everyone to pray for David and me and to be good neighbors and friends to us. I could see that David felt better after the service, but that last plea from Father Charles had worked to ruin the connection I was trying to make with God. I did not find it comforting to be the object of pity. I felt like I had swallowed a three-pound rock and it had settled in my stomach. Until now, I had felt older than my years, and I realized that having Becca with me, and being engaged, had made a big difference. Here, in the eyes of the congregation we had grown up with, I was still the child they remembered. I was the good twin always watching out for poor little David.

David was also five days shy of twenty-two, but he would never be seen as anything but a disabled child in their eyes. I once again resolved to myself that I would prove that I was up to handling the responsibility that had fallen upon me. In a few years they would see that I had been able to do it all. I knew we had their pity, their actual help was something they said they would give, but it would very rarely materialize.

Out of curiosity, I scanned the pews to see if Jessie was there. No such luck. Maybe she came to an earlier Mass.

"Did you like the service, too?" David asked.

"Sure," I lied. "How about the movie now? We can get a big popcorn and hot dogs there for lunch, and then we'll have dinner at home later."

"Sounds good to me," he said. "Oh, wait, I see Izzy coming with her parents for the next service. I want to say hi to her." He was gone without waiting for an answer.

Izzy? I didn't know he was calling her that. I liked it; he could say it correctly. I stayed at the car and watched David limp his way over to his "girlfriend." Her face lit up to match the joy I saw on David's face when he greeted her. Her parents were also obviously glad to see David. I watched from across the parking lot as if it were a TV show on mute. David pointed to me, and then he and Isabella's mother walked back to the car together.

"I told Mrs. Romano how you ate all her lasagna, and she asked if we would come to dinner on Friday and she would make it again," David said.

"Can you come?" she asked. "It would be our pleasure to have you both. David said your fiancée is away for the week, so by this coming Friday, you boys might like a nice home-cooked meal. David said you approved of my Italian cooking."

"David was telling the truth, I did love your lasagna. We'd be happy to come to dinner on Friday," I said. She didn't need to know our fridge and freezer were stuffed with home-cooked meals.

"Oh, and Friday is our birthday!" David said.

"Is that right?" Mrs. Romano asked.

I'd been hoping David wouldn't say that and answered, saying, "Yes, but *please* don't make a fuss, we are in no mood to party, it's just too soon. Dinner with your family will be a nice way to celebrate. Just no party hats or blowers, okay?"

"I completely understand, Aaron. But I'm happy you won't be alone that night. So we'll see you at about seven then, okay? Isabella will be so pleased."

"It will be our pleasure, we'll be there with big appetites," I said. "Thank you for the invitation."

Mrs. Romano gave David a kiss on the cheek and headed back to her family. David couldn't stop grinning.

"Thanks, Ari, you are the best."

He gave me a hug, and I hugged him back. I felt my old wonderment that David could so easily express his happiness without self-consciousness. It was one of the special gifts he had that us "normal" people rarely displayed.

Because of the time difference, Becca and I spoke on the phone late each night just as I was ready to fall asleep. I thought I'd get to see some friends from high school that week, but most had taken jobs out of the area after graduation. Only my friend Max, who had gone to college locally at Hofstra, was around, and he was working during the day and was with his high school girlfriend and their daughter at night. Max and Shelby hadn't planned on parenthood before marriage, but it happened, and they were living together in her parents' two-family home. The baby was six months old, and they wanted to save enough money for a small wedding by the time she was old enough to walk down the aisle with them. There were no apologies for this little miracle.

One night after dinner, I took David with me to visit Max and Shelby. David was fascinated with their baby, Zoey.

"When did you two get married?" he asked. I kicked myself for not warning him beforehand about that.

"Well, David, we're planning on getting married at the beginning of next year," Max said.

"We're thinking of having a small wedding on Valentine's Day," Shelby said.

"Oh," David said, "I thought you had to be married before you have a baby."

I started to say something, and Max held up his hand to stop me.

"That is definitely the preferred way of doing things, David. Zoey was a bit of a surprise to us. But she was a wonderful surprise."

"Yeah, she's so cute," said David. "Can I hold her again?" David and Zoey kept each other occupied for most of the night, while Max and Shelby and I reminisced. I looked forward to Becca getting to know them. They were still a great couple; I was grateful we hadn't grown apart during college.

Dinner on Friday with the Romanos came as a relief after being without Becca to keep the talk casual at our house. With only David and me at the dinner table all week, talk invariably turned to the empty seats at the table, and most nights we didn't eat that much.

Mr. and Mrs. Romano fit the stereotype of a loving Italian couple. They touched each other with affection often, and at the moment Mr. Romano was keeping his hand on his wife's upper back. Mr. Romano was tall with a girth that showed his appreciation for Mrs. Romano's excellent cooking, with a heavy emphasis on pasta, cheese, and rich homemade sauces. He wore his suit jacket open. I doubted it would close with much room to spare. His face had enough wrinkles in it to show that he worked hard and worried hard and wore a toughness that would not allow him to show his sadness in public.

Mrs. Romano obviously didn't allow herself to indulge in much of the food she proudly served to her family. Standing about a foot shorter than her husband, she was a trim woman with short brown hair and a quick smile that said, "I care, and I'm happy to know you." She wore a necklace bearing the names of her children. In addition to Isabella, the Romanos had two younger sons, seven and ten, who made dinner an adventure of sorts. The boys, Joseph and Anthony, could barely sit in their chairs as they gave us a blow-by-blow description of how their team had won color war at camp that day. Each boy had won his event, and they were bursting with pride. Then, out of nowhere, Joseph said, "Y'know, David, you talk kinda like my sister does."

The Romanos and I looked at each other, and I wondered who would speak first. But David jumped in.

"That's because we both have 'velopment disability," he said.

"Yeah, Joseph, you know that," said Isabella. "That was a dumb thing to say."

"I didn't mean anything by it," said Joseph.

"Don't worry, Joe," said David. "We all say wrong things; sometimes. I sure do."

"Joseph, why don't you and Anthony clear the table while I get dessert?" said Mrs. Romano.

"Hey, he's the dope, why do I have to help him?" Anthony said.

"Anthony—" his father started.

"I'm clearing, I'm clearing," Anthony said, grabbing his plate and mine and bringing them into the kitchen.

On the ruse of going into checking up on them, Mrs. Romano followed them into the kitchen and came out with a round chocolate cake decorated with flowers and the words, "Happy Birthday David and Aaron."

"We had to have dessert anyway," she said, "I hope you don't mind."

"No, no, not at all, thank you," I said.

"Hey, how did you know chocolate's my favorite?" said David. "Can I have the blue flower?"

Very carefully, Mrs. Romano cut David his blue rose slice.

"Now we're really twenty-two, right, Ari?"

"Yes, David. We're both twenty-two. This cake is delicious, again, thank you," I said. I choked down the cake, thinking of past birthdays with my family. I envied David a bit. He was able to enjoy the cake with gusto.

chapter seventeen:
aaron

ONCE BECCA GOT home, the next two weeks went along without too much drama. She had ordered her dream gown and gushed about the plans she and her mother had made. I put in my best effort to show interest and made sure never to disagree with her. Fortunately, the room they liked best would only fit 150 guests comfortably, so it would not turn into a circus like the last wedding I attended. That one, with about 300 people, was insane. They even had Ziggy the Chimp dressed in a tuxedo and riding a bicycle, amusing the guests who liked that sort of thing. Becca and I agreed, no chimps and no pumped up dancers to get the people to behave in a way they would regret the next day. Fun, but dignified, was our goal.

I had not yet started work, and I was able to handle most of the responsibility for David. I took David to his physical therapy, and Jessie made him work hard and like it—truly a new phenomenon for David, who had always been on the lazy side.

He came out of each session tired but exhilarated by all the strength he was gaining in his leg. Jessie had a way to measure his progress, and he could see his numbers rise. It seemed as if he had a crush on Jessie, although he and Isabella were getting to be very good friends. Each night he and Izzy now talked on the phone, and with Becca home for me, he would spend Saturdays with Izzy's family. It wasn't the same, but I think it really helped him to be part of a whole family again. And I could tell he liked the fact that he was bigger than Joseph and Anthony.

After the second week of therapy, David said that Jessie agreed there was no reason for him not to sleep upstairs. The stair climbing would be some useful extra exercise. I could no longer avoid the situation I had known was coming.

"Well, the thing is, David, I haven't been sleeping in our room upstairs. I've been in Mom and Dad's room," I said.

"Okay, if you like that better, I guess I can stay in our room myself. I always did when you were away at school."

"Um, David, Becca and I have been sharing Mom and Dad's room. You know, because we're engaged."

"Oh," said David. "I see." He mulled that over for a while and just as I thought I had dodged that bullet, he said: "Isn't that why your friends had their little Zoey?"

"It's a little more complicated than that," I said.

"Ari, I'm twenty-two just like you. I know about sex. And I have a girlfriend, too."

I got a sick feeling in the pit of my stomach. The three-pound rock was back again.

"David, please tell me that you and Isabella are not having sex," I said. "You have not been together long enough for that. Having sex is a very big deal emotionally and physically, and neither one of you are ready for it. I want you to promise me you will behave like a gentleman and take things very slow with Izzy. Most important, you are not to do anything she doesn't want you to. With a girl, *No Means No*. Do you understand me?"

"Relax, Ari. We are not having sex. Dad told me a long time ago a rule for when you're kissing a girl."

"What, what was that?" I asked.

"He said you can't get in serious trouble if you both keep your hands above the waist at all times."

"That was excellent advice that Dad gave you."

"But you don't follow it with Becca, do you?" he asked.

"That's a very personal question," I said.

"It's not more than your questions. Now *you* should answer *me*."

How was I going to answer this without lying? I couldn't. I told David that we had kept to Dad's rule for the first year, and it was only when we had really committed to one another and had talked marriage that we went any further. I also emphasized that we were very careful with birth control.

"You mean you use a condom? They taught us about condoms in school. But they said they do not always work," David answered.

"Well, Becca and I take double protection. She gets a pill from her doctor, and I use a condom also. The pill is very important, and you can only get it from a doctor. I really don't know if Izzy's doctor will prescribe it for her."

"You mean because she's not smart enough?" David said. His eyes narrowed, and it was clear he was both frustrated and embarrassed at the conversation having taken this turn, but at this point there was no going back.

"I'm afraid so," I said softly.

"That's not fair," he said. "Izzy and I are a couple, too. We are people just like you and Becca. We are the same age as you, too."

"It may not seem fair, but it's the safe thing for now. You and Izzy are a couple, but we both know that you are not just like Becca and I. Both you and Izzy need more help with the grown-up parts of life, and sex is for grown-ups. You are going to have to promise to come to me and talk about it if you and Izzy are even thinking about having sex. Another thing, Izzy and her family are very religious, the church doesn't allow sex before marriage, and I'm sure her parents believe that, too. And David, please, please keep following Dad's advice. He would say that to you if he was here."

I realized that this conversation was nothing compared to the one I was going to have to have with the Romanos, and soon.

David slammed his fist on the couch and limped off to the kitchen. I followed him.

"About the room," I said. "Would you mind very much if we converted the guest room into your room from now on? You can come with me now and show me whatever you want to move there. I'll take care of the whole thing."

Despite his disappointment, David went along with it. We picked out all the things in his room that made it special for him. He eventually admitted that he liked the guest room better because of the bigger bed and the television, especially since we had hooked up the DVD player. He wanted the Mets comforter, and I promised to get him a bigger one as soon as I could.

• • •

On Saturday, I drove David to the Romanos and instead of just dropping him off, I parked the car and got out.

"Where are you going?" David asked.

"Oh, I just want to ask Mrs. Romano some cooking questions. Now that we're almost out of casseroles, I want to do some cooking for Becca."

Fortunately, Izzy was outside, sitting at the picnic table and drawing a picture, and David went to join her. Mr. and Mrs. Romano came to the door when I knocked, Mr. Romano looming over his petite wife. They were surprised to see me. Mr. Romano started to look worried, but Mrs. Romano's face kept its visage of motherly concern.

"Hi, do you two have a minute? I need to talk to you."

I'd prepared myself with two Xanax before getting there, so I was feeling somewhat relaxed. We sat at the kitchen table, and I gave them a recap of my conversation with David about him and Isabella.

"You see, David and Izzy—it's not just the platonic friendship we had assumed it was," I said.

Mr. and Mrs. Romano seemed stunned at first. Izzy always referred to David as her friend, they insisted. She had never shown them any signs that the relationship was more than that. Not able to meet their eyes, I picked at a paper napkin until it was in shreds while I told them that I was pretty confident he was playing by our father's rule, and I told them what he said about staying above the waist, all the while continuing to shred more napkins.

"David told me that Izzy shared the same feelings, and I believe him. I'm afraid the friendship thing is not going to last forever. David knows that Becca and I are in an adult relationship," I said, "and he's frustrated that as my twin what is acceptable for me is not acceptable for him."

"That can't be a new situation for him," said Mr. Romano, sounding as if he was trying to convince me I must be mistaken. "He must have had that a lot growing up."

Taking another napkin to shred, after pushing all the other little pieces of paper into a ball about the size of a golf ball, I said, that while that was true, neither one of us had a girlfriend when I was still in high school, and that he hadn't been privy to how my love life was going during my college years. Not being on the soccer team didn't quite compare to sex.

"Besides," I choked out the words, "he has a man's feelings."

At my speaking the word *sex* out loud, I saw Mrs. Romano jerk involuntarily and then she attempted to make a shift in the conversation.

"Can I get you a cold drink?" said Mrs. Romano. "We're running out of napkins."

The three of us saw the mess I had made in front of me and laughed weakly.

"Sure, if you have any soda, that would be great."

Mrs. Romano went to the refrigerator and peered inside, although I suspected if she had to, she could name every single item inside without a glance.

"Would chocolate milk do it? We don't keep soda in the house."

"That sounds great." I sipped at my chocolate milk and very self-consciously reached for a napkin to wipe the chocolate mustache I felt on my face. I sensed that the Romanos were looking at me, waiting for more.

"Well, as I said, I talked to David very seriously, and I strongly emphasized that he should never do anything against Isabella's wishes. I'm just afraid they are going to be two consenting, not-quite adults."

As Mrs. Romano busied herself by nervously wiping the kitchen counters and table, Mr. Romano opened the back door to check on the kids. They were sitting on the picnic bench kissing.

"What the hell is going on here?" he said. "David, get off of my daughter!"

"I . . . I was staying above the waist," he said.

Mrs. Romano and I had followed him outside, and David looked at me, his eyes begging me to help him, to take his side and explain they weren't doing anything wrong.

"Ari, we were just kissing."

"Aaron, please take your brother home now," said Mr. Romano.

Izzy started to cry. She ran to her father. "Please, Daddy, don't be mad. Don't make David leave."

Mr. Romano ignored Izzy, shaking off her hold on his arm and turned to address his wife.

"We are taking that trip we've been putting off. This settles it."

"Louie, please . . ." said Mrs. Romano.

Keeping his voice low enough so that Izzy couldn't hear, he said to me, "Aaron, I'm sorry to put you in the middle here, but my wife and I have talked about getting Izzy's tubes tied. We may have to go out of state to have it done. It's not legal here, but it is in the South."

Mrs. Romano stood wringing the dishtowel she still had in her hand. Mr. Romano and I stood awkwardly, and then he took me aside and very quietly said that perhaps I should consider taking David for a vasectomy. Shit, that had never crossed my mind. It was such a drastic move, and David would never agree.

Not quite knowing how to answer him without things escalating into a more volatile situation, I chose not to acknowledge that I had heard him.

"David and I will be going now."

"Please stay," said Mrs. Romano. "We need to talk some more, come back in the kitchen. Izzy and David, please go in the living room, and watch some TV with the boys, okay?"

"Aaron, is there something else you want to tell us?" she asked.

"Well, if we can talk calmly," I said, looking at Mr. Romano and waiting for him to nod in agreement, "I am worried about something. I think David may wish he could have a baby. David says they know how it works. They were taught about birth control in school."

"Why do you think that he wants a baby?" asked Mrs. Romano, her voice rising even higher and starting to shake. I saw she was holding back tears.

"Well, we saw some friends of mine who have a six-month-old. She's adorable, and David didn't take his eyes off of her the whole time he was there. Compound that with the loss of the rest of our family, and I'm worried that David could believe that having a baby would help make up for what we are missing."

"*Dio mio!*" said Mr. Romano, "Carmella, this is a calamity!"

"Please, this is just a suspicion of mine. David has never voiced any such plan."

"Maybe I should take Isabella to see the doctor," said Mrs. Romano.

"That's your call, but I felt I had to talk to you about this, and I'm sure you will want to talk to your daughter. I don't think you need to panic. I could be wrong about David's wanting a baby. But we have to consider everything. They are both high-functioning, but in my opinion neither one should ever be a parent."

Mr. and Mrs. Romano agreed. They said they were proud of how much their daughter can do for herself, but even if Isabella wasn't fully aware of her limitations, they were very realistic about them.

"Last month we heard about a couple similar to David and Izzy who did have a child. Their son was born without any developmental disabilities, but it was a disaster," said Mrs. Romano. "Eventually, he was removed by social services when he was three because of neglect. They didn't know what they were doing, or what could happen, and neither had parents who could help them. They loved the baby, but just couldn't care for him properly. Imagine how traumatic that was for both the child and his parents." She was literally shuddering picturing it. "We can't let that happen to our kids."

"Please," I said, "Their feelings for each other are real. David is still grieving; he needs to stay friends with Izzy. I hope you won't ban him or anything like that."

"We can't answer that right now," said Mr. Romano. "I'd like to see them take a break from each other for a while."

• • •

I found myself looking for another napkin to shred. This was one of the most difficult conversations I ever had in my life, and I'd had about as much as I could handle.

Shortly, David and I got in my car and headed for the nearest Carvel to get hot fudge sundaes. As we ate the ice cream, I told David he would have to stay away from Izzy for now.

"But we were just kissing!" He stood up as he shouted this,

spilling the rest of his sundae on the floor. I said a mini-prayer of gratitude that there were no other customers in the place. I calmed him down as best I could, promising to talk to the Romanos again and begging him to be patient and do what Izzy's father had decreed.

"Remember, Mr. Romano said 'for a little while,' he did not say forever."

When I got home, David stormed off to his room and slammed the door. I climbed the stairs to our bedroom to find Becca and bring her a vanilla thick shake. I told her about my talks with David and the Romanos. She turned as white as the shake.

"David is having sex?"

"No, I didn't say that. But I'm afraid he could be headed there. It means we have to be vigilant when Isabella visits here not to leave them alone in his room."

"You should never have taken him over to Max and Shelby's; that was really dumb of you!"

"Rebecca, I can't shield him from all babies. Don't start blaming me because my brother has normal male urges."

"But he's not a man. He'll never be a man!"

I tried to calm down her down. She sipped her shake slowly, and I hoped that its sweetness would help.

"He understands about his disability, but his emotions are strong. I think his having Isabella as a girlfriend is a good thing. For now, they are sticking by that rule my father gave him. Don't worry; I will stay on this. The worst thing is that Mr. Romano freaked out."

"You'd better take care of this," she said. "There is just so much I can cope with, Aaron. You'll excuse me, I was planning on finishing my grad school apps."

I watched my fiancée run up the stairs. I had hoped for support; instead I got anger from her. I opened the refrigerator and reached all the way in the back of the bottom shelf for the beer I had stashed there. It was still a nice afternoon; I took the beer and my iPod out to the hammock and allowed myself to eventually drift off to sleep.

chapter eighteen:
aaron

T.S. ELLIOT SAID, "April is the Cruelest Month," but for me it was August. I had recently started my management-training program at the executive offices of Livingston Bank in Manhattan. I'd been a monthly-ticket-holding member of the early morning commuters club on the Long Island Railroad platform for a week already. I was now, of all things, a banker. I was one of ten new management trainees. We were ensconced in meetings on loan criteria, investments, bank policies, customer support, ad infinitum. I found this all incredibly dull and wondered how the other trainees felt.

My time of mourning was for all practical purposes ended. I had to join the world again, and it was harder than I'd expected. As I looked around at the others waiting for the train, it struck me that banking is among the last professions where men still have to wear suits, and it was hot as hell. I looked enviously at the computer geeks breezily cool in their T-shirts and khakis and the women in their colorful, sleeveless summer dress. Unfortunately, I hadn't mentioned dislike of pit stains during my placement office interview.

It had never occurred to me to consider comfort-wear when I was picking my major. Dad had worn a suit, because lawyers are the other group of people who haven't traded status fashion for common sense when it comes to dressing for work. My economics and finance courses were interesting, so how did they lead me to banking? It hit me like the train. I was too busy with Becca the last two years to give my career the serious thought I should have.

After a week, it becomes rote. The car doors open, and we push our way solemnly into the train, no different than cattle going to market, just a little low mumbling instead of loud mooing. We avoid eye contact rather than acknowledge the indignity of the system we are trapped within. The LIRR air conditioning is anything but reliable. I sigh with relief that the metal pole I grip as I stand in the packed car is frigid to the touch. The mass of bodies here generates more heat than the air conditioning does cold, but it would be much, much worse if such a battle of the elements were not taking place. I try to stand as still as possible, mentally marking a circle around me not to be violated. That morning, I swear I saw a middle-aged man looking back at me in the mirror while I shaved. Becca even fixed my tie knot when she kissed me goodbye. Who were we, Carol and Mike Brady, minus the bunch?

David was set to start Waldbaum's on the fourteenth, one day less than a year to our wedding date, Becca reminded me. His cast was off, and he was walking well, thanks to the PT. Izzy was on a completely different work schedule, so my hopes of arranging for a carpool with her parents were shot to hell. But at least the kids did get to see each other at work a few days a week. Becca took a part-time job at the Plainview Library, and between her and me we could transport David to and from work.

● ● ●

I missed my parents and sister every day. David missed them, too; he said it often, but he really doesn't dwell on things too deeply. He lives more in the present. I was out of Xanax and feeling more anxiety. David's doctor had bumped up his antidepressant prescription after the accident and provided him with his own Xanax to keep him calm. I wasn't low enough to steal David's pills. I remembered what the doctor said about it being an addictive narcotic, and I couldn't deny I already had a weakness for liquor and feared I had an addictive personality.

It had been close to three months since my brother and I were orphaned. The calls of consolation and offers to help had tapered off. Becca was an enormous help. Although I wouldn't say anything, her phone calls from home were like little knives jabbing into my heart. I was jealous that she had parents. I know, it's almost evil of me, but it hurt to be reminded. After my third week of work, on a Saturday while David was working and Becca was shopping, I decided to call Colin for a much-needed boost.

"Aaron, I was just thinking of you, how are you?" said Colin.

"Eh, not great. I started work the first of the month, and already I feel like a bored old man wasting my life in business."

"Do you think it's the job or the stress of your situation?"

"The stress is probably most of it. It's too early to tell about the job, but I'm not loving that either."

"Aaron, anyone in your place would be feeling down. Are you getting medical help?"

"What do you mean? I was taking Xanax, but I'm out of it now."

"You know I can't prescribe, but I would say you may need an antidepressant to help you cope for a while. It doesn't mean it's for the rest of your life."

"But I'm depressed for a reason. Antidepressants can't change that!"

"Aaron, people with real, terrible problems suffer from depression. You can be helped with medication. There's no shame in that. It won't make you forget your problems, and it won't bring your family back, but it will help you cope. You can see your family doctor and have him start you off with something and ask him to recommend a psychiatrist."

I spoke to Colin for a while longer and decided he was right. My doctor had Saturday hours, and I made a quick call. That's one good thing about being a pathetic figure, the receptionist told me to come right over, and I walked out of his office forty-five minutes later with a prescription for Prozac and for the Xanax I had come to rely on. A quick trip to the drugstore, and I was home before Becca. I hid the meds in a cup near the kitchen sink that no one used anymore so that I could take them in the morning before work. Becca didn't need to know, I decided.

"I'm so glad I took this library job," she told me. "I love when I get to work in the children's room. I've definitely decided to concentrate on elementary education in grad school."

She was, however, unimpressed with Plainview.

"I can see why they named it 'Plainview;' it's really a colorless town," she said. "All there is are strip malls and houses in rows that look exactly alike. Its major claim to fame is the JCC, and that's in an old school."

I laughed, even though I had learned in the third grade that it had been named that because it had a view of the Hampstead Plains way back in the 1600s.

"Not every town can be like LA," I said.

"No, but we could live there." She muttered it so softly that I was able to ignore it. I looked down at my watch and realized it was seven-thirty. No call had come from Becca's mother.

"Speaking of LA, did your mother say she wasn't calling tonight?" I asked.

"No, she probably went out, it's Saturday. Maybe she's beginning to feel more comfortable with me here," she said.

But another hour passed, and Becca started to get worried.

"You know, this is the third day in a row she hasn't called. I think I'd better call her." She asked me to sit closer to her on the couch so that I could hear the call, too. Her father picked up. "Is something wrong at home?" asked Becca. "Is Mom mad at me?"

"No, Mom is not mad at you Rebecca," he said, "But I am glad you called. I have some upsetting news to tell you. Please try to stay calm."

"What is it Daddy? What are you talking about?"

"Um, you see, a few days ago, Mom found a lump in her breast during a self-exam, and her doctor did a needle biopsy right there in the office. It was malignant." He whispered that last word.

"What did you just say? Wait, Daddy, I'm putting you on speakerphone so Aaron can hear this. Now repeat what you just said."

"I said Mom has a lump in her breast. The doctor found it was malignant, but Bec, there are more tests to be made. She didn't want to call and upset you. I was going to call you later."

"Is she home now?"

"No, they are keeping her in the hospital for now."

"I'll be on the next flight I can get. I'll call you when to pick me up at the airport."

"Hold it, you don't have to do that. No one is going anywhere. They think they caught it early."

"What do you mean, *think* they caught it early? Did they or didn't they?"

"She's having exploratory surgery Monday."

"I'm flying out tomorrow, Dad. Don't try to stop me. Mom needs me." She hung up and buried her head in my chest crying hysterically.

I put my arms around her and tried to reassure her that her mother would be okay. No one could empathize better than I could, and Becca's having gone through the past ten weeks must have seriously amped up her fears.

I sat on the bed, watching her pack. She took practically everything she had brought, folding each item neatly, despite being panic-stricken. I became more anxious with every shirt and sweater she put in the suitcase. All she left was her Pennsylvania cold-weather clothing. Finally, I slipped out to the kitchen and popped two Xanax, and when I returned she was just zipping up her bag. I knew there was nothing I could do to slow down her frenzy.

Next stop was the computer where she booked a one-way ticket to LA.

"I can't say when I'll be back. I have to stay with my mother as long as I can since I really do have the time now to spare. I'll call the library in the morning. If they won't give me a family leave, I'll quit. I'm just doing it to pass the time, anyway," she said.

That night we made passionless love in a consoling way. We needed to be close, but it already felt as if the entire country separated us. Her thoughts were with her family in California while I worried about how I would handle everything with her gone again and David working. I could drop him off at the store early, but who would take him home on Wednesday, Thursday, and Friday? I didn't dare say anything to Becca; I could just imagine her wrath if I brought up the subject. I tried to think of a solution. Would David's manager let him change hours? Maybe he could take the bus. Was he up to that? I wanted to believe he was capable of more than my parents had let him do. I didn't have the luxury to be so protective of his every move.

Becca kissed me goodnight, turned over, and quietly shed tears for her mother. After an hour of watching her twisting and turning in bed, taking a tissue now and again to blow her nose and wipe her eyes, I saw her get up and take a Benadryl tablet to make her drowsy enough to fall asleep. I'd gotten used to not sleeping ever since the accident. I lay in bed, thoughts racing, and now I had this new worry about Becca leaving on a one-way ticket. I had to put up a strong front, hiding my fears about managing David. The doctor said it would take a few weeks for the Prozac to kick in. I wished I could stay in bed in the fetal position until that happened, but tomorrow morning I had to take Becca to the airport and then teach David how to use the bus. A terrible weekend, I thought, already dreading Monday morning, too. Although we had inherited enough money so that I didn't have to work, I wouldn't even consider that. For now, we were leaving that money in the bank until we decided on how to use it best. My parents were hard workers; I went to college for a purpose, and I just couldn't take staying home all day. Even if my job was dull, it was an escape.

chapter nineteen:
aaron

NOW IT WAS my turn to call Becca every night. I called at eleven my time, since I had no trouble staying up late. Fran was stable and being prepped for a second surgery the next week. They'd discovered some more lumps and cancer cells in both breasts, and one side of the lymph nodes. She was having a double mastectomy. Becca did a lot of crying, and I tried my best to comfort her.

About three weeks later, Becca got a few thick envelopes in the mail. One was from Hofstra, one from Stony Brook, and one from UCLA. Damn it! She wasn't sure about staying with me. She'd lied. What was she doing applying to grad school in California?

I didn't wait until night to call. It was only nine there, and I was likely waking someone, but I didn't care. Becca answered the phone.

"Hello? Aaron, you're calling early. Is everything okay? I don't think I could take another catastrophe."

"That depends on your definition of catastrophe. You got replies from the colleges you applied to."

"Oh, no, you mean I didn't get in?"

"No, I mean you got into Hofstra, Stony Brook, and, oh, yeah, UCLA," I said, ice dripping in my tone.

"Oh. Well, I applied there because my mother wanted me to."

"Oh, I see."

"Aaron, you haven't even asked how my mother is. She has to go through chemo starting two days after her second surgery!"

"Well, at least she's alive," I said, and then immediately tried to take it back. "I didn't mean that, Becca, I'm sorry. I meant that chemo is tough, but at least the doctors are treating her aggressively."

Uncomfortable silence followed. I had a clear picture in my mind of Becca's face showing absolute rage. She said nothing at first, then, "Aaron, I was just covering all my options applying to UCLA, but now I think it's really not a bad idea."

"What do you mean? What about us? It's a two-year program, right? I thought the wedding was set for next August."

"It was, but that was all before my mother got sick."

"But, but, she'll get better. Don't you think? I thought the prognosis was good."

"It was good at first, but it's not as good anymore. Anyway, that's not really the point. No one knows what will happen tomorrow, and we have a bigger problem here. Look, I have to go now. I'll call you back later. But I really don't think this is going to work, Aaron."

"What's not going to work? Us?"

"I'll get back to you later tonight. I've got to go to the hospital now. Goodbye."

I stared at the phone. I was angry with her, but I hadn't been expecting her to break our engagement. Now I didn't know what to think or what to say to her. I paced the room. Then I went to the kitchen and made myself a bowl of ice cream, heavy on the whipped cream. She'd probably been planning this since she got home, I thought. She was just waiting for an excuse to start an argument, and I had definitely given her one. I wanted to go for a walk, but I was afraid to miss her call. Finally, I called Max; with call-waiting I'd be safe.

"Max, I just spoke to Becca. Now she's planning on going to grad school at UCLA, and I think she's breaking our engagement."

"Because of her mother's cancer?" Max asked.

"Well, that's what she's saying. Shit, Max, I don't know what to do."

"Buddy, you can't argue with cancer. It always wins. If Becca wants to break it off, it's better now than later. You'll be okay, Aaron. Shelby and I are here for you. I want to say don't jump to conclusions, but you have to prepare yourself for what you think is coming. To be perfectly honest, Shelby didn't think Becca had what it takes to help you with David indefinitely. You can do this; call me later and let me know what happens, okay?"

• • •

Three hours later, Becca called. It sounded as if she had her whole speech already prepared. It was a foregone conclusion.

"Aaron, I never realized that our lives had become all about you and your problems. But now I see that I'm not allowed to have a problem, because if I do, it won't be as bad as yours and it won't count for anything. I can see it now; if my mother doesn't survive this, you'll think, 'Well, at least you still have your father and sister.'"

"What? No, Becca, that's not true. I just thought we had agreed that you were going to grad school in New York. I thought the plan was for us to be together. You know I can't move David now."

"Can't or won't?"

The conversation went downhill from there. Becca contended that her mother needed her now and maybe for the next few years. Things have changed, she said. She wasn't going to be across the country when her mother went through fighting cancer or, God forbid, died of it. And I wasn't the only one with a sibling. She needed to be there for her sister, too, and for her father. She gave me an ultimatum: We could postpone the wedding, put it on hold, and if by that time I was ready to move out and we still wanted to get married, we could then live near her family.

"Why do have to live in that house? Maybe a move would be good for you. You can put the house on the market, and you can prepare David to leave New York. LA is a good place to live. You don't even like your job, and you can get a new one here."

"But David says he is in love with Isabella, and it's mutual. How can I separate them?"

"It's them or us, Aaron."

We were both mute then, waiting for the other to say something.

"Aaron, your silence says it all. You are always going to put your brother's happiness before your own, and definitely before mine. I don't want to come in second in my own marriage. I'm glad I applied to UCLA. I'll send the ring back to you by Fed Ex tomorrow. Please send me the envelope from UCLA."

Damn. I needed her. "No, please don't, Becca. I do want to marry you. Can't we work this out? I love you."

"Not enough, Aaron. And I'm sorry if this sounds cold, but I want to make a clean break. I have too much stuff going on now. Don't call me again. I can't be your friend now. Call your buddy Colin if you need to vent. I'm sorry it didn't work out. We tried, but life has just become too hard for us. I loved you, and I wish things were different, but I have to say goodbye."

I hung up the phone and stared at it for a while. Already our love was in the past tense. My instinct was to call her right back, to text, to email, to send her flowers, candy, jewelry, anything I could think of to get her back. Instead, I lay on the couch with my hands behind my head and replayed the scene, beginning with the thick envelope from UCLA in the mailbox. I sat there feeling as if I'd just had my right hand amputated—helpless and horrified. How was I going to cope with this life I had now by myself? I'd counted on Becca to make me the man I needed to be. To have a woman by my side to help me as my mother had helped my father, and to love each other as they had. And, yes, to help me with David. It was a Saturday so, David was at work. I felt like a failure. I was alone, all alone, almost comically alone if it hadn't been so tragic. Even Ollie and Stan missing, hiding wherever they went when they heard loud voices.

Taking stock of the situation was pitiful. I had no family but David, who was in love with a woman who loved him back, and somehow I had to get her parents to accept that and treat her as an adult, even though they saw her as a nine-year-old child, at best. My now ex-fiancée was in California. At least I wouldn't bump into her on the street. No New York City accidental meet-ups for me. She had promised to be with me for life, but she had sure changed her mind about it fast enough, and I knew she'd have no trouble finding a replacement for me. She was cheerleader pretty. If only her mother hadn't gotten sick. But that was messed up of me. I didn't really care about her mother's cancer. I only cared about it because it screwed up my life, not because it threatened Fran's. No wonder Becca broke it off with me. I was a shithead.

I had to go pick David up at work. No time to wallow in my pain. As soon as he got in the car, I started talking.

• • •

"David, listen, Becca won't be coming back from California. There isn't going to be any wedding."

"She dumped you?"

Ouch. "You could say that. She says she has to take care of her mother now, and, well, things just went from bad to worse. It's over."

"Mom didn't like her anyway," he said.

"What? Why do you say that?"

"I heard her tell Dad."

"Are you just saying that to hurt me?" Now my anger was aimed at David. My hands tightened on the steering wheel. I had to be immune to his bluntness, but I couldn't. Becca had been good to him; he could have at least shown some sign of caring instead of making me feel like a fool.

We pulled into the driveway and I turned on him. "Thanks for making me feel better," I said, slamming the door behind me.

David shrugged. "I was just saying what Mom said." He went into his room and put on the videotape of *Star Wars* he'd been watching.

I went into the family room and scrounged up an old LP of my Dad's and put it on the his old turntable. The song was *Paint it Black*, by The Rolling Stones. I always played it at full volume when my mood was the blackest.

With the Stones blaring, I went into Dad's office and found his stash of Johnnie Walker Red in his bottom drawer. There was about half the bottle left, so I didn't bother with a glass. I plopped onto the couch in the family room to finish off the booze. I took off my jeans, and pulled my mother's afghan over me, clutching the bottle. One of the pillows smelled of Becca's girly shampoo, and I took it and threw it across the room. I sipped at the scotch until the bottle was empty. The music had stopped, but I was in a stupor by then, and I drifted off into an alcohol-induced sleep.

Later, I woke to the sound of a bunch of voices. I kept my eyes shut and tried to shut them out as well.

"Aaron, Aaron, wake up son," said some man.

"He's really out," he told David.

I scrunched deeper into the couch, hoping they would leave. Then David jumped on the couch, rudely forcing me awake. "C'mon, Ari, time to get up."

"Daaaave, whaaat is going onnn?"

"You wouldn't wake up, so I asked Mr. Stillman to help."

My head was spinning. I saw the bottle, and bent over the couch to push it underneath, but then I couldn't get myself back up. David was laughing, but Mr. Stillman looked serious. If I hadn't been so out of it, I'd have had the sense to be embarrassed.

"C'mon, Aaron, sip the coffee and get it down," said Mr. Stillman. He had asked whether I had taken any pills with the whiskey, and when I admitted taking a couple of Xanax, he called his pharmacy and was assured that he should just keep me awake for the next three hours and then to watch me in the morning. The pharmacist didn't seem half as worried as Mr. Stillman. I heard him call his wife after coaxing me to drink the coffee.

"Honey, I'm going to sleep here with the boys tonight," I heard him say. "Aaron is three sheets to the wind, drunk, he can barely talk. He said something about Becca and the ring. I think she broke up with him. I don't want to leave him and David alone. Okay, I will. Yes, if there is the slightest reason to, I will. I'll be home in the morning."

"You don't hafta stay here, Mr. Stillman. I feel *fiiiine*," I said.

"Don't worry about it, I could use the night off. I think Mrs. Stillman wanted me to clean the grill tonight," he said.

David took something to eat and then went to bed, tired after a day at work on his feet bagging groceries, and Mr. Stillman and I sat and talked for a long time. I started to sober up and found he was a good listener. It felt almost like I was talking to Dad. He said I'd undertaken a hell of a lot in the time since the accident, and he didn't think any the less of me for breaking down tonight, especially after having my heart stomped upon and my whole life plan with Becca shattered in an instant.

"That is something heroic you did, putting David's interests before your own," he said.

"Well, what choice do I have? I'm no hero. My parents left me in charge of him." Then I got up and walked across the room, grabbed a photo off the piano and showed it to him. It was Mom holding up the award she had won in college for an advertising competition.

"Mom sacrificed her whole career for him, and Dad took his own ambitions down a few notches, too. David is happy here in his own home, I can't move him across the country. He, uh, he is in love with a girl he met at school. I think she's what has prevented him from really crashing emotionally, but her father won't let David see her because he caught them kissing."

"Maybe you could use a little help with him," he said.

"Well, I just lost the help I was counting on, not to mention the love of my life," I said. "Besides, your family has helped me, too."

"I meant professional help, like from the ACDS," he said.

I shook my head vigorously. "No, I can handle David. I was just drowning my sorrows tonight."

"As long as you didn't drown yourself," he smiled. "Wow, look at the time, it's two in the morning, let's get some sleep. I'm going to curl up on this couch. Go on upstairs to your bedroom. Maybe you and David can join my family at church tomorrow morning."

"I don't know if I'll be up for it."

"We can go to a later service. Let's talk tomorrow, get some sleep now."

I wasn't dead set against it. I had some new issues to discuss with God. But I was afraid I'd be sick in the morning.

● ● ●

At Mr. Stillman's urging, the next day David and I got ready for the one o'clock service at church, and Mrs. Stillman had promised to make her famous brisket for dinner, insisting we join them. My stomach was still a little queasy, so Mr. Stillman suggested I stick to some light toast and a little jelly for breakfast, and I would be okay. He seemed to have some expertise in these matters.

We were sitting with the Stillman family before services started until David spotted the Romanos and moved over to sit next to Izzy. I felt confident Mr. Romano would not act up in church and scored one for David for getting to see Izzy.

I attended the service in my own way, using it to have a téte à téte with God about my life and how I needed him to help me, to at least prove that he could if he wanted to. *Just help me to do the right thing for David without completely destroying my own life,* I prayed. *You had better have had some very important need for my family to take them from us like that,* I raged at God silently. *If you would help me to see that, to believe that, I believe I would have a better chance to make a good life for David and myself, but right now I'm afraid I'm going to make a mess of things being on my own. I had counted on having Becca to help me, but she was obviously not your agent on Earth for me. At least she was good enough to send back the ring.*

I'd known guys who lost both the girl and the ring they'd spent three or four thousand bucks on.

It arrived early Monday morning before I left for work. Just a small Fed Ex box. When you're staring at the ring that lit up your fiancée's face and it's not on her finger, there is no denial the engagement is off. I let myself wallow in it all the way to work, but it was a busy day at the office, and I didn't think about it again until I came home and found it on the counter. I started to open the pill bottle for a Xanax and then stopped. I didn't want to get in the habit of reaching for the Xanax whenever I felt bad. That's not what the doctor had prescribed it for. The Xanax wasn't going to change what had happened. Should I really take a pill every time something went wrong? I debated with myself, and then swallowed one pill, deciding after all that this was a legitimate time for pharmaceutical assistance. I felt the Prozac was justified, but I was worried I'd get addicted to Xanax and abuse it. I'll quit using it soon, I told myself, just not today.

chapter twenty: david

AFTER CHURCH AARON took me to show me the bus route to and from work. We waited at the bus stop, and when the driver opened the door, I slid in a special card that Aaron gave me to use instead of money. I had to turn it around, and it took me a few times, but I got it and the driver was nice about it. He said, "Take your time son, it's a slow day." We got off at the stop near our house, and Aaron made me lead the way home to make sure I knew it.

"Now do you have your key?" Aaron asked when we got to the door.

"Um, I thought you had it."

"David, you have to be able to take care of this traveling yourself!"

Aaron was mad at me. "When I said I wanted to practice, I meant everything. Here."

He shoved his own key in my hand, and after just two tries I got the door open. The alarm went off.

"Well, what do you do when that happens?" Aaron asked. He was mad again.

"I forget," I said. "Stop being so mean to me!" I let the alarm keep ringing as I ran to my room and shut the door. Aaron must have gone to the machine and stopped it. I was so glad he didn't come into my room after that. About an hour later, he knocked.

"Sorry, kid, I lost my temper," he said. "Let's not worry about the alarm. We just won't set it on the days you have to take the bus home. Just make sure to lock the doors when you come home."

"Sounds good to me," I said. I was glad Aaron had cooled off. Mom always hated that alarm and only set it because Dad made her.

"Well, we're due at the Stillmans for dinner at five," Aaron said. "I'm going to pick up a dessert to bring. Do you want to come with me?"

"Don't, Ari! I'm way too old for a babysitter! Mom left me home alone all the time." I was telling a little bit of a lie. Mom hardly ever left me home alone, insisting she wanted my company when she needed to go shopping or somewhere when I wasn't in school. Still, she had left me home once in a while. All I did was watch TV or play video games. I wouldn't use the stove.

When Aaron got back, I was just where he left me, lying on my bed watching TV.

"So Thursday I have work and you don't," Aaron said.

"Yeah." I was watching a show and didn't want to talk.

"What do you want to do about that?" Aaron asked.

My show was over. I got up and yelled, "I already told you. Don't need a babysitter. I can stay by myself alone!"

"What are you going to do all day?"

"I don't know. Maybe I will call my friend Hunter. He might come over. His mother could drive him."

"Doesn't he have that volunteer program they offered you?" Aaron said.

"I'm not sure; I think not on Thursdays."

"Well, why not call him now? You can make plans in advance."

"Okay, okay, but you're being silly. I can stay alone."

"Please just give him a call."

So I called Hunter, and I was embarrassed that his mom talked to Aaron after we made plans for him to come here. They decided it would be better for Aaron to drop me off on his way to the train at Hunter's house. It didn't matter to them that I'd have to get up so early; they didn't want the two of us to stay here alone. They decided that I'd do that every Thursday. Hunter was free then, and so was I. No one asked us if we wanted to do that, either. Aaron just waved off my complaint when he got off the phone.

"Well, it's all settled. I'm going to drop you at Hunter's house on the way to the train tomorrow, and on Thursdays you can hang out together."

"Oh. Wonderful," I said, trying to show sarcasm, but he didn't catch it. "And what about Fridays, did you plan that day, too?"

"No, Hunter has his program on Fridays. Is there another friend you can call?"

I threw down a magazine onto the coffee table. "I'm not a baby. I'm staying home alone on Fridays. That's it, Ari, no more making arrangements for me."

Aaron tried to talk his way out of it. It's all new, he said, it would be that way if Mom and Dad were here. But we both knew he was lying because Mom would be home with me. I liked Hunter good enough, but I didn't like getting put in a "play date" like a little boy. Finally, he gave in and said I could stay home on Fridays on a trial basis.

Truth was, Hunter and I did have a good time on Thursday, and I was glad to be going back there. His mom was a great cook and made the best macaroni and cheese for lunch. Hunter had some new video games, and before I knew it Aaron picked me up and we went home and had dinner. Aaron was pretty quiet at dinner. I think he missed Becca.

"So what are you going to do tomorrow?" he asked me.

"I'm not sure; if the weather is nice, I might take a walk or go to the park," I said.

I could see Aaron get nervous. "Well, make sure you lock up the house and bring your key," he said. "You don't have to bother with the alarm."

"Aaron, I took the bus by myself on Monday, Tuesday, Wednesday. I was home alone for three hours then. When are you going to trust me? You are worse than Mom!"

I didn't wait to hear his answer. I left him with the dishes to do, and I locked myself in my new bedroom until it was time to go next door for dinner. Now I was glad I'd moved into the guest room. It had a lock.

chapter twenty-one:
aaron

I HEARD DAVID turn the lock on his door, and something in me just snapped. I had just been dumped by my fiancée, and now, instead of cooperating, David was giving me shit. I stomped into the family room, clenching my fists and fighting the urge to turn back and break the damn door down. But tolerating David and not pushing him into a meltdown of his own was so ingrained in me, I resisted the temptation to retaliate. Instead, I plucked a framed photo off the fireplace mantle of David and me taken when we were ten years at one of the many Special Olympics tournaments where I had been his helper. My arm was around his shoulder, and he was grinning from ear to ear, having just won two medals. For the first time, I looked closer at my own face. My mouth was smiling, but my eyes were not. I was looking slightly away from the camera and could imagine that Colin might have some opinion about that. I took the photo and stuck it inside the piano bench under a bunch of old Beatles music and Fake books my mother had. Then I took another photo down from the mantle and sunk down into Dad's favorite recliner. It might have been the first time I sat in that chair since we were home. The photo was of Mom, Dad, and Caroline at my sister's Sweet Sixteen. I was only six, but I remember they made a huge deal of the party, holding it at a restaurant, and leaving David and me with a sitter. Without warning, the tears came. This was it. I was really alone in the house with David, and now there would be no Becca I could hang on to. No lifeline, no normal partner. Oh, make that typically developing, that's how Mom and the association referred to the siblings of their disabled children, or for that matter, every other child without disabilities. They couldn't admit that their kids with Down syndrome or other disabilities weren't normal, so that meant even I couldn't be considered normal, just not the same as David, the *beloved*.

But Laurel and Jonathan had already had their normal lives when they decided that Caroline, or me in her stead, as it had turned out, should live my life revolving around David. They had fallen in love, gotten married, and had a beautiful, normal daughter for ten years before we came along and messed everything up. But how was I ever going to have a normal life? I wasn't. The people who would help me were gone. I had deluded myself into believing that Becca loved me enough to accept David, too, but I now believed that if her mother's illness hadn't happened, she would have broken up with me for some other reason.

I still needed my parents and sister. The memory of their bodies lying under the sheets in the hospital came back to me, and I began to feel a splitting headache coming on. The funeral; everyone crying. I had to hold myself upright, stand up and shake hands. I had relied on the Xanax then to get me through it, but the memories were still so recent, so painful. I had been denying my broken heart up until now, allowing the joy of my love for Becca let it take second place, and filling my conscious thoughts with caring for David, making sure he was able to go on. Yet, now could I honestly go on with my life? Had I been kidding myself this whole time?

I got up from the recliner and headed upstairs. First, I listened at David's door. He was playing a video game. Good, maybe that would keep him busy for an hour or two. I was afraid if I had to see him at that moment, I would lash out at him with all sorts of names.

I popped two Tylenol, and then I crept into my childhood bed and pulled my old Mets comforter over my head. I murmured all the resentment toward him I was feeling. "You retarded pain in the ass. Why did they have to die and burden me with you? I can't believe you have a love life and I don't. I never will with you attached to me; we might as well be Siamese twins. You're going to scare every woman away from me anyway."

As my tears poured down and my nose filled up with mucous, I went through a box of tissues before I slowed down. I breathed deeply and slowly for several minutes, using a relaxation technique that Colin had taught me until I was able to shift gears a little. *Shit, it's not all your fault, David. Your life's been ruined, too. You just feel protected because you have me.*

I pulled the comforter down and saw that the moon had replaced the sun and dark enveloped the house, just like my mood. I decided I needed the night to myself, and I went back to the master bedroom, no longer shared with Becca. I stripped off my clothes and crawled back into bed in my T-shirt and boxers. I heard David coming up the stairs, and I prayed he was just looking for something in our old room. Then I heard him knock on the door.

"What is it, David?" I said, staying under the blanket and keeping my back to him so he wouldn't see that I'd been crying.

"Umm, I'm sorry Ari, please don't be mad at me."

"I'm not mad . . . I just have a headache."

"I'm hungry, are we going to have dinner?"

"David, I really don't want anything. There is a leftover roast beef sandwich in the fridge that I got at the deli. Can you eat that? I need to sleep, okay?"

"Well, okay. Just don't be mad, please?"

"It's fine, David, I'm not mad. I'm just too tired to eat now. Good night."

It was true. I couldn't stay mad at him. Yeah, my life now officially sucked, but his always had. I was feeling so sorry for myself, my engagement yanked out from under me and having David be so obstinate about everything I had worked out, it was all too much. I quietly went into the bathroom, took two more boxes of tissues from the linen closet, and spent the next six hours just crying and wallowing in self-pity until I finally fell asleep. Tomorrow, I vowed, I'd go back to being the mature, responsible Aaron. Tonight, I'd indulge the loss of my innocence and my freedom.

• • •

It was taking a village to replace my mother. On Fridays, David promised to stay in the neighborhood, and Mrs. Stillman kept a discreet eye on him. Mrs. Reilly from down the block took the same bus home from work as David, and she walked him home. That was one thing less to worry about. She was an exceptionally kindhearted woman. Unfortunately, her big heart matched a very big body, and her family worried she would eat herself into an early grave.

The day after Labor Day weekend, I was sitting in a meeting discussing loan criteria at work when the department secretary, Joanna, tapped me on the shoulder. She had taken a message from Winthrop Hospital. "They said you should go there, your brother David has been hurt." I jumped out of my seat. This had to be a nightmare. How many hospitals do I have to go to? Was I dreaming? The meeting could have easily caused me to doze off. I looked around me, to see everyone in the boardroom wondering what Joanna had told me. It was no dream.

"My brother was in an accident, I have to go."

Murmurs of "good luck," "let us know," "hope he's okay" came from around the table and rang in my ears as I ran down the hall, not even stopping to take my bag. I ran to the subway and then had to wait twenty minutes for the next train to Mineola. It felt like two hours. I reached for my little stash of Xanax, popped two, telling myself it was an extreme circumstance, and was glad I hadn't thrown them away yet. You'll know when it's time, I told myself. When the train came, I found a seat where I could be alone and breathe slowly and deeply to calm myself. Luckily, it was well before rush hour.

As soon as the train pulled into the station, I went into high gear, sprinting the two blocks to the hospital's emergency room. When I got there, my breathing was so heavy they thought I was having an asthma attack. Finally I got out the words, "David LeShay, all I know is he was brought in here."

"Oh, okay, and you are?" the nurse asked.

"I'm his brother and legal guardian," I said, about to hyperventilate.

"Are you all right? Can I get you something?"

"Can I please see David, where is he, what happened?" I asked, and the nurse promptly disappeared.

Just as I was about to make a scene, she returned. "Mr. LeShay, is it? Your brother is going to be fine. He broke a bone in his wrist. From what I hear, he's quite the hero. He hurried to the aid of a woman who was falling. She only suffered minor injuries due to his quick action."

I opened the double doors and walked slowly through the ER. They said he was in Room 42, so I moved through the corridors methodically. Although the curtains were a different fabric, the ER sections brought back memories from Pennsylvania, and I started to feel somewhat lightheaded and nauseous. A nurse saw me and asked who I was looking for, and she was nice enough to bring me over to David. This time, he was sitting up and eating Jello. What a relief.

So David was a hero. Great, I thought to myself that I'd never hear the end of it. Still, I felt a hundred times better, except for the guilt of sticking him with Mrs. Reilly. I was told she was resting comfortably and had only a few scrapes from the incident. I stuck my head in to see her and promised her a ride home as soon as David was ready. He was no longer in his cubicle, and the nurse led me to see him. He was having his wrist casted by our friend Dr. Axe.

David told me the details. He and Mrs. Reilly were walking home from the bus, and she tripped over a stick and started to fall. David quickly held out his arms to catch her, and the result was that she broke his wrist, and he'd scraped up his knees in the process. He'd be out of work for about six weeks, and he only had two weeks' sick pay. Later we learned that they would allow him to go on disability for the following four weeks. It was an absurdly small amount of money, but David's job was not about the money he made, even though his paycheck truly thrilled him.

Dr. Axe, cheerful as ever, was quite surprised to see us there.

"I'm glad you like me, Davey boy, but you didn't have to go to such extremes," he said.

"I was trying to catch Mrs. Reilly from falling, but she's as big as you are—ohh," David covered his mouth and turned red, but the doctor thought it was the best joke he'd heard in years.

"I'm astounded that all you broke was a wrist," he said. "I saw Mrs. Reilly."

"Well, when I saw she was falling on top of me, I kind of rolled away," David said.

"Davey, don't ever let anyone tell you you're not smart. Why, you're a bloomin' genius and a hero, too. You prevented your neighbor from getting seriously injured."

"We've had our fill of accidents this year, Doctor," I said.

• • •

That night, unable to sleep and feeling very sorry for myself, I took out my mother's journal again. It went on from our birth to describe all the differences in our development, and I could almost hear the joy in her voice every time David had a real growth event. Oh, sure, she was thrilled and saddened for all three of our successes and setbacks, but I could sense the tone change when she wrote about David. He was truly her life's project. There were some intimate descriptions of times with Dad, but after reading one, I skipped the others. TMI—Too Much Information! Then I read her last entry. It was written the night before they were to drive to my graduation.

Aaron is really graduating college tomorrow. That means we're finally done with college tuition. We told Aaron and Carolyn they were on their own for grad school. We still don't know if he'll be coming home with us. He said he has some options for after graduation, but he won't tell us about them yet. He wants to talk about it in person. I feel worried and happy at the same time.

David is off-the-wall excited about going to his Senior Prom. The whole Special Ed class of graduates is going. I just hope the other seniors leave them alone and don't pick on them. I'll have to remember to call the school and make sure they have a chaperone positioned right by their table that can prevent any nasty kids from making trouble.

I feel really lucky that Carolyn is joining us on this trip. It's so rare these days that the whole family is together when it's not a national holiday. Still, it's a LeShay holiday, and I'm so happy we'll be celebrating together. Well, it's getting late. Time to go to bed. I'll write all about our weekend in my next entry.

chapter twenty-two:
aaron

SO NOW DAVID was out of work for six weeks, and I was going to have to find some help. I took the day off to find a temporary day-program he could go to with his broken wrist. I had no choice but to admit I needed the help of the ACDS. I looked in my mother's phone book and found the name of the woman she went to most often with questions about David. She had been at the funeral—Helen Schatzberg.

Her daughter answered, and she sounded like she had Down syndrome.

"Hi, may I speak to Helen please," I said.

"Yes, may I say who's calling?" she asked.

"My name is Aaron LeShay. I'm calling about my brother David."

Helen picked up the phone very fast and sounded out of breath.

"Aaron, you must forgive me for not calling you since the funeral. How are you? How is David? How can I help you?"

"Well, you see, Mrs. Schatzberg, I'm in kind of a jam. Remember my fiancée from the funeral?"

"Yes, lovely girl. Please, call me Helen."

"Well she was lovely, but not for me anymore."

"Oh, so what did the bitch do?"

"Excuse me?"

"I'm sorry, sometimes I fail to censor myself. Please forgive me. Do you need some help with David?"

"Just temporarily," I said.

"Of course, how can I help?"

"David had a minor accident, but he broke his wrist and can't work. I was wondering if there was a day program he could attend just for the next six weeks or so."

"You live in Westbury, correct?"

"That's right."

"Okay, let me make a few quick calls, and I will find him a program he can attend during the day. I suppose you'd like it if transportation were included?"

"Yes, please, if you can."

In less than an hour she called me back and told me that David could join a delivery team of the ACDS Meals on Wheels program. Program participants put together meals for seniors and other housebound individuals and delivered them with a smile, she said. It was a win-win situation and rewarded both the givers and the receivers. They would pick him up at home at nine tomorrow.

But nothing was easy. David didn't like the idea. He said I was treating him like a baby.

"I don't need to be watched, I can just stay home on my own."

"But you would be part of a program that needs people to help others who can't get out of their homes or who can't cook for themselves. I would think you would be proud to do that. Isn't Hunter in that program? Maybe you can do it together?"

He tried to cross his arms, then put his hands on his waist and assumed the David stubborn position I knew so well.

"I don't want to."

I wasn't going to let him get away with that or try to talk me into feeling guilty for being overprotective. I still felt guilty that he had broken a bone under my watch, and I wouldn't leave him alone again so soon.

"Then I can't even say how disappointed I am in you. I didn't question that you chose a job to make money when you really have all you need from the life insurance. But I know that Mom and Dad would not want you sitting on your ass all day instead of doing something worthwhile."

"Well, why do they need me? Don't they have enough people?"

"Helen Schatzberg explained that two people are taking family vacations now, and they absolutely need your help. Try it for the rest of the week, and if you really don't want to continue, we'll discuss it then."

"Are you ordering me to do it?" asked David, trying to cross his arms again, but wincing when he put his good arm over his broken wrist.

"Let's just call it a strong suggestion."

"Well, okay, I'll try it for this week. Then if I don't like it . . . "

"You will like it, I swear!"

That night, I tossed in bed worried that the ACDS was going to start coming after me and wanting to get more involved in David's care. I was doing all I could, Becca had thrown me a curve ball, but I was determined to be up to the challenge. *There's nothing more dangerous than well-meaning middle-aged women with a cause and a catastrophe to clean up after,* I thought.

• • •

I decided to go in late to work and see that David got off the next day. An ACDS staffer drove a white minivan that said *Meals on Wheels* on both sides. Inside the van it had been set up in the back with a cold area and a hot area for the different meals. David's partner was Don. He explained to David that together they would carry the food and deliver it to the person on the schedule. They even gave David a Meals on Wheels cap and a badge. Before they drove away, I saw David laughing and smiling at Don. Yes! He was going to like this after all.

chapter twenty-three:
david

MEALS ON WHEELS was very cool. Don was funny and told lots of jokes, and our staff driver, Rick, knew the whole route back and forth and he really liked talking to all the people we visited each day. The people were glad to see us at every house we went to. Sometimes they would make us late, telling us stories about when they were young, or about their grandkids, or grown children. They always showed us pictures, and though we were bringing them meals, a bunch of them baked cookies for us. They were really good.

One woman, Adrianna, was only twenty-seven, but she was in a wheelchair and even though she had help from people in her family, she needed us, too. She lived in a ground floor apartment by herself, and her wheelchair had a motor. Her parents lived in Florida and wanted her to move in with them, but she wouldn't go. Her nearby family members—two brothers and six cousins, she told me—took turns helping her. An aide came to help her get ready for bed each night and to get dressed each morning. She told us they didn't have time to do the cooking and shopping, and since she qualified for Meals on Wheels, then she should use it. In fact, they did very little shopping for her, and Rick offered for us to take a list and money from her and go to the store so she would have something to eat when she was done with her meals. We did it for a few of our clients.

Adrianna was very thin. I didn't know why her family didn't bring her food. It made me feel sad. One day I wrote down the address and asked Aaron if we could visit her on a Saturday. Aaron had been very sad since Becca left. I thought that what made me feel good might make him feel good, too.

Aaron said we couldn't just show up, and so he looked up her phone number and I called her. Adrianna was surprised it was me and was confused when I asked if my brother and I could visit.

"But I have meals for the weekend," she said.

"We just want to see you. I want you to meet my twin brother."

We got there at two on the dot, and Adrianna was waiting for us. It looked like she had fussed getting dressed; she looked pretty. Her cousin answered the door. I could tell she was one of those who thought people with Down syndrome were just sweet retards, and she talked to me like I didn't speak English, that crazy loud and slow talking voice that so many people used.

"Hi. How nice of you to visit Adrianna today," she almost shouted, saying each word slowly. "I'm her cousin Roberta."

"I'm David, and this is my twin brother Aaron," I said, keeping my voice low, so that maybe she would stop yelling.

"Hello," Aaron said. "David has been talking about your cousin, and when he suggested we meet her, I was happy to come here with him. I hope we're not interrupting your visit."

"Oh, no," said Roberta, while staring at Aaron. "In fact, I think I'll run some errands if you're going to stay with Adrianna. Is that okay with you, dear? Do you want to use the restroom first?"

"I'm fine. Will you stay for a while?" she asked us. "I can ask Roberta to be back by four, okay?"

Aaron looked over at Adrianna in her chair. "Take your time, Roberta, we'll visit with Adrianna for a few hours," he said.

I felt really proud of Aaron. He was acting like the good guy I knew him to be from before Becca dumped him.

"I hope you don't take offense at this, but you remind me a bit of Clara, you know, Heidi's cousin in the wheelchair? Have you read that book?" Aaron said.

"Of course, but I don't know many men who admit reading

it. Isn't it more of a girl's book?"

"I never thought so, but I'm the sensitive type. Anyway, that was my roundabout way of asking if you'd like to get some fresh air. I know a nice park not too far from here. We could, um, walk there."

"David, your brother is as nice as you are. Sure, would you just mind grabbing a sweater from the coat closet?"

Aaron went to the coat closet and found the sweater she described.

"I'm sorry to be so nosy," he said. "But wouldn't you be better off putting the bar lower in the closet so you can reach it. It's actually a tension bar. I could move it for you later."

"Ha, I've been asking my brother to do that for two years. He said he'll do it when he can."

"Well, I'll do it today, but let's go to the park while the sun is out."

I helped steer Adrianna's wheelchair, and we followed Aaron as he led the way to the park, several steps ahead of us. When we got there, we found a shady spot by a pond with a bench for Aaron and me. There were white ducks, geese, and even a pair of swans swimming around. I wanted to feed them, but Aaron pointed out signs that said it wasn't good for the birds to do that. I watched them dive for food. It was so funny the way their bird butts stuck out of the water.

Adrianna didn't know that we were the twins she had read about in the paper, and we didn't know why she was in a wheelchair. Just two years ago she had a car accident, too. A drunk driver hit her, and she was alone in the car. She had only one more year of college in social work and wanted to go back and finish soon. She didn't feel she could go back to the dorm to live and said she just wasn't ready. Her lawyer was still working on getting her case, she said. She had two older brothers and the cousins who helped her. She said she felt like a burden to them.

"We don't have any family but each other," I told her. "We have no one to burden. I have a girlfriend, I told you about Izzy, right? Aaron had one, too; they were going to get married, but she changed her mind."

"David, you left out the part about her mother getting breast cancer," said Aaron. "They live in California, and Becca felt obligated to stay with her."

"Oh, so are you still in touch with Becca?" Adrianna asked.

"Well, no. That wasn't the only thing, but that's what started it. Who knows what would have happened if her mother had stayed healthy?" Aaron said.

Aaron and Adrianna talked about our lives and how everything had changed. I mostly watched the ducks and stuff. I think of all three of us, I was probably the happiest. I had Aaron who loved me and took care of me. Adrianna didn't feel the same way about her brothers and cousins, and Aaron, well, he was still unhappy about Becca, and he'd told me that after a year or two he was going to look for a different job.

At three-thirty Aaron said we should go home and he would lower her closet bar for her, so that's what we did. We got some soda and chips at the deli on the way there and were relaxing in the living room when Roberta came back.

"Hi," said Aaron. "We were just about to call and have some pizza delivered. Would you like to join us?"

Roberta looked surprised and didn't answer at first. "Oh, thanks, I wish I had known in advance. I have plans with a chicken," she said. "You know, once you defrost those things, they have to be cooked and eaten."

After she left, we got the pizza delivered. We all liked mushrooms and even splurged on garlic knots. Then we got ready to go.

"Well, my aide is going to come in a little while to help me get ready for bed," Adrianna said. "Thanks for a wonderful day. They should call it Friends and Meals on Wheels."

I felt so good after she said that. I gave her a big hug. "Adrianna, you are my favorite client," I said. "Thanks for letting us visit. I'm glad you got to meet Aaron, too."

"It was a pleasure, m'lady," he said, and made a swooping bow that made her laugh. "I hope we can do this again some time."

"Any time," she said.

In the car, Aaron and I talked about Adrianna and how lucky I was to have fully recovered from the accident.

"David, that was a good afternoon. Meeting Adrianna was good for me. She proved what they say about life going on, whether you are ready to face the challenges or not."

"Yeah, she doesn't act sad about her problems," I said.

"And, Adrianna has a lot of people who work together to help her with her physical disabilities, but I'm not convinced they make her feel that they are glad she survived if it means being in a wheelchair and requiring help. In some ways, we are luckier than she is, David," he said. "Thanks for bringing me today."

chapter twenty-four:
aaron

THE MORNING AFTER we visited Adrianna, I took my Prozac and was about to take the Xanax, but instead I thought of that brave young woman. I decided this was a good time to stop the Xanax, and I poured the remaining pills down the toilet and flushed. But the next week I was back to feeling blue again. David was staying over at Hunter's house, so I let Max talk me into going to a bar, since Shelby and the baby were visiting her favorite aunt in Connecticut for the weekend. Max and I got bombed. He loved Shelby and Zoey, but at twenty-two his life was done, he said. What did he have to look forward to?

I argued that he had what most people want very badly. "Don't screw it up, Max, you still have a lot of life to look forward to."

I didn't think I'd ever meet a woman who would agree to have David live with us, and my parents' will and my conscience wouldn't let me have it any other way. Even if it hadn't been in the will, I couldn't see warehousing him in a strange house by himself. No, I was the one who was done.

We'd been smart enough to go to a bar that we could both walk home from. The bar was surprisingly upscale; they'd just renovated the place. I wouldn't mind bringing David's physical therapist Jessie here, I thought. She was hot, and I loved her accent.

Max and I spent a few hours at the bar and went through an entire bottle of scotch. I felt that numb-drunk feeling from my school days, and all I could think was, "Hell, I deserve this." We were too drunk to even hit on girls.

Besides, even when he was drunk, Max knew he couldn't do that, and I didn't want to leave him alone. It was good to bond over our troubles together. It felt like high school when I would complain about being ignored by my parents when David had any kind of issue, and he would complain about being ignored by his parents, period.

The good thing, he said, was that his parents loved Zoey, and he and Shelby were getting along better than ever. Zoey had brought a new dimension of love to their little family. Staying home with her as a newborn, they each had lost a semester of college, but they would graduate in January, and then they would have their wedding, with tiny Zoey as flower girl.

"We want to have Zac pull her in a little red wagon down the aisle," he told me. "Obviously we are not having a church wedding, so we can include our dog and do what we want. I know the odds for high school sweethearts making a marriage last are against us, but we both want it to work."

I gave him a bro hug and said my money was on Zoey and Zac making it down the aisle, and he and Shelby growing old together. At about midnight we staggered out of the bar and made our ways to our respective houses. The next day we both paid for our binge with hangovers and traded ways we could manage it. I put an ice bag on my head, took three Tylenol, and sacked out on the couch.

• • •

The Trick-or-Treaters finally stopped ringing the bell around eight-thirty. David and I had spent all day and evening answering the door and giving out candy to every kid in the neighborhood. I would swear many of them came twice, but who could blame them? We'd picked the best candy—everything chocolate. We didn't mind, they were very cute and looked like they were having so much fun.

Later, just before I was about to turn in for the night, I turned the calendar page. Not counting Veteran's Day, the next holiday was Thanksgiving. How were we going to deal with that? David was already asleep downstairs, and I carried a glass of red wine with me up to bed and took a pad of paper and pen to make a list of things to be thankful for. I titled it:

WHAT WE ARE THANKFUL FOR DESPITE
THE ACCIDENT:
1. *David and I have each other.*
2. *David's leg and his wrist are fully functional thanks to his hard work with Jessie.*
3. *I'm getting used to my job and don't hate it as much as I did in the summer, and I'm getting good experience to find another job in a year.*
4. *We have no financial worries.*
5. *David is able to keep working at Meals on Wheels just on Fridays, and he has developed nice friendships with Don and with Adrianna. He is getting to feel more confident that he can help another disabled person and "make a difference" in her life. He has definitely made progress since high school.*
6. *It has been good for me to reconnect with Max and Shelby, and little Zoey can always get me out of a funk.*

Then I made a list: WHAT I AM NOT THANKFUL FOR
1. *The loss of my family, obviously.*
2. *No Becca, no girlfriend, no prospects.*
3. *Having this stupid holiday looming at me that will make me feel worse than ever.*
4. *Having to take on huge responsibility so young, even though I would never bail on David.*
5. *No social life beyond Max and Shelby.*
6. *Requiring antidepressants to keep up my spirits.*
7. *Mr. Romano banning David from seeing Izzy.*

What the hell was I going to do about Thanksgiving, anyway? Make a turkey for just David and me? How would David take it all? I guess we could pretend the holiday didn't exist, but advertising makes that almost impossible. It was so depressing.

My doctor had given me the name of a psychiatrist who would not only prescribe medicine, but also talk to me about my life, and I decided to give Dr. Shannon a try with this dilemma. After I brought him up to date on my life and how I was feeling, the first thing he did was concur that I should continue on Prozac, and he suggested a stronger dosage.

"There is no shame in taking this medication. You've had a true disaster, and it will help you carry on with life. Just make sure you use it exactly how I prescribed, promise? And what about the Xanax? Are you sure you want to discontinue it?"

"Yes, I'm sure," I said. "I know I can get into a problem with alcohol. Xanax is another addictive substance, right? I just don't trust myself with it. Xanax gives me artificial relief that fades when the pills wear off. It's not worth it. I have too much responsibility to use that crutch. Now can we talk about stuff that's going on?"

"Certainly, what's on your mind?"

"So, Thanksgiving is coming up, and I'm really bummed," I said.

"I can understand that. What are you going to do?" Dr. Shannon asked.

"I was hoping you could help me find an alternative to eating turkey sandwiches. I guess I thought we'd be invited somewhere, but all our possibilities are going out of town. There's no one to go to."

"Well, the standard suggestion would be to volunteer in a shelter, but I don't think that's what you need. Why not make your own Thanksgiving? You need to establish a new kind of gathering, one that emphasizes friends as much as family. Hard as it is to hear, but Mom, Dad, and Carolyn are unavailable. Did your parents ever invite other people for holidays?"

"Not too many since my grandparents died. Occasionally we'd have a friend or acquaintance that had nowhere to go, and my parents would include them."

"What did you think about that?"

"I thought it was nice."

"So then do it. You can make your own Thanksgiving. It's an American tradition to be nontraditional, don't you think?"

I laughed. "Well I'll have to do some thinking and see who I come up with."

But Dr. Shannon didn't want me to put it off. He encouraged me to think beyond the usual cast of characters of family that we didn't have. So, right there we came up with a pretty substantial list to invite. First, Max and Shelby and Zoey were on their own, as their parents were going to see their own elderly parents—whoever was left–and they were all in Florida. Next, I thought of David's physical therapist, Jessie. She might not have anywhere to go, being from Australia, and this would be a great excuse to see her. I'd seriously been thinking about wrenching my back.

David's friend Hunter and his mother lived alone, I wondered if they might need someone to share the holiday with. And David wanted to ask his Meals on Wheels client, Adrianna. Even though she had siblings, it didn't hurt to ask. She had told him that she usually "tagged along with her brother to his in-laws on holidays," and she had not sounded happy about it. I also remembered that Dr. Axe had no pictures of family on his desk at his office, just a photo of his dog and cat cuddled together. I pictured his beefy hands and could not remember ever seeing a ring there. He'd come to David's rescue twice, and we had grown fond of him. I didn't know how he felt about socializing with patients. But, as Dr. Shannon said, the worst he can do is say no thanks. There was also a new guy at work, Rashi, who had just transferred to my office from India. He was funny and smart, and we had started having lunch together.

Dr. Shannon encouraged me to invite all these people to our house for Thanksgiving, the sooner the better. "You've got a good number and quite a diverse crowd. Even if they don't all come, I'll bet it would be an interesting evening, and it'll keep your mind off of your parents and sister. I predict your invitation will brighten the holiday for your guests, who may also be feeling isolated."

"But I can't cook a Thanksgiving dinner; I don't know how," I said.

"C'mon, Aaron, You've certainly heard of caterers. Just pick up the phone."

Our house was made for entertaining. The dining room table could easily fit up to sixteen with all its leaves, and amazingly, everyone we invited accepted the invitation. We had eleven people in all, a very respectable number. By the time we were asked to be guests by Colin and his wife, we had already received yeses to our homemade invitations. We made construction paper turkeys tracing David's hand and mailed them out right away. Who could say no to that? Everyone volunteered to bring something, so with the catered turkey and all the side dishes, we ended up with an amazing feast.

chapter twenty-five:
aaron

JESSIE WAS FANTASTIC. She had insisted on coming early and helping play hostess. "You blokes need a woman's touch for this," she said. I could actually feel myself falling for her, imagining that she was my date, and it felt good. She was about four years older than me, and I hoped that didn't matter to her. I definitely felt a spark between us. I hoped she did, too.

The caterer brought the dinner in disposable serving ware, and Jessie brought several bottles of Australian wine, plus little paper turkey nameplates to put at each seat. I did a cartwheel in my head when I saw she had placed herself next to me.

"These wines are the Australian brands people here don't know about," she said.

Along with the turkey, cranberry sauce, gravy, and potatoes—sweet and white mashed from the caterer—we had exotic dishes from our guests. There were poached pears in wine sauce from Adrianna, sweet and sour turkey meatballs from Dr. Axe, blueberry-apple meringue pie and pumpkin pie from Max and Shelby, cinnamon-raisin noodle pudding from Hunter and Suzanne, and Rashi brought some traditional Indian goat curry and nan. We used Mom's good china and crystal and the sterling silver she had inherited from her grandmother.

"Our Mom used to tell us that her mother said the silver 'fell off a truck' during the Great Depression, right, David?" I said.

"Yep, she told that story every holiday," David said. An awkward silence followed. "Ahem," said Dr. Axe. "As I seem to be the elder statesman here, I'd like to thank our hosts for bringing us all together on this holiday."

"Hear, hear, L'chaim, cheers, skol, God's blessing." Everyone clinked wine glasses around and across the table.

"To Aaron and David," Max toasted, and the glasses clinked for a second time.

David and I were probably the only ones actually missing our parents. Well, Jessie said she would have liked her "oldies" there to show them a great American tradition, but it wasn't as if it were a holiday that they had ever celebrated together.

Everyone took a turn moving us to tears of laughter or poignant sadness. Sometimes it was both. We all got very quiet as Adrianna told us about her original dream to be a dancer.

Rashi broke the silence. "I knew it, you have the true grace of a ballerina."

"Well, what most people don't realize is that ballerinas have to go through as much pain as football players. That drunk may have trashed my dancing plans, but he relieved me of the terrible foot pain that I'd had for ten years." Her own laughter gave us permission to join her.

Jessie had us in stitches with her tales from down under. She regaled us with tall tales about her pet koalas taking rides in their family kangaroo's pouch and being punished as a child by being forced to have nothing but shrimp on the barbie for every meal for a full week.

Zoey was, as my Mom would have said, delectable, as she delighted herself and everyone else with trying every new food on the table. David and I made her a pilgrim hat to wear for the occasion. Max and Shelby gave us a preview of what they planned for their upcoming Valentine's Day wedding and portrayed the horror of what they expected from their much more conservative families, complete with some hilarious impersonations.

David gave a very funny imitation of the ways so many of the shoppers at Waldbaum's give him instructions. "They take one look at me and start to talk slower. 'Now those eggs are break-a-ble so please pack them in a sep-a-rate bag, all by themselves, with no other items,' they say. Hey, I have Down's, but I know what eggs are!" he said.

Rashi had us choking on our food with laughter, telling us how Americans take their opulence for granted. "The women in my country have a color-coded system with their dots that we keep secret from you Americans, but they warn us when they haven't been able to wash their saris in two weeks, and we keep a safe distance," he joked.

Dr. Axe, who insisted on being called Norman, was a great addition to the gathering. He was a fount of doctor jokes and gruesome bone-breaking stories that he told with such glee and humor that he had all of us laughing at things I would never have dreamed could be funny. Norman boasted that he once had a work tidbit published in *Reader's Digest*. He also told me something in private that greatly eased my mind. I was showing him my Dad's book collection after dinner, and I got up the nerve to ask him if he knew a good urologist.

"Why, are you having piddle issues?" he asked.

"No, it's not for me. I was thinking it might be best if David had a vasectomy."

"Whatever for?" he asked.

"The usual reason, Doc. David has a serious girlfriend. So far he says they are still virgins, but I don't want to take any chances."

"I guess no one ever told you about Down's and sterility, then?"

"Sterility?" I asked.

According to Norman, almost all Down syndrome men are sterile or have a very low sperm count. Izzy and David's chances of having a baby are almost none. The genetic anomaly was not meant to pass on to future generations. That made sense, scientifically speaking. Still, when I said I was concerned that almost zero was not zero and that there had already been talk of marriage between the two of them, he suggested that Izzy could get a shot of Depo-Provera a few times a year that would ensure no pregnancy would take place. Advances in birth control had come a long way, especially for people who had a hard time keeping up with the pill or the diaphragm and condom, all of which required usage either daily or every time there was intercourse.

I was so relieved that I wanted to call the Romanos at the ski lodge. I thought this might alleviate some of their worries and make them more accepting of the kids as a couple. But I forced myself to wait until the next week. Certainly nothing was happening now.

Zoey was the first to loudly signal that it was time for the evening to end. I learned from her that once a baby is cranky, you've got to put her to bed, and Max and Shelby wanted her sleeping in her own crib to ensure that they could sleep in on their day off. I had driven Adrianna and put on my coat to take her home, but Rashi stepped in and insisted that it would be his honor. I really liked hearing his accent. He had such a unique way of saying things it amused me.

"No, no, my friend," Rashi said. "You have completed the tremendous task of hosting a most elegant holiday dinner. Please allow me the honor of escorting this lovely lady back to her home."

Adrianna blushed, but allowed Rashi to guide her wheelchair ever so gently down the path and lift her like an antique porcelain doll into the car. Again I was reminded of Clara from Heidi, only now Rashi had stepped into the role of Peter the goatherd. Hmm, I thought to myself, he even brought goat curry.

By ten, only Jessie, David, and I were left. David was yawning and could hardly keep on his feet. Jessie took him by the arm and led him to his room.

"You, mate, are just about done in. How about I help Aaron finish up here? Thanks for invitin' me, Davey. Everything was aces."

David, having had his one glass of wine, which was honestly one glass too many, was in no condition to insist on staying up and practically fell asleep before he could change and get under the covers. I crept in about fifteen minutes later after hearing him snore and pulled the blanket over him so he wouldn't wake up cold in the middle of the night.

"Aww, you are such a ripper of a brother to David," Jessie said.

"Ripper?" I asked.

"It's good, it's all good. You are one special mate, Aaron LeShay." She put the plate she had been scraping into the dishwasher; turned toward me, put her arms around my neck, and the rest followed. We kissed gently at first, each of us making sure the other one wanted this, and then, as Jessie would say, it became quite "pash." I prayed that this wasn't the wine talking. Then I took her hand and led her into the living room where we got comfortable on the couch. Wow, I'd forgotten what it felt like to kiss someone new. It was fantastic! We continued kissing for some time, and then Jessie stopped, slid away a few inches, and cleared her throat.

"Let's take it slow, mate. I could fall hard for you, and the last time I did that, I ended up with a big bad hurt. Let's finish in the kitchen now and talk s'more. Is that okay with you, Aaron?"

I kissed her chastely on the lips and said, "That's perfectly okay, Jessie. I could fall hard for you, too." Oh, I was thrilled to hear her say that. "And I also know what it feels like to have your heart stomped on. I'm all for taking it slow. Now," I took her hand and pulled her up off the couch, "let's finish cleaning up before I'm stuck doing it all by myself."

Never was cleaning up so much fun. We laughed and teased one another, and in what seemed like an instant we started to become the best of friends. I guess all we needed to light that spark was a change of venue. At midnight, my mother's cuckoo clock tweeted the end of the day and the beginning of another.

"Oh, listen there," said Jessie. "I just may turn into a pumpkin pie. I think it's time for me to go home."

"Not until we make a date," I said, putting my arms around her waist. "Let's see, it just turned Friday. What are you doing Saturday night?" I said, and kissed her.

"Mmmm, you tell me," she said.

"I'll call you tomorrow with a plan that doesn't include leftover turkey. How about I pick you up at seven, okay?"

"That sounds perfect," she said. And just as I was about to lean in for another good kiss, she pecked me on the cheek and was out the door.

• • •

I went to bed dreaming about Jessie. Maybe this is what I needed after all. A woman a little older than me, more mature than Becca, someone like Jessie who had been making it all alone in a foreign country. She could be the solution to my problems, and even if she wasn't, kissing her made my head feel light and my pants quite tight. Her auburn hair flowed thick and wavy over her shoulders and down her back, framing a small, round face with big green eyes. A patch of freckles spread across the bridge of her nose and decorated each rosy cheek. To me, she was perfection.

I planned a romantic and fun date. We started out at the restaurant near the old Jones Beach Hotel and then went to Newbridge Road Park for some cozy ice-skating, holding hands mandatory. After all, I told her, if I fell and injured myself, I knew a great physical therapist. Then we drove north to the Vanderbilt Planetarium where they had a midnight laser show to classic rock music. We finished off one of the bottles of Australian wine in the car before going in, and that helped enhance the show, which can otherwise be kind of corny. We came out of the planetarium, and the late autumn night was full of real stars. Being at one of the higher points on Long Island made them seem as close as the ones that had been merely light bulbs inside the show.

"Can you believe if I was 'ome, I would just be getting up," Jessie said.

"I'd like you to feel this is home. Are you planning on going back to Australia for good eventually?" I asked, trying to will her into saying "no."

"I'm not sure, Aaron, it all depends."

"On me?"

"What was that we'd said about takin' it slow?" she said. "I'm sensing a very abrupt speeding up 'ere. I can't know what's ahead for me just now."

"You're right, but honestly, in your gut, do you think there could be a real future for us? I mean, would you fight that or welcome the possibility?" Before she could answer I moved closer for a kiss and held her tightly but comfortably in my arms.

"What can I say, I'm not sure about anything at the moment." She closed her eyes in pleasure as I began kissing her neck and nibbling on her earlobes.

When I came up for air, I said, "Just say whether you think

it's at all a possibility or that you've completely closed your mind toward it; give me a hint."

She stopped me from coming in for a third kiss and said, "Aaron, I am not closing my mind or my heart to the possibility of us being together in the long run. And it's not fair to ask me that right after you've made me toes curl. But if this does get serious, I want to get there slowly, so let's go 'ome now, okay?"

"Whatever you say, luv," I said, trying imitate her accent. "If 'ome you want, then 'ome it shall be."

We parted with a date set for the following Saturday night.

"How would you feel about dinner and a movie with David and Izzy, or would that be too weird for you?" I asked Jessie when I called to confirm our date.

After hearing what Dr. Axe told me about David and Izzy's very poor prospects of becoming parents, the Romanos had started allowing supervised visits. I was sure they would agree to her joining all of us at the movies.

"No, sounds aces! David is such a dear, and I'm eager to meet his little woman friend. He's told me a lot about that Isabella. You pick a film that would be good for us to see together. You know, I have a little niece with Down's—my brother's daughter. Melinda, she's a dear. Don't worry so much, we'll all have a good time."

"Great, I'll make all the arrangements."

chapter twenty-six:
jessie

A DOUBLE DATE with David and Isabella, this should be interesting, but I was sure I could handle it—no worries. I work with all kinds of people, and I love helping them heal. That's why I went into PT. I sound like a bloomin' saint, don't I? But it makes me feel that I'm not just taking up space on this planet. So don't start any canonizations just yet, right? Working is one thing, but going out socially in public—well, I'd just have to see.

We got to a nice-looking Italian restaurant that seemed a notch above family-friendly and was right next door to the cinema. The hostess took one look at us and quickly showed us to a dimly lit booth in the corner, somewhat out of sight of the other customers.

"It's so good to see you. I'm so sorry about your family," she said. "Here's your regular booth." Aha, so they came here often.

When we walked through the main part of the restaurant, I noticed several people look up and then look away. I might just have been sensitive to it, but I know I saw one couple shush their little girl and pull her hand down as she started to point at us. Hmm, second twinge.

When Aaron said, "Look, David, they have your favorite, spaghetti with red clam sauce," I was certain that he'd picked this place for more than its convenient location to the movie. I always remember me mum telling me when I was a girl never to have spaghetti on a date, because it's impossible to eat without looking like you've got worms hanging out of your mouth. "A sure turn-off for your bloke," she'd say. Izzy's mum must have given her the same warning; she ordered veal Marsala, a pretty neat dish, and when I saw her struggle a bit with the veal, I quietly helped her cut them into more manageable pieces. I chose the stuffed shrimp, mindful of Mum's advice. Aaron watched for my reaction as David slurped the pasta, and the sauce gave him a bit of a red beard, trailing a few dots of sauce that nearly blended with his red shirt. I also watched my own food so that I wouldn't make a mess of myself. Truth, I really did have to look away at times while David ate, although he was enjoying his food immensely. Even though I'd expected it, it still was a bit of a turn-off. I hoped our booth gave us enough privacy. No wonder it was their regular. Then I thought a bit about my niece Melinda; at her age, this wasn't really an issue yet, but someday I knew it would be.

"This was the best," David said, when his plate was empty. "Izzy, how was yours?"

David and Izzy are such a sweet twosome and clearly very fond of each other. It did get a little dicey for us though when Izzy bluntly asked Aaron, "So are you two, like, um, serious now?"

I saw Aaron get a little flustered, so I jumped in and said, "You know how it is, Izzy, we're still getting to know each other, but it does seem like something could percolate. We're just taking our time and seeing how the coffee tastes when it's brewed."

"Izzy and I have been friends, one, two, three years, and a little more," David counted on his fingers.

"That's right," Aaron said. "You're old friends, but Jessie and I haven't known each other long. Yep, we're just like coffee when you first start to make it. The coffeemaker immediately starts bubbling, but when it settles down and you take a sip, you know if you've got it just right, or it's too bitter and you run to the sink and spit it out."

Aaron looked pleased with himself for being able to run with my coffee metaphor. But Izzy and David thought the image of spitting out coffee was hilarious.

"Aaron, you are funny," Izzy said.

"I hope you don't spit out Jessie," David said.

At that the four of us had a full-blown snicker at Aaron's expense and mine, but it was all right good fun.

The picture Aaron chose was a James Bond flick, and again, I think he did it intentionally, knowing it would be hard for David and Izzy to follow. Like most folks, I want complete silence at a movie show. I even work at keeping my popcorn quiet. But Aaron knew that wasn't going to happen. He found seats for us close to the front so that the kids' voices wouldn't carry when they asked questions. Then it was pretty much a show and tell for two hours. It was a good thing I didn't really care about the movie and that the audience was sparse, because I was getting irritated despite knowing they couldn't help it. I slunk deep in my seat, the pre-show warnings about not talking flashing in my head, expecting to be ousted by an usher any minute. With each scene David or Izzy would ask Aaron what was going on.

"Why is that guy so mad?" David would ask.

"What's that lady trying to hide?" Izzy wanted to know.

Aaron kept them down to a low whisper, but if it had been anyone else doing that, I would've taken a swing at them. I made a mental note not to go with them to a movie rated more than G again and made sure we left long into the credits so that I could avoid the glares of any audience members we had disturbed. Later, I told Aaron I knew what he had been doing.

"Did I pass your test?" I asked, after David and Izzy had been brought home and we were on the way to my flat.

"Was it that obvious?" he asked. "Are you mad at me?"

"Mad? You were too blatant about it for me to be mad. But from now on, let's eat spaghetti at home and the same thing for Bond movies. Let's watch them on a DVD. If we go out to a flick with them, it'll be a Disney picture. Did you know the *Little Mermaid* was filmed in Oz?"

"Really?" Aaron believed that for a moment, and then realized I was twitting him.

"Oh, the cartoon?" he said, laughing at his own gullibility. "So it did bother you, their behavior?" He got serious for a moment.

"It bothered me that it might be disturbing to others, especially at the cinema. But I think it's all manageable. I'd certainly be happy to go out with them again. Don't worry so much, Aaron. Coming in to see my flat?" I asked when he pulled up at my door.

"Sure, um, do Aussies have the same 'third date rule' that we have?"

"Aaron, I don't date by the rules, certainly not that one, tho' I know it's somewhat of an expectation with Americans. Besides, this is our second date, and we agreed to take it slow, remember?"

Aaron's face fell as if I had just taken away his sweets. I smothered my laugh and maintained my self-control so he would know I meant it. There would be no knickers kicked off tonight.

"But we can still have a good snog and talk some more, you game?"

"Absotively," he said.

Aaron spent the first ten minutes taking inventory of my flat.

"This place is great. It looks like a little piece of Australia," he said. "Umm, I already asked you if you are planning to eventually move back home, didn't I?"

It wasn't a casual question. He seriously wanted to know if we had a future, or was there heartbreak in store for him if we fell in love? I could tell he'd been thinking about it and did not want to get burned by geography a second time.

"I don't have any plans to go back home for good," I said, which was the truth. "I like the faster pace of the States. I was set to stay here when I was engaged to Nick, and I haven't really changed my mind. But I'll just have to see how things go. I keep my photos and my mementos of home, but I want to make my own place in the world, and I still hope I can make it here. Of course, I'll always stay close to my family. But two of my brothers have left Australia, and we keep tight, so I know that wouldn't be a problem."

Aaron grinned uncontrollably. I really should get him in a poker game.

"That's good to hear. As we told the kids, I know we're still in the percolation stage, but I'd hate to find we had the perfect blend and then lose it. You know I have to stay close to David, right?"

"Yeah, I figured that out. Don't worry about it so much, Aaron. If we're meant to be, we'll work it out."

We naturally gravitated to my overstuffed couch, and as we sank into it, we wrapped our arms around one another and got to the snogging part of the evening. It was hard to stop there, but at midnight, I claimed I was going to turn into a pumpkin again and led him gently to the door, leaving him with a soft kiss on the lips and a promise to see him again very soon.

chapter twenty-seven:
aaron

JUST WHEN YOU survive one holiday, the next one is biting you on the ass. Christmas was flourishing in every shopping center, mall, street corner, building, school. Santa's helpers were ringing bells on corners and sitting with dampened laps from crying babies forced by their loving moms to have those special photos. I felt my tension grow as soon as the sales began the day after Thanksgiving. I also found myself wishing I hadn't thrown away the Xanax; I had stopped for at least two months. Again, David and I were faced with coming up with a new way of celebrating. Mom had handled each holiday with aplomb. We never saw all the work she put into it. I really didn't want a repeat performance of Thanksgiving. As well as it turned out, I wasn't ready to do it so soon again.

Jessie had promised to spend Christmas with her family in Australia, and she wanted me to come. David had been invited to stay with Hunter, but he wanted to be with me.

I didn't want to be away from him on Christmas either, but I was torn. Jessie and I were getting very serious about each other, and I decided I needed to put myself first for once. Finally, I chose a compromise: I would spend Christmas with David and have David stay with Hunter while I went Down Under and spent New Year's with Jessie and her family. Our intentions to take it slow had been impossible for either of us to keep. The "coffee" was the best either of us had ever had, it brewed perfectly and quickly, and we were in love. We'd been seeing each other almost every night for a month now. Her family wanted to meet me, and I wanted to meet them. It was an expensive trip for a five-day weekend, but I'd been frugal with our inheritance and I felt I deserved this splurge. David and I would spend a quiet Christmas together.

We tried our best, but Christmas was rough for us. We bought a tree from the vendor our family had always gone to, and I had to smile, because for once, I let David buy the big tree, instead of being more practical the way our parents had been. Following LeShay tradition, on Christmas Eve I went into the attic and brought down the ornaments we hung every year. Each year we had added a new ornament, but not this year. Mom always chose the new ornament. Most of the ornaments had stories to go with them, and I tried to take the place of Mom and Dad telling them this year.

David pulled out one of the newer ones from the box.

"We got this at that shop near your college, right?" he said.

"Yeah, it was at the Amish Farmer's Market. It was August, but they already had these and Mom wanted to commemorate my going to F&M."

"It's pretty," said David. "But I was sad when you left."

I nodded my head, but I didn't want to talk about that now.

When we came to the ornament Carolyn had made as a girl scout that said *Twin's First Christmas,* we choked back our tears at first, but as David let his tears out, I followed and we both had a good cry. Once the tree was decorated, we had a pizza delivered, put on comfy sweats, and settled in for a few hours of video games. It wasn't exactly your traditional Christmas, but at least we were together.

That night, David and I managed to sneak back to the tree to put down presents. David had been there first. He had put two presents for me, and a present for Izzy. I also had two presents for David, plus I had bought a few things we could use together, from Santa—a few new video games, matching funny slippers, and a new TV for the kitchen. Our parents didn't believe in watching TV while eating together, but now I really thought it would help us get through mealtimes. I planned to bring Jessie's gift with me to Australia.

After we had opened and admired all the presents on Christmas morning, Mrs. Stillman came over with two tins of homemade cookies for us. She asked us to join them for Christmas dinner later that day, and we accepted the invitation. A quiet Christmas might work for lovers, but it's not the best for brothers. After she left, David and I agreed one tin was enough for us so we decided to give Adrianna one.

We got dressed and took the Santa Star cookies in the Rudolph the Reindeer tin and drove to Adrianna's house. We didn't call ahead because we wanted it to be a surprise and figured we could leave the tin if she wasn't at home. It felt good to get out of the house for a little while. It had started to be a white Christmas, but the snow had quickly turned to rain.

We rang the bell, and Rashi met us at the door.

"Well, Christmas Greetings," he said, "what an honor for you to grace us with your good cheer on this holiday."

"Hey, Rashi," I said, clapping him on his shoulder. "We didn't expect to see you here. We came to bring Adrianna some of our neighbor's Christmas cookies."

Adrianna wheeled herself up to the door. "Well, don't all stand there in a clump, come on in," she said.

We ended up sitting around the table and eating the cookies. The four of us watched as Rashi set the table and poured us hot chocolate. He seemed very much at home at Adrianna's place.

"So now you know our little secret, my friend," Rashi said. "The lovely Adrianna and I have been keeping company. I am indebted to you, and to you, David, for making the introduction."

"You're welcome," David and I said almost simultaneously. We left them after about an hour to have their romantic Christmas, and we had a nice holiday dinner with the Stillmans. The fantastic food and teasing banter were a good distraction from thoughts of our own family.

chapter twenty-eight:
david

THE SIGN IN the window at Zale's said *SALE! Genuine CZ Diamonds—Make this a New Year's Eve to Remember.* One of the guys at Waldbaum's drove me to the mall during lunch. I couldn't believe it, I had saved almost sixty dollars of my pay, and right there was a real engagement ring for fifty-four ninety-nine. I knew Izzy would love it, but I wasn't sure if she would say yes. I went into the store to buy it.

"Uh, the ring in the window, please," I said.

"You want the CZ diamond solitaire?" the girl behind the counter asked.

"Yes, it's for my girlfriend."

The girl turned away from me and went to her co-worker and whispered. I could feel myself turning red. Those women thought I was stupid.

"You know, that's an engagement ring, sir," said the second girl.

"I know. Can you put it in a box?"

"What size do you need? Do you know her ring size?" the first one asked, smiling too much.

"No, not sure. Let me see it . . . please," I said. It was hard not to get angry and say something nasty to her.

She shrugged and handed me the ring. I put it on my own

hand and it fit on my pinky. That should be right, her hands were smaller than mine.

"This seems like it will fit her."

"Well, if it doesn't, she can bring it back and we can adjust it."

I didn't see how they could change the size of a solid ring, but I was not going to ask. "I'll take it."

She put it in the black velvet box, and it shined as bright as a star. I gave her all the money I had.

"Sorry there's so much change, but it's all here," I said. The change rolled across the counter and some of the coins fell on the floor. I had thirty-five dollars in bills, but the rest was in change. Both of the salesgirls were rescuing the coins that had fallen and were counting it, and if they looked at each other, they would burst into giggles, but we got it all counted at last. I'd have to skip lunch, good thing my friend was going to drive me back to the store; he was waiting for me. I told my friend everything had gone great and I had finished my Christmas shopping. When I got home, I put the box all the way in the back of my night table drawer. Aaron would never look in there.

After Christmas, I was invited to spend New Year's Eve at the Romanos with their whole family. Izzy must have begged them for it, and they were allowing me to come over, as long as we all stayed together, and I slept downstairs. Hunter understood my canceling on him. Of course, Mrs. Romano made a terrific dinner, then the family sat together in the living room and watched the parties in Times Square and all over the world on TV. They even showed Australia, but we couldn't find Aaron. At midnight, the Romanos gave all of us, even the little boys, who they had to shake awake, sips of champagne, and toasted 2005 to be a better year. I really wanted to be alone with Izzy. It had started snowing at about 11 pm. There was about an inch of fresh snow on the ground, and I asked if Izzy and I could go out and catch the first snow. Mr. Romano nodded yes. He could barely keep his eyes open.

We bundled up in our winter coats and boots, Mrs. Romano plopped hats on our heads, and we walked down the driveway. Snow makes everything look so new and bright. It was still coming down, but in small, light flakes, and of course, we tried to catch some on our tongues. We held hands and slipped and slid down the driveway until we got to their bench under the big oak tree. The tree covered the bench from getting snow on it. I took out the ring box and just like in the movies, I got on one knee, and asked, "Izzy will you marry me? I love you."

"Oh . . . oh, David," she said. "Get up, my parents might see you."

"You didn't say yes yet," I said.

"Please, just get up. If my Dad sees us, there will be big trouble."

I got up and took my place at her side on the bench again. It was cold, but we didn't care.

"David, I say yes. I do want to marry you, and I love you, too. But I'm sure my parents will say no. I'm too young and too, you know . . . "

"I know, but we're in love. Just because we aren't as smart as some people doesn't mean we can't be in love. I wish my parents were here. Mom would let us. We'll find a way, I promise."

"David, let's be engaged in secret for a while, okay? I'll hide the ring. But we should wait to tell my parents or your brother."

"Yeah, they will wreck this for us. And right now, I feel so happy."

But first she tried it on. Hiding behind a large bush, just in case some parents or little brothers were peeking out at us, she held out her hand and I slipped it on her finger. I don't know which sparkled more, the ring or her eyes. We kissed and held each other. I told her that if we stay strong, someday we will get married. Then she put the ring back in the box and the box deep into her inside coat pocket to be taken to a good hiding place.

chapter twenty-nine:
aaron

I WAS VERY excited to spend New Year's with Jessie, but I was unprepared for the toll the long plane ride would take on my stomach. The pilot apologized for the unusual bouts of turbulence, but I got hit with airsickness like never before, and I was still suffering from it when the plane landed in Australia.

After giving me a tight hug, which almost caused me to heave again, Jessie took a closer look at me and gasped, "You're as green as a pickle, what's the matter?"

"I didn't take that flight well." Speaking brought another wave of nausea. "Hold that thought," I called, running for the nearest restroom, where by now dry heaves were all I had left inside me.

Using breath spray for about the tenth time that day, I slowly made my way back to Jessie. Without attempting a kiss, I clasped her hand tightly in mine, and having made my way through customs quickly, we made it to her car, only stopping for me to retch once more.

"Jessie, I'm going to make a terrible first impression on your parents. I look and feel like shit, even though I'm so glad to see you." I had pictured this moment very differently in my mind before the flight.

"No worries, Aaron. I'm going to tuck you right into bed. We'll make the intros tomorrow."

I doubted this would be possible, but Aussies are much more laid back than Americans. Jessie went in ahead of me, told her family that I was done in by the long flight and that she was taking me straight to the guest room. They would have to meet me tomorrow. Jessie and I had decided in advance not to push things and to sleep in separate rooms while guests in her parents' house. Miraculously, they listened to Jessie. My mom would have been in that room with a cup of tea and some crackers ten minutes after any guest of mine had arrived sick, but maybe Jessie's being twenty-six made a difference.

Jessie got me all set up and then brought me some tea and crackers. She definitely had the mother instinct in her. *Good to know for the future.* She gave me some antacid and slipped me a sleeping pill. The whole time, not one member of her family stuck a head in the door. I took her remedies, pulled the covers over my head and was soon sound asleep.

The next morning I woke to hear Jessie and her mother talking about me, nothing serious, her mom just wanted to know what I ate for breakfast. I got up feeling 100 percent better, slipped into the shower, and I even used the blowdryer on my hair to look my best for Jessie's family. I dressed in my nicest summer clothes, which felt great because it was winter back in New York. I strolled into the kitchen and apologized for my disappearing act the night before.

"Don't give it another thought, mate," her father said. "You're not the first one of our guests to arrive here green around the gills. That flight is a killer for some people. You just rest yourself on the deck, breathe in some of our special Aussie air, and you'll think you're in paradise."

New Year's is a huge family affair at Jessie's, with her parents, siblings, in-laws, and cousins holding a barbecue in a Sydney park during the day and then after sunset watching the kind of fireworks we have on the Fourth of July.

At the barbecue our party grew as the day went on, as more friends and families joined us. As I helped myself to another serving of chips, I saw a little girl who had Down syndrome digging a hole in a corner of the children's play area by herself. She must be Jessie's niece, I realized. I went over to her.

"Hello, Happy New Year, my name is Aaron, I'm a friend of

Jessie's," I said. "Are you one of her nieces?"

She looked up at me, her light blue eyes slightly crossed behind thick glasses. "Jessie is my aunt, and you talk funny," she said.

"You are right about that. I'm from the United States. You knew right away I'm not from around here, didn't you?"

"Well, duh," she said. "Anyone could tell that."

While I was trying to think of something I could say that would further this stalled conversation, Jessie rescued me.

"Aaron, I see you've met Melinda, my brother Ernie's youngest daughter." Then turning to her niece, she asked, "Melinda, why are you sitting here diggin' a hole? Aren't you hungry? Don't you want to play with your cousins?" Jessie asked.

"No, not just now." Melinda carefully finished the perfectly round three-inch hole and decorated its edges with smooth white pebbles. "I'm kind of busy now, I'll come later."

I knelt down beside Melinda. "That's a very pretty hole you've dug. I like the way you've decorated it."

"Thanks, my Mum is going write some special things I did this year, and then next year we'll dig it up. It's a . . . "

"Time capsule?" I offered.

"Yeah, that's it. I forgot." She looked down and seemed embarrassed.

"Well, I think that is one great idea. I may even make one for myself when I go home."

She looked at me in frank disbelief. "Do you have a little girl like me?" she asked.

I swallowed hard. "No, no, I'm afraid the only family I have now is my brother David. He's back in the States with his girlfriend and her parents."

"Where are your parents?"

"Um, they're in heaven now. My sister is there, too. I can't see them anymore."

"Oh, that is a small family. I have two brothers, Mum and Pop, my grannies and grampas, and aunts, and uncles, and cousins. See?" she said, standing and sweeping the area with her arm to demonstrate.

"Yes, you're very lucky, and I am too, to be spending the holiday with all of you."

Jessie came back to me with a beer.

"C'mon, Aaron, the guys are getting up a game of soccer. Why don't you show them how the U.S. does it?"

I was hesitant to step into that kind of situation, but what the hell, it was all in fun. I turned to Melinda once more.

"Do you want to come watch us play?" I asked.

But she shook her head. "No, maybe later."

At that, Jessie pulled me by the hand, and we made our way over to the soccer field where they were choosing up sides.

"Ere's one more for you mates, don't forget my man Aaron."

Well, when in Australia, do as they do, so for the first time in a very long time I found myself deeply engrossed in a friendly, but kind of edgy family sports competition. It brought to mind the iconic Kennedy family and their famous football games on the lawn.

Aussies play hard and always seem to be celebrating— holiday or not. The five days were over in a flash. Jessie told me her parents had expressed their concern over her getting serious with me and ending up with the package deal I now presented, but they seemed less freaked out than Becca's parents had been. They knew it was up to Jessie, and when they saw us together, I think they accepted that Australia would no longer be her home. If our romance kept going, as it appeared it would, Oz would be a place to visit, and we in turn would always be glad for them to visit us.

On the last night, Jessie's father, whose nickname was Punch, coined for his famous holiday punch, which I agreed had a knockout effect, asked me to join him on the porch. It was a balmy summer night, and the constant loud crackle of the mosquito zapper provided some unusual background sounds.

He offered me a can of Foster's and held his out to me for a toast. We clinked cans, then each took a long swig of the beer.

"Here's to makin' new friends," he said.

"Yes, and thank you for everything. You've all made me feel welcome here."

"No worries, Aaron, my Jessie thinks you're aces. She looks so happy when she's with you, her eyes glow. I didn't see her look like that with the last guy. He was, umm, as you say it, a schmuck."

"She makes me very happy, too, Punch," I said. "I'm going to do everything I can to see that we stay together. I love her, you know."

"I can see that mate. Just don't hurt her, and we'll be fine," he said.

• • •

"I never thought David would be the one responsible for my meeting my soulmate," I said to Jessie as we tried to get comfortable for the long flight. "Meeting your family proved to me that you didn't just sprout up from nowhere so perfect. They are a cool group of people."

"Well, they fancied you. They thought you might someday keep me from being an old maid," Jessie said with a teasing smile. She was wearing the locket I'd given her and had put a picture of the two of us inside it.

"They are certainly very intuitive. Because, someday, that's exactly what I hope to do."

As I napped on the plane, my mind kept drifting to little Melinda. When I saw she had Down syndrome, I had just automatically assumed that I could make friends with her, and although she hadn't been rude, she had certainly not been swept away by my charm. Up until tonight I'd thought of myself as an undisputed expert and friend to all people with Down syndrome. Now I was beginning to doubt my skill and wonder if it was limited to David.

After that trip Jessie and I agreed we "were engaged to be engaged," or "working towards it," as Jessie put it. With one broken engagement apiece already, we were both cautious, and we wanted this one to work out. We were well aware that we each fit the rebound lover category, and we had to make sure that this wasn't the case with us. It was hard to believe we'd only been together a short time, so we agreed to make this year the one to test and see if next New Year's Eve we could possibly start planning a wedding. My mother had given me some advice about getting married when I was in college. I remembered it as we talked.

"No quickie marriages, Aaron," she had said. "You should date a minimum of a year before becoming engaged. That way you can see how compatible you are. Will she feel she's a football widow during the season if you want to watch the games? Will she want to go to the beach every weekend when you'd rather go play golf? It may sound silly, but a married couple has to be able to have fun together and apart. It's often the little differences that pile up and bring upon the end of a marriage." Thanks, Mom, we will take your advice.

chapter thirty:
aaron

YOU NEVER KNOW when it's going to hit you. As I was picking out Valentines for Jessie, I saw the rack with Valentines–Sister. Carolyn had never had a true love, and she never would. I talked about Carolyn to Dr. Shannon that week.

"She never had a chance," I said. "At least my parents had a good life together. It was too short, but they crammed a lot of love and life experience into those years, and they didn't leave us until we were old enough to take care of each other. But Carolyn, sometimes it makes me so angry that she was cheated out of a life. She would have been a wonderful wife and mother. She was a great teacher. We got incredible tributes from her school and her students. What a waste."

"I guess it goes without saying that she was a wonderful sister, too," Dr. Shannon said.

"Definitely. She was ten when we were born. She'd wanted my parents to have another baby for a long time, so when, as she put it, she was doubly blessed with David and me; she always claimed we were worth the wait. She wasn't the kind of kid to get jealous, and there certainly had to have been extra attention paid to David as soon as he was born. But she was really a second little mother to us, and we were her favorite playthings."

"And Valentine's Day makes her passing harder on you?" asked Dr. Shannon.

"It does. It was the one thing she hadn't achieved in life, and she was beginning to lose hope. She had a career, good friends, a good education, she had nice things, but she had no man to love and share her life with."

"It's the survivor's guilt again."

"I guess so." I sat up and saw Dr. Shannon looking intently at me. "I guess it never can leave me. For the rest of my life I'll have it."

"You started out your life with it, didn't you? With David?"

"Yeah, I guess so."

"Aaron, it's natural for you to feel guilty. If you didn't feel anything, you'd be a sociopath. I'd never tell you to deny those feelings. Remember, everyone has something they would change in life if it were possible. Yours was being a twin to a disabled brother. Your feelings are honest; I want you to go with them, to recognize that you've earned them, and to work through your emotions. Time will make the pain less acute, but you'll always feel the loss, and that's because you did have good relationships with your parents and Carolyn. Think about it, feeling blue is better than not caring at all. You already know that the best way you can honor your family is to live a good life and to help your brother to lead his life as well as he can, too."

Going to Dr. Shannon did help some. I spent that night quietly thinking about my parents and Carolyn, and then on Valentine's Day I took Jessie, David, and Izzy to Max and Shelby's "Fun and Frivolous St. Valentines Day Wedding and Frolic," allowing myself to feel the true joy of the occasion. It was a sensational affair. Instead of doing his job with dignity, a beribboned Zac raced down the aisle, pulling Zoey in her wagon. The dignity of the service was further dampened when Zac peed on the pile of rose petals that Zoey threw down at the end of the aisle, instead of strewing them idyllically one or two at a time. An acting student dressed as Cupid hired for the occasion, swooped in with a pooper-scooper, shot a paper arrow in the air above Max and Shelby, and the wedding went on.

Jessie and I had a great time. We danced to every number and feasted on such nontraditional wedding foods as deep-dish pizza, mozzarella sticks, steamers, and an ice cream sundae bar next to the chocolate fountain shaped like a heart. Max and

Shelby looked fantastic. He wore a thrift shop white top hat and tails with red bow tie, and she looked amazing in a white-fringed flapper dress, also scored at the Junior League Thrift Shop in Roslyn. Long white gloves, a beaded cap, and a candy cigarette on a foot-long holder completed her fantasy outfit. When they led us in the Charleston, every wedding guest—dressed in the suggested red, white, or pink—could have been mistaken for dancers from a Broadway musical.

I had been anxious for the time to come for me to give the Best Man toast, but once the first buffet was being set up and the DJ silent, the clinking of the glasses began, and after Max and Shelby kissed lovingly, it was my turn.

"Max and Shelby, you've been together a long time, and it's been my privilege and pleasure to see your love for each other grow right from the beginning—tenth grade to be exact. I'll never forget the time in junior year of high school that Max cut Social Studies because he'd forgotten Shelby's birthday. I had to divert the teacher as he snuck out the door to run to CVS to get something passable. You still owe me for that detention, Max, but maybe in honor of your wedding I'll dissolve the debt. Who knows, Shelby might have kicked you to the curb if you hadn't shown up with the card and the cheesy statue of two lovebirds, and we might not be here today, so I guess it was worth it. Shelby, I'm sure Max will never forget your birthday again.

"Zoey is an incredible expression of your love for each other." She and Zac were curled up asleep in the wagon. "And you are so lucky to be starting this new phase in your lives together, knowing that you have everything you need to make a marriage work. You have love, respect, kindness, forgiveness, and as everyone can see from this wedding, you know how to have fun. I know you two will never forget that without fun in your life, nothing else really matters. Thank you both for giving me this honor, and thank you for being my best friends. I promise to always be there for you, too. Max, you are one very lucky man. I love you both."

I lifted my glass to Max and Shelby, then to Jessie, who was looking at me as if I were her prince, and to David and Izzy, who had been allowed to come to the wedding as long as we agreed to keep tabs on them. It was hard to believe I could feel as I did, so happy for my friends, and in love with a beautiful and exciting woman. *How could my life be going on and going well after what had happened? How could I be laughing and telling jokes after losing almost my entire family? It didn't make sense to me.* I tried to shake the thought away and threw back my head, downing the glass of champagne in one big gulp.

chapter thirty-one:
aaron

A WARM SUNDAY in early April was enticing people to linger on the lawn after Mass. Women were sharing photos of new babies and grandbabies, and men were saying things like, "Time to get the lawn mower fixed," and "I think I might take out the grill and fire it up for dinner." After exchanging pleasantries to a few other people, we had stopped to talk to the Romanos after Mass. Jessie was with me. David and Izzy had found each other beforehand, and after a few minutes of talking together in private, they came up to us, hand in hand.

"We don't want to hide anymore," Izzy said.

"We are in love, and we want to get married," David said.

Izzy slid her left hand out of her pocket and showed us the engagement ring on her fourth finger. Her right hand was firmly clasped with David's left.

"David gave it to me New Year's Eve. I know you think we're not smart enough to get married. But we don't need to be smart to know we love each other."

I immediately went into panic mode, blurting out the first thing that came into my head. "But you just don't earn enough to live on your own as a married couple. You're both so young. You each make minimum wage. It's just not enough to support yourselves." That was obviously the wrong answer, since even David could immediately shoot me down.

"But you said I have surance money from the accident, didn't you? You even said I had enough not to work, remember?" David said.

"Yes, but as I told you, I'm your guardian. I'm in charge of managing your share of the insurance money to make sure it lasts you throughout your life." I knew that argument wouldn't hold water either, but I was struggling to say anything coherent at that moment.

"Don't I get some say in how my money is used? Aaron, I want to be with Izzy, and she wants to be with me. Don't you want me to be happy?"

"Isabella, you wouldn't want to leave your father and me and your brothers, would you?" asked Mrs. Romano.

Izzy didn't answer; she just looked down at the ground and kicked at some rocks.

Then Mr. Romano said in his most intimidating voice, "Look, there's no need to go on with this discussion. No engagement, no marriage." He gestured like an umpire calling a runner to home plate safe. "We agreed to let you two be friends, and that's where it has to stop."

Everyone started talking at once. I sensed David's temper boiling inside him from the expressions on his face. I could see he was trying hard to maintain his calm, but he was going to lose it unless I could stop him. In a minute he would explode and throw a tantrum that would completely blow his case of being mature. I had to spare him that humiliation. Also, we were drawing attention from the churchgoers who passed us on the way to the parking lot. Mrs. Romano noticed it, too, and whispered in her husband's ear, but I was close enough to hear her.

"Louie, people are starting to stare at us; if you don't stop, you'll have Father Charles here. Please lower your voice," she said.

"Everybody stop talking," I said. Then, lowering my own voice and hoping the others would follow suit, I said, "We are all overreacting. David and Izzy have told us some surprising news. They are not willing to continue forever with their relationship as it is now. They are serious about one another, and they want to move forward. They deserve our full consideration of this."

I spoke pointedly at Mr. Romano, trying to match the authority in his voice. "Mr. and Mrs. Romano, do you agree that we can neither say yes or no at this time?"

Mrs. Romano nodded and elbowed her husband in the side until he said quietly, "We'll think about it." I believed David had calmed down just enough for him to catch his breath and take this "we'll see" for an answer for now. He was undoubtedly using all his inner resources to control his anger. He then turned to Izzy instead of coming with Jessie and me.

"Izzy, we may have to fight to be together. Will you?" he said, loud enough to make sure we all heard him.

"Yes, I will, David," Izzy said, and she put her arms around him and hugged him tightly. It was clear to me that she had matured these past months from the giggly schoolgirl to a young woman who had deep feelings for David.

Nobody spoke further. Instead, each couple moved away. Izzy and David stayed in an embrace, forming a small triangle of very anxious people.

"Aaron, that was brilliant," Jessie whispered to me. "You diffused that situation so fast. You handled it perfectly."

"Well, extreme times . . . " I said. "I think we should go home now and make a plan to get together and talk it over with the Romanos soon. I'm going to see if that will fly. Will you back me up?"

"Definitely," said Jessie.

The Romanos were huddled together, and David and Izzy were about one hundred feet away, keeping a united front. Izzy's brothers had become bored and found a pile of rocks on the edge of the parking lot to play with.

Jessie and I walked over to the Romanos, and I called over to David and Izzy to join us.

"David and Izzy, you are going to have to give us some time to talk about how or if we can make what you want happen in a way we are all comfortable with," I said. "Mr. and Mrs. Romano, I need some time to talk to David alone, and I'd like to talk with you another time. I'm sure you also want to talk to Izzy alone."

Everyone agreed that would be the next step, and David and Izzy looked slightly triumphant that we hadn't just dragged them off in opposite directions. Izzy clenched her hand tightly, holding onto her ring while she reluctantly let go of David's hand and followed her parents to their car. Jessie and I decided to go back home with David and stop for take-out Chinese food.

"Mr. Romano, a moment," I called before he got into his car. We met in the middle of the parking lot; there were just a few groups still mingling on the lawn.

"First of all, I hope you believe me that I'm as shocked as you are. David had not confided this plan to me. Let's talk to them and see if they know what they want or have made any plans. We've been focusing on their getting married. Maybe we can push them back a bit and agree to their being engaged for the time being. I know you're against it, but honestly, it just may be *a fait a'compli*. They are adults despite their disabilities. We have to convince them to allow us into this decision-making, simply because they are adults. Before any wedding can take place we would have to be certain that we have everything set, including outside supports from Social Services that could possibly make it work. We need to keep supervising them. It can be a long, long engagement." I was talking so fast I ran out of air. Mr. Romano took advantage of my taking a breath to again voice his opinion.

"I cannot imagine Carmella and I ever agreeing to Izzy marrying David," he said. "She's not really an adult; it's like two children getting married." Then he added, "This may be a solution to your having to care for your brother, but it's not the same for Carmella and me."

Those words literally made my head spin. I had been trying so hard to honor my parents' wishes. I wasn't trying to get rid of David—or was I?

I inhaled and continued. "They would not be the first couple with developmental disabilities to marry. They are legally adults, even with their limitations. We may need to get some advice from ACDS or OMRDD. I don't believe that their marriage in any way lessens my commitment to care for David," I said, hoping that would serve to end that part of his argument. "Let's try to stay calm, and if after another year or two we all believe that this is what they want and we can support them, then we can try to make a suitable arrangement. They will have to be patient while we work out the details. We'll talk later, okay?"

As soon as Jessie and I got into the car with David, he started shooting questions at me.

"What did Mr. Romano say? Are you going to take us seriously? Because we are not kids. We are in love. Will you be on our side, Ari?"

"David, take it easy," I said. "First of all, I am always on your side, and I do take you and Izzy seriously. The two of you have behaved maturely and properly for all this time. It would be very bad if you changed now and acted like children. There are lots of things to consider and work out so everyone is comfortable with what we decide. You are going to have to help me by being honest when I ask you questions and practicing your best patience. Is that a deal, pal?"

"Yes. I always trust you, Ari. I'll be patient as I can. But this is my life, so you have to respect my wishes, too. We weren't asking permission from you, we were telling you what *we* had decided."

A great guardian you turned out to be, I told myself. *He's already rebelling.* I felt like a villain, stopping two people in love from getting married.

David was right, it was his life, but I knew in my heart they could not live as a married couple alone together. Additionally, I could not stomach the idea of my living in the house with them. David was hard enough to care for. I didn't want to be responsible for Izzy, too. I didn't know if they expected to live with me, but the house was half David's. Of course, I was also afraid I'd lose Jessie. That couldn't be her plan for the future. The question in my mind was could there be another way? I didn't want to continue this conversation, so I turned on the radio and David settled back in the car, perhaps content that he had the last word.

When we got home instead of eating the take-out Chinese food we had picked up on the way, David went into his room and closed his door with a force just this side of slamming.

"Let him be for a while," Jessie said, grabbing my arm as I started to go after him. "Let him sleep on it tonight. You can hash it out in the morning."

• • •

In the morning, David gave me the silent treatment. I went upstairs and called the Romanos. They each picked up an extension phone so we could all talk, and we came to an agreement that we would respect their wishes to be engaged, but explain to them it was way too soon to make any wedding plans. Then I was ready to talk to David. He was sitting at the breakfast table, and I poured myself some coffee and then sat across from him.

"David, can we please talk about it?"

"What?"

"What? The man on the moon! Don't give me what, you know perfectly well what! Your engagement."

He lifted his head slightly from the newspaper comics he appeared so focused on.

"What about it?"

"First of all, I have to apologize for not saying this sooner: Congratulations. It's really something that you and Izzy like each other so much."

"WE-ARE-IN-LOVE," he said, stressing each word.

"Okay, I believe you. The Romanos believe you, too. But you and Izzy surprised us, and we responded badly."

David started to smile. "Yes, you did," he said.

"I accept that you are engaged. I'm just asking you to enjoy being engaged and concentrate on what that means and the commitment you would make to each other should you get married."

"We ARE getting married."

"That may be true down the road, but for now, let's just see how the engagement goes. Use your engagement to get to know each other better. You've been good friends for a while, but being engaged is different. Not every engagement works out, you know. Look at Becca and me. You two are an engaged couple, but we're not ready to help you set a date and start planning a wedding, and whether you and Izzy know it or not, neither are the two of you."

David let that sink in for a while. He closed the comics, stood up and said, "I'll take that for now. We're not trying to rush it. But one day, we'll be married. Will you be my best man?"

"Always, David, always."

chapter thirty-two: david

WE DIDN'T GET what we wanted, but Izzy and I knew they all would give us a hard time. We decided to not plan a wedding—for now. It makes both of us happy to see the ring shine on her finger and to know we are really engaged.

Izzy's parents seem most against our having a baby. They took her to the doctor, and he gave her a patch to wear that she has to change every month. The patch will not let her get pregnant, but her parents told her that they would be very upset if she and I had sex before marriage and that the patch was just to be super safe. They reminded her that sex before marriage was a sin according to the Church. That was fine, we wouldn't do anything like that until we were married. Aaron had told us that Dr. Axe said that because I have Down syndrome, our chance of having a baby is almost zero, but the Romanos didn't trust that.

"Miracles happen every day, and this is not a miracle we want to see," Mr. Romano had said.

Izzy promised them we would not do anything to make a baby, and I promised Ari for the millionth time that we were keeping to Dad's rule. I didn't think he believed we would, so I had to keep telling him we didn't want to have a baby. I do love babies, especially little Zoey, but I don't know what to think about having one of our own.

"I think we would be better off with a cat or maybe a dog," I told Aaron. "Besides, if it would take a miracle, I don't believe that it would ever happen. The time I needed a miracle was when the accident happened."

One thing that being engaged has done for us is that her parents and Ari treat us more like a couple. They don't plan family stuff without checking with us and without inviting both of us hardly at all now, and that's much better, although they still won't let us stay home alone together, which makes me mad. Still, I feel much more grown up now, and I know Izzy does, too. I just wish I had my Mom and Dad and sister here. It's very weird to make such a big change in my life without them. Aaron's going to want to get married someday, too. Maybe to Jessie. Since Izzy and I are engaged, he won't have to worry that he's leaving me alone. Like Aaron and Izzy's parents say, we'll have to work things out so everyone is satisfied.

chapter thirty-three:
aaron

IT WAS OFFICIALLY spring, and the trees and flowers were beginning to take on their most lush and colorful qualities. The grass was changing from brown to green. Jessie and I went out together often, and I could hardly believe how good I was feeling. Just as they did every year, our azalea bushes bloomed right in time for Mother's Day. I cut some flowers, and David and I brought them to the cemetery together, telling her we were sending hugs to her in heaven and that she was the best mom ever.

I was coming close to accepting the reality of the accident and feeling as though I could make good lives for myself and for David. Slowly over the weeks, I realized the knots in my stomach had untangled. By the time summer had taken over, I was feeling warm inside and out. Jessie had made the difference, and I wanted to tell her.

"Jessie, you've brought me through to the other side," I told her at dinner that night. "I didn't even realize what a fog I was in before. Thank you for being so great with David, too. Becca thought she could do it, but it fell apart. I wish I could give you the kind of romance my parents had. It was like out of a storybook the way they told it. They were married for ten years before they had us. You know what you're getting into, and it doesn't seem to scare you."

"Relax, Aaron, I understand that we'll care for David. It's okay. Hey, tell me about your parents, will you?"

"Well, they had loved to tell us, and anyone else, the story of how they met and fell in love. I heard it repeated so many times, I can tell it in my sleep.

"Dad always started, saying, 'We both transferred to NYU our junior year and met at a new student mixer. I knew the moment I met her that it was going to be trouble. I mean, she was way out of my league.'"

"Then Mom would cut in. 'As soon as I introduced myself, his face turned bright red, and he practically choked on his own name. I thought he might either be having a panic attack or would soon be making a mad dash away from me. Turns out he was blinded by my beauty,' she'd say, striking a sexy pose."

"Dad said, 'She looked up and smiled at me, and that was it.'"

"Sweet," Jessie said.

"Mom told us how she doodled his name, surrounding it with valentine hearts as if she were twelve instead of twenty. They said that every love song on the radio was just for them. Break-up songs gave Mom a twinge of fear, she said, but she shook them off quickly. They were both so head over heels without a worry between them. The next two years were perhaps their happiest. Always together, they sampled all that New York City had to offer. They went up to the Cloisters and the Bronx Zoo and down to Chinatown and Little Italy. They dined on all the local delicacies and routed out exotic stores and kinky galleries. Washington Square Park and the Village were always teeming with activity. They didn't have to cope with anything more than deciding what time to go to the movies. I wish we had some of that."

"Aaron, we can't relive their lives. I love you, that's all that matters to me," Jessie said.

chapter thirty-four:
david

IZZY AND ME knew her parents and Aaron would be very mad, but she was sure her parents would never, ever let us get married. We liked kissing, but we wanted to do more. I really did, and I told her that the only way for them to treat us as adults was to do what adults in love do and get married. We were tired of my brother and her parents always telling us what to do. Izzy had never disobeyed her parents on such a big thing before. We saw a movie on TV about Las Vegas and that you could get married there. We were scared, but excited, too. A friend at Waldbaum's helped us buy the tickets with the credit card. We decided that if we got married, they would have to let us be together.

So instead of going back to lunch, we did a secret plan. We walked to the train station and took it to the airport. After being pointed in different directions, we finally found it, and Izzy went up to the ticket counter.

"Two round trip tickets to Las Vegas, please," she said, clutching my hand for courage.

The ticket officer glanced at us and said, "Photo ID please."

I knew this was coming from the last time I went on vacation with my family. Izzy and I showed him our non-driver's photo IDs that we had gotten on a field trip with our class in school. The agent gave us tickets and told us what gate to go to. He politely pointed out the signs we should follow.

"Checking any bags?" he said.

We showed him our two small suitcases. We had bought them on a lunch break and brought clothes from home, hiding them.

"You can carry them onto the plane with you if you like."

Izzy and I looked at each other and nodded yes. That was one less thing to worry about.

The ticket man pointed us to a large winding line. "You have to go through security first. They'll tell you what to do. Just show the agent your ID and boarding pass, and follow the line."

The security guy looked at our ID's and squinted at each of us, and then he scribbled on the pass and nodded us through. Other people were making announcements about electronics, belts, and money. We watched what everyone else did and put our overnight bags on the conveyor belt and our shoes and sweaters and wallets in a gray container. Then we waited on another line where we put our feet on yellow painted outlines of shoes, and one at a time we went through what looked like a Star Trek transporter. I even made the guard laugh, 'cause I said, "Beam Me Up, Scotty." We had to hold still and keep our hands up, but just for a few seconds. Then we could put on our shoes, collect our stuff, and go to the gate. We were glad that no one was paying attention to us, and we talked to other people as little as possible.

The whole aisle had different stores, most with foods to buy. We got chocolate-covered popcorn. We got to the gate just in time. A few minutes later, we were able to go onboard.

After we landed, we kind of just followed other people to a line for a bus to take us to the Las Vegas strip, and what we saw made our eyes pop. It was another world there. Everywhere was lit-up signs, with arrows showing you the way to "fun, fun, fun." And the people—the people were dressed in everything from bikinis to evening gowns all sparkly and showing more of their bodies than cloth. There were amusement parks for kids and pools with giant slides. It looked like Disney World without Mickey and the other characters, but we had no time to play. It was hot, and we immediately looked for a place to stay. We didn't know what to do. We held hands tightly and looked for someone to ask for help. We walked into a casino and took the elevator up one flight just to see what it was all about. When the doors opened, we saw two signs, each with an arrow pointing a different way. Toward the left, it said *CASINOS*, toward the right it said *CHAPELS*.

"Well, this must be it," I laughed and tried to make Izzy relax. She still looked very nervous. Lucky, people were very friendly. Izzy didn't want to go right to the chapels.

"Let's find a place to stay first," she said.

We asked a man in the casino if he knew a place that didn't cost a lot. It was just another block over, so we walked there and checked in, again using Izzy's credit card.

We asked the man at the desk if there was a wedding place near enough for us to walk to.

"Lose your money in the slots?" he asked.

We weren't sure what he meant, so we just nodded. He gave us directions to the Viva Las Vegas Wedding Chapel. There was a brochure on the counter, and it was just two blocks over. We got to the chapel, and the man in charge was dressed in a tuxedo that couldn't close over his giant belly. His face had deep wrinkles that looked like he had drawn them in with gray clay. He looked at Izzy's credit card, looked us up and down, and asked her if this was really hers to use for whatever she wanted. He was so scary looking we almost left, but we were afraid to do that, too. We stared at him, and we both nodded our heads yes, and then he signed us up for the one hundred ninety-nine dollar traditional wedding special. We didn't want the Elvis impersonator. If our own priest couldn't marry us, we could at least be married by someone who dressed like him.

They led us to separate dressing rooms where they fitted Izzy with a white, lacy wedding gown and me with a white tuxedo and a red bow tie. Somehow they made their clothes look like they fit us. It all happened so fast, and before we knew it, I was up at the altar, and a woman with really big red hair and eye makeup that made her look like a raccoon was playing the wedding march. They even provided a fake father to walk Izzy down the aisle.

Izzy looked beautiful in that dress, and she said I was handsome in my tux. When the minister asked us if we would agree to love each other and take care of each other all our lives, our guilt over running out on our families was forgotten. We looked into each other's eyes and said, "Yes, I do!" and then he said we could kiss, and we were married. They took a bunch of pictures and gave them to us to take home. They even gave us wedding rings, although my finger started turning green on the way to the motel. We'd have to get better ones. We didn't want to charge too much on the credit card. We decided to stay just one night in the motel. I couldn't stop looking over my shoulder, expecting a red-faced Mr. Romano to pick me up by my shirt collar and throw me as far as he could, but he was never there. We stopped at the drugstore to buy a condom, just as they had told us to do in school. I actually bought more than one condom, just in case one ripped, and then after a wedding dinner at The Golden Nugget Buffet for just eighteen ninety-nine each, we went back to the motel to spend the night.

I won't tell too much about our wedding night. I'll just say that it was the best time we ever had. We got undressed to our underpants and for the first time, I put my hand on her bare breast. She smiled and kissed me and then she put my other hand on the second breast. I sighed. This was even better than I've seen on TV. We fumbled around under the sheets for a while and even though we kind of knew what to do, it wasn't as easy as the pictures in the book. We weren't even sure if we actually "did it." It didn't matter; we laughed our way through.

I think the best part was being able to sleep close together in the same bed, knowing that nobody would bother us or barge in. Now we were more than best friends, we were husband and wife. I felt so happy. I just wished Mom, Dad, Aaron, and Carolyn were there to see it—the wedding, I mean. I wondered what they would have said.

The next morning before getting on the plane, we each called home to tell them we had gotten married. Izzy's father started yelling and her mother took the phone and told her to get home as soon as she could. Aaron was silent for once. I told him we were about to board the plane, and all he said was, "Good, I'll see you soon."

chapter thirty-five:
aaron

ABOUT A WEEK after David's wrist was healed and he and Izzy were both at work, I got a call from David's manager. My stomach did a flip-flop when I saw Waldbaum's on the caller ID on my cell phone. The short of it was that David and Izzy had come to work, but had left for lunch and not returned, and they were an hour and half late. Their manager wanted to know if I knew where they were. I had no idea, but as we spoke, I was packing up my desk and getting ready to bolt from the office. He told me that Isabella's parents didn't know either, and Mrs. Romano was out driving around, checking all the places the two might go for lunch and lose track of the time.

When I called Mrs. Romano, she was beginning to panic. She was afraid that someone evil had lured them into going with him. Maybe they'd been told a puppy was missing, and they went along with a kidnapper who would either ask for ransom, or worse, hurt them in unspeakable ways.

"They're both too trusting," she cried.

The same scenarios had crossed my mind, too, but I tried to convince Mrs. Romano this was highly unlikely. I suggested they may have been distracted by the beautiful weather and walked to the duck pond to feed the ducks, one of David's favorite things to do.

"No, I checked the duck pond near the store. They weren't there, and no one had seen them," Mrs. Romano said. "I've checked everywhere. I don't know where they are; I'm telling you, someone enticed them away."

I asked Mrs. Romano if Izzy had enough money to travel somewhere with David.

"¡Mierda!!" she said. "She has a credit card she's supposed to use only in emergencies."

Neither one of them had a cell phone. I'd tried it with David, but after he lost two of them, we gave up. I think Izzy had a similar experience.

I asked Mrs. Romano to go to the Westbury train station and see if they were there. If the ticket booth was open, the seller might remember them; if not, maybe the man at the newspaper stand saw them. She called me back in twenty minutes.

"They got on the train," she said. "I can't imagine the two of them navigating their way in New York City. They're probably lost and scared and too proud to call and tell us."

If only Mrs. Romano had been right. She called the credit card company and found out that the card had been used to buy two round-trip tickets to Las Vegas. VEGAS! There was only one reason they could have for going there. David had seen TV shows about all the quickie wedding chapels there, and they had decided not to wait any longer. The next morning David called and told me that he and Izzy were married.

"We didn't believe you would ever let us really get married," David said. "We felt we were ready."

"Oh. So you decided that and went against what we all agreed?"

"If my parents were alive, they'd kill me," I told Jessie.

I had failed to be the guardian my brother needed. I was as disappointed in myself as I was with David.

Mr. Romano called me and bellowed, "We have to have the wedding annulled." But, being a lawyer's son, I asked if he and his wife had legally become Isabella's guardians at 18 as my own parents had with David, and I literally stopped Mr. Romano mid-bellow, leaving him stammering.

"Tell him we never dreamed it was necessary. Izzy always listened to us before she got involved with David," I heard Mrs.

Romano saying in the background. It was the first time she had made any complaint about David to me.

Izzy was a legal and independent adult over twenty-one. Intellectual disability does not automatically make a person incompetent. As court-appointed guardian to David, I did have the power to bring the matter to court and try to have the marriage annulled, but I wouldn't do it. Maybe my parents would have done so, but David was still my brother, and I could not do that to him. I tried to explain my reasons to Mr. Romano, and for the first time I heard some very salty language from the distraught Italian father who had expected that his slow daughter would always do as he told her.

The issue for me was now that they were married, they would expect to live together, and the question was where? They would probably want to live in our house with me, and I worried that I'd lose Jessie if that happened. *Damn David! Why does he have to screw this up for me?*

"Do you think they had a wedding night?" Jessie whispered to me.

"Please, don't put any pictures in my head," I said, covering the phone.

I also worried about that miniscule possibility that David might not be sterile. I decided to make an appointment for a test the next day. That was one thing I would insist on. I would steadfastly refuse to agree to their sleeping together again until the results of that test were in. I could understand why they had eloped, but I was angry over the fact that David had lied to us and they had gone against our agreement.

When Mr. Romano finally agreed to get off the phone and meet the plane at LaGuardia, my ear ached from the conversation. I felt so conflicted. Should I behave like a brother or a parent? Could I really risk David's animosity if I tried to undo his marriage? What would my best approach be at the airport, and how were we going to get out of there without a huge public scene?

When we saw the Romanos, they looked as if they had seen a ghost and just sat together staring at each other blankly. We approached them cautiously.

"Well, genius, what happened to the long engagement? What

happened to their waiting a year or two? They barely waited a few months," Mr. Romano said.

"You're not going to help us, are you?" Mrs. Romano asked me. "We're being punished. The Church was right. Giving your daughter birth control tells her she can have sex, use it, even if you tell her she shouldn't. We did the wrong thing, and now we're being punished."

"Please, Mrs. Romano, don't blame yourself. I don't think God works that way. Do you truly think he's got the time to send out punishments to every person who doesn't follow the tenets completely?" Jessie said, putting her arm around her and supplying her with tissues.

Stuck in the baggage claims area, the only place where non-ticketed passengers could meet arriving family, Mr. Romano got up and paced back and forth, constantly stopping at the board to see if the arrival time had changed. It was half an hour before their flight was due in.

"Did they get married by an Elvis impersonator?" Jessie whispered to me. "Maybe you can tell them that everything that happens in Vegas stays in Vegas so they aren't really married here."

Finally, she said, "Well, your twin brother finally did something before you did."

"Jessie, I know you're trying to see the humor in this, but I just can't."

After that, she stopped her attempts at changing my grim expression and went to a Dunkin' Donuts, bringing back coffee and those sickeningly sweet vanilla creams that we loved to eat. She pulled me over to a high table with bar stool chairs and coaxed me to indulge in at least one pleasure before the newlyweds arrived and things got even stickier than the donuts.

"Seriously, I know you're upset, but if the Romanos weren't so off the wall, would you still feel the way you do?" Jessie said.

I couldn't give her anything but a blank stare and a shoulder shrug.

"Look at the facts; they love each other, don't you believe that?" she said.

"Well, yeah."

"They've known each other all through school, and their love grew out of friendship, which is a damn good way to start. If it can be ensured that no children result from their marriage, is it so terrible for them to have a physical relationship that is consensual and legal?"

"But my parents specifically said they want him living with family for the rest of his life in their will. Of course, they had pictured this all happening when they were in their eighties and Carolyn had grown children, but their plan backfired. Still, how can I not follow their last wishes? What would they do if they were here?" I looked at Jessie and then answered my own question. "This would never have happened if they were here."

"But they're not here. It's time to make your own decisions and stop trying to step into their shoes and be them. You are Aaron, not your parents. You have to trust your own judgment and help your brother."

"But what about the 'living with family' they put in their will?"

"Well, isn't a wife family?" said Jessie.

"You don't think they can live together on their own, do you? That would be disastrous."

"So you will get them help. It doesn't have to be you giving all the help. Call the ACDS and ask what they can do. This can't be the first time this has happened. I think the biggest problem you have to deal with is Izzy's parents. They seem to be shattered."

"That's for sure." I looked over at the couple. Louie had taken the seat next to his wife Carmella, and their heads were bent down close together. At first I thought they were discussing what to do and then I saw the rosary in Carmella's hand. They were probably praying for a miracle.

chapter thirty-six:
david

WE WERE SCARED to see Izzy's parents and Aaron when we landed. We had on our only clean shirts. They said "*I GOT MARRIED AT VIVA LAS VEGAS.*"I think it made them even madder. Soon as we got to them, it got crazy. Izzy's Dad grabbed her arm, and he and her mom kept telling her how disappointed they were at how she ran off and didn't care about what they thought. Only Jessie was calm. She was standing with Aaron a few feet away. She spoke first after I slowly joined up with them.

"Congratulations, David," Jessie said.

Then Aaron kind of exploded. "Yes, congratulations, David. Congratulations for running off and scaring the shit out of us for two days. Congratulations for breaking your promise. Congratulations for showing me I can't trust you. Congratulations for putting us in a position that no one is ready for."

Then Jessie put her arm around Aaron and pulled him away. She got him to sit in a chair. Aaron looked like he wanted to punch me. Izzy and I were already crying. I walked away from Aaron and sat next to my wife, and then her father started screaming at me.

"So, David, this is what you do after we invite you into our house? You just couldn't wait to get your hands on our daughter. I'd like to get my hands on you! You just couldn't wait to . . ."

When Aaron saw that, he ran over to protect me.

I stood up still holding Izzy's hand and pulled her up gently.

"We are in love! We are adults, and we wanted to be married! We are legal now!"

Izzy's father's face got even redder and couldn't get any more words out.

I tried to stay calm and said, "We are sorry we worried you. But we are not sorry we are married. We love each other and want to be together."

"Well, we will see about that," said Mr. Romano. "This isn't over."

"Louie, calm down now. We've caused a big enough scene. I want to go home now. Izzy, you're coming with us," said Mrs. Romano.

"But, but David is my husband," Izzy said through her tears.

"Yes. I want to be with Izzy," I said.

"Excuse me, I have a suggestion," Jessie said, bringing Aaron over to us. "We clearly are in a fog over what to do next." I started to speak, but Jessie said, "David, shush, please, let me have my say now. Why don't we go to the church and talk with Father Charles? I rang him up earlier, and he's waiting for us in the rectory. I say we need an objective voice here."

Mr. Romano didn't like that. "You did what? You have a lot of nerve telling us what to do; who do you think you are?"

"Hey, Louie," said Aaron, "Jessie's part of our family, and you have no right to speak to her that way. She is probably the one person here able to think clearly right now, and she's right. We're going to meet with Father Charles now, before we do any more damage with hurtful accusations. Are you all coming?"

"Yes, we are," said Izzy's mom, Carmella. Mr. Romano gave her an angry look but didn't say anything.

"I'm going with David," Izzy said. "Okay?" she asked Aaron, giving him her best smile.

"Sure, Izzy," Aaron said.

"Now, everyone take a few deep breaths," Jessie said. "Father Charles will help us figure things out. David and Izzy gave us all a big scare, but we're all glad to see that they are safe and unharmed. That's the important thing!"

"And we love each other!" I said.

"Yes. They do love each other, and now we need to figure out what to do next," said Jessie. "I hope we can do it calmly and remember that not only do David and Izzy love each other, but we all love them, too, right? We seem to be forgetting that."

Aaron and Mrs. Romano nodded, and Mr. Romano muttered something else, but Izzy and I held hands and stuck together and then got in the back seat of Aaron's car.

No one talked on the ride to church. I held Izzy's hand and whispered to her, "We are really married, don't worry." Aaron's face color had returned to normal except for the tips of his ears, which were still a bright red.

Then Jessie turned around to talk to us. "Well, you two must have had an adventure, eh? I haven't been to Vegas, but I hear it's a spectacular sight, all neon and sparkles, is that right?"

"It really was like that," Izzy said. "We were scared at first, but people are very friendly there. We asked for directions, and they showed us where to go."

"What was the chapel like?" she asked. "Was it nice?"

Izzy dug into her purse and took out the photos. "Here, you can see it."

Jessie went through the pictures. "Wow, you two look great, don't they, Aaron?" She tried to show him the photos, but he wouldn't look.

"I'm driving, Jessie. I'll see them later," he said.

"The chapel was decorated nice. You really found a pretty place," Jessie said, giving Izzy back the pictures.

"Thanks," she said. We were almost at the church, and I was getting more nervous, knowing we were in for more of her father's yelling.

When we all entered Father Charles's door, there was a woman with him.

"That's the lady from the 'sociation," I told Izzy. "She'll be on our side. This is good."

"I asked Helen to join us," Father Charles said. "As President of the ACDS, I think she will be able to give us some good advice. I hope you don't mind."

"Not at all," said Mrs. Romano. "Helen, it's so good to see you. Thank you for coming, we could really use your input now."

"I hope I can help you, Carmella," she said.

Just seeing that lady actually made Izzy's mom smile. I started to think things would be okay.

chapter thirty-seven:
jessie

THE DRIVE TO the church was, to put it mildly, difficult. Aaron was gripping the steering wheel and would not engage in conversation no matter how hard I tried. I was beginning to think that maybe David and Izzy could have a full life, much different from what their folks had ever expected. Their elopement was such a bold move. I knew from private talks with Carmella that Izzy's never marrying and having her own life was one of the biggest disappointments they felt as a result from her brain damage. Maybe they could grow to accept this. I wondered what Father Charles would say about the birth control. It was a worry, but I felt there must be some dispensation in this case. Carmella had told me she heard about couples like David and Izzy having children and then losing custody to the state. She said that was a major concern of hers, but it didn't seem to be a big problem if David couldn't, well, provide. No, there would be no babies, no matter what the Church says.

When we got to the rectory, I never saw anyone so relieved to see a friend, as I was to see Carmella greet Helen. She had told me about Helen from the many meetings, fundraisers, and events she chaired, and that she had helped arrange for support services in marriages between "individuals," as they were called, and she might be able to help us work it out. What was done was done. Now we had to make the best of it. Introductions were made all around to Helen, and then we arranged ourselves in the Father's living room. Each couple stuck together like glue. David and Isabella squeezed next to Aaron and me on the couch. I put my arm around Izzy to make room for them. Izzy had found an ally. Louie and Carmella took two adjacent club chairs, and Father Charles and Helen sat together on an antique wooden bench, facing all six of us.

Father Charles started the discussion.

"Jessie has filled me in on what has been going on the past few days. Before we talk about what's next, I think we should clear the air about what happened. I sense there are still some pretty angry and disappointed people in this room."

"That's right, Father," said Louie. "I would never have believed my little girl would take off and put me through two days of wondering if she were dead or alive."

"I'm not a little girl," Izzy said.

Father Charles stopped it from escalating. "Izzy, no matter how old you are, you will always be your father's little girl. Do you and David want to apologize for giving your families such a terrible scare?"

"We already did, Father," David said.

"Could you do it again now, while we are all calm and able to listen, please?"

Izzy and David nodded their heads. Holding hands, David spoke for both of them. "We are very sorry we made you all worry. We didn't think you would ever say yes, and we were ready to get married. We are in love."

"Yes, I'm very sorry I worried you," Izzy said.

"So we have both an apology and an explanation now," Father Charles said. "Louie, Carmella, Aaron, do you feel you can forgive David and Izzy now?"

"What choice do we have? They did what they wanted to do, and Aaron is the only one capable of undoing it in court, and he refuses," Louie said.

"Aaron, is Louie telling the truth?"

"Yes, Father. First, I want to answer you and say that I do forgive David and Izzy. I think I understand why they ran off, although the way they did it was very inconsiderate, but I forgive them. As for what Louie says, it's true. I am David's legal guardian, and if I felt it necessary, I could ask the court for an annulment—not that it would be automatically granted. The Romanos never saw the need to become Isabella's guardian, and she is a legal independent adult. I'm not going to challenge David now. I want to give them a chance."

"And developmental disability is not automatic grounds for incompetency," Helen interrupted.

Aaron continued, "I just want to see that he and Izzy get the social services and support they need to succeed. As long as there are no children. We are all strongly opposed to that happening. Father, this is a special circumstance. If they need birth control, will the Church object?"

"I wish I had an easy answer for you, because the Church is not as flexible as you might believe it should be. In the case of two consenting adults, as David and Isabella seem to be, birth control is not permitted."

"But why, Father?" I asked.

"Because the Church believes every life is precious and that if these young people needed help caring for their child, it would be the obligation of the couple's parents to step in and help raise that child."

"Oh, dear," Carmella said under her breath.

"But the point may be moot," Helen said. "Having Down syndrome often makes a male sterile."

"What is that?" David asked Aaron.

"It means you can't father a child. And tomorrow morning we are going to the doctor to find out for sure."

"Father, we have sinned," Carmella said. "We provided birth control to our daughter even before this happened."

"Carmella, I appreciate your confiding that. Let's talk about that a little later. Now, I think we should get back to the question that is really of import. David and Isabella eloped and got married without the consent of their parents and guardian. They have always gone to you for support and guidance up until now, and for such a significant decision they turned away from the people who love them the most and chose to do what they believed is right for them. I'm sure you feel anger, but I'm sure you also feel hurt, even betrayed, am I right?"

David and Izzy squirmed in their seats.

David stood up, still holding onto Izzy's hand. "We had to, Father. They would never let us get married. We didn't want to wait forever. We are in love, and that's the truth!"

"David, I'm sorry, but your running off without calling to tell Aaron and Izzy's parents is exactly why they have strong doubts about you being ready for marriage," Father Charles said.

"Father, may I say something now?" asked Helen.

"Certainly."

"David and Isabella are not by any means the first couple with developmental disabilities to get married. After all, what is marriage but the commitment that two people will love each other throughout their lives, stay together, help one another, and remain faithful to each other? They have already made that commitment. Does anyone here doubt they are sincere?" She paused for someone to speak, but the room remained silent. "They've known each other almost four years and were good friends before romance came into the picture. Granted, running off and eloping was not the best thing for them to do. But they did it. Now we have to help them succeed."

"I made copies of this article in *The Washington Post,* which was recently written about a couple very similar to these two young people. It might make you feel better." She passed out papers stapled together to everyone. We all looked through them and held onto them. Proof that it had worked with another pair. It was in the newspaper.

"The young man has Down syndrome, and the young woman was born with hydrocephalus, which caused brain damage. They, too, fell in love and got married. Their parents recognized that they wouldn't be happy if they were separated, and they celebrated their love with a wedding. They weren't Catholic, and the young man chose to have a vasectomy. The couple was sad that they would not have children, but they agreed that the two of them made a family. They receive support services and live in an association-run apartment. They admit that they have some problems and see a couple's therapist once a week. They also have the unlimited support of their parents, who see their children living lives they had never thought possible. I think with some help David and Izzy could be as successful as this couple. But they need your blessing and your support.

"I know that these families do not want to go against Catholic tenets, but Aaron is taking David to find out if birth control is even an issue tomorrow morning. Whether or not it is, I'm prepared to help you all to find a way to accept this young couple's marriage and to continue to be a very close-knit family." As she finished her speech, she tugged at her sleeves, straightened her blue suit jacket, sat up very straight, and looked around the room, almost daring anyone to argue with her.

"Aaron, Izzy and I want to live in our house with you," David said.

"Would that be okay?" Izzy asked.

What could he say? "Of course you can."

David and Izzy smiled widely; then they both tackled Aaron with a big hug.

"Well, if all this can be worked out, it sounds like a very reasonable solution to me," Father Charles said, "I feel Helen has given a compelling argument against our, as we say, tearing asunder what God has joined together. Louie, Carmella, what are your thoughts?"

Louie looked down and kicked the floor. Then he muttered, "I guess I'd go along with it. But does this mean we have to get on a long waiting list with the agency?"

"I'm afraid it could take some time before we can get the ideal situation for them. I will look for an opening in our supported apartments and will try to move them to the top of the list, but there are people who have been waiting ahead of you," Helen said, "In the meantime..."

"In the meantime they will stay with me," Aaron said.

"Although this is still very upsetting for us, we do have to realize that while we think of Isabella as our little girl, she is also a woman capable of love," Carmella said. "David is a wonderful young man, and I don't believe he would ever hurt our daughter. Louie, I do think we have to go along with it."

Helen embraced her and let Carmella's tears fall on her shoulder. "I'm very proud of you, Carmella. It is so hard to allow our children to grow into adults, and when marriage comes into the picture, we feel that they are leaving us. But Isabella will always come to you for advice, support, and company, because you're her mother and she loves you."

"That's right, Mama." Isabella gave her a hug and reached out her hand for Louie to take. "You and the boys will always be my family, too."

"Can I make a suggestion?" Father Charles said. "I think that until David takes that test, it would be better for Izzy to sleep at her own home tonight. By tomorrow you will know what you will do. David, Izzy, would you please go to your separate homes tonight?"

"Yes, Father," they said together.

"But after that test, I want to be with my wife," David insisted.

chapter thirty-eight:
aaron

THE DOCTOR'S VISIT would have been funny if we weren't stricken with fear and embarrassment. Instead, it was as tense as it could get. There we were, hoping for the opposite results most people want. Getting the sample in the cup was, to put it delicately, a sticky situation, and our being twins didn't make it any less embarrassing. I'd helped David through a lot of things, but no guy wants to do that with his brother. Yet, what choice did I have? I actually had to show him porn magazines. It's not the first time David had done the deed, but I physically had to direct his penis into the cup, and there was almost no time between his first "Aw, aw," and the spurting out of the sample. I held onto the cup and tried to think of anything else but what was actually happening. When we emerged from the room, I felt as if all eyes were upon us, and I felt so sheepish, I'm surprised I didn't bleat.

We lucked out with the test. David had zero sperm, and so it was all up to me to carry on the LeShay name. Izzy started moving her things into the guest room that afternoon. I think her parents were numb at this point. No more attempts were made to stop her and keep her home; they helped her pack and drove her over. They only live about two miles from us. While they were busy unpacking and organizing, I told them I was going out to pick up a few items, and I drove over to the cemetery.

• • •

I leaned over and pulled out some weeds around the gravestones. I kicked myself mentally that I hadn't stopped to get some flowers. I momentarily considered 'borrowing' from another grave, but immediately nixed that idea. I need God on my side, although I still had very strong doubts he was paying any attention to me.

I had only been back a few times since the funeral, and always with David. We usually assured them we were fine. Now I had a different message for them.

"So, maybe you know this already, but David and Izzy eloped, to Las Vegas yet, to add to the drama. We had David's sperm count tested, and there's no chance of him becoming a father. I have no choice but to help them to make this marriage a success; it's legal. Trouble is, now I'm in charge of both of them because they're living with me, although I'm sure they don't see it that way. I think David believes now that he is married, he suddenly can do anything he feels like. Not only that, but I know Izzy's parents are going to be a constant presence in our house. I'm not sure I can do this, and I'm afraid it will scare Jessie off."

Once I said the words, "I'm afraid," I lost it. I sat down on the ground in front of the three stones and prayed to them. "You were always there for me, so I'm asking you, not God, to help me find a way to keep David and Izzy happy without losing either my mind or my girlfriend. "God, please feel free to give me any help you can," I said raising my head upwards to address the heavens.

I sat there for about half an hour, just talking about life and how things were going. Mostly I talked about David and about Jessie.

"It's harder than I thought, guys. David knew what he wanted, and he went and got it. You know, he's sweet as can be, but he doesn't realize that this puts more on my shoulders. Will Jessie stick it out with me now? How much will she tolerate? I really think I want to marry her, but I can't rush into it because of David. And they're living with me. Although Jessie has her own apartment, she'd been staying with me most nights. When it was just David, I thought Jessie would be okay with him living with us, but now, I really don't know what to do. I can't ask her to move in with me and the happy couple; it's just too much. What should I do?"

Of course, no voice sounded to answer me, but I got a bit of comfort from my attempt at including them in the situation. Eventually, I got up and told them I would bring David and Izzy here to tell them their happy news.

"We'll bring flowers, too. I wish you had them all the time," I said.

I decided to stop and bring in pizza, salad, and antipasto for our first dinner as a family of three. Jessie had gone home by that time. Now I was the third wheel. I'd just have to roll with the punches until a better solution came along. One thing I was certain, this was not going to be a permanent arrangement.

David and Izzy were thrilled with the dinner. Of course, now I was the dinner fairy. Things had always appeared magically for them all their lives, and now it was me who was performing the tricks. I just didn't know if I had the strength to do it any other way. That night, as I lay in my parents' bed, I could hear David and Izzy giggling together and, well, acting like honeymooners. It was not what I wanted to hear. I put on my iPod headphones to drown out any other sounds, and eventually we all got a fair night's sleep.

The next day, David and Izzy went back to Waldbaum's and apologized for running out. They were allowed to return to work on probation, and best of all, they were given new hours, and they would now work there at the same time. I could have kissed that manager! I could take them there in the morning, and they would take the bus home together with Mrs. Reilly.

The second week of our new family unit, David and Izzy surprised me by having dinner ready for me when I got home. The spaghetti was a little underdone, a little too al dente, and the garlic bread was black around the edges, but the sauce was delicious.

"MMM, what kind of sauce is this?" I asked.

"Mama Romano's famous," David giggled.

"Mama brought it over, and these meatballs," Izzy said.

These kids are certainly getting a lot of help from all of us, I thought. I'd have to talk to Carmella about how we can get them to be more independent now. Maybe she'd give them some cooking lessons.

Jessie came over most nights, but I didn't feel comfortable leaving David and Izzy alone in the house overnight, and somehow it just didn't feel right to us to sleep together with them in the house. Most nights, Jessie left to sleep at her own apartment.

"We've got to figure out a way we can be alone together, you know what I mean?" I said to Jessie.

"Oh, I agree. I feel like a teenager, hiding from my parents if I want to snog with my boyfriend. What about Carmella and Louie? Would they help?"

"It's a thought, let's wait another week, and I'll ask them," I said. "Louie seems to be adjusting."

"Right, it's not fair that it's all on you," Jessie said.

"Well, I think Louie still feels I could really have their marriage annulled, and since I won't do it, why shouldn't I have the burden?"

After another week of frustration I gave Louie and Carmella a call. My luck, Louie picked up.

"Hey, Louie, it's Aaron, how are you?"

"Just fine, what do you need, Aaron?"

Already he was anticipating my asking a favor. Oh well, best to rip off the band-aid.

"I was wondering if perhaps Saturday night, if you and Carmella aren't busy, if you and the boys can stay over. Jessie and I need some alone time. We'd go to her place."

"Oh." Silence. "And you need to stay there overnight?" he asked.

"That's what we'd like to do if you don't mind," I said, trying to put "pity me" into my voice.

"Hold on, let me see what Carmella says."

He left me hanging for a good ten minutes, then Carmella came on the phone and offered to be there on Saturday at 6 pm. "We'll take all the kids out to dinner, then we'll go home to your house. The boys can stay in your old bedroom, right?"

"Right, and I'll have fresh bedding for you and Louie in the master bedroom."

"Great, thanks, see you then."

Sunday morning we all met at church. Carmella pulled me aside.

"Listen, Aaron, you can count on us every other weekend to stay with the kids at your place. I hadn't given a lot of thought to how this was cramping your space. You know Louie and I don't believe in premarital relations, but it's none of our business what two adults do, and it's not up to us to make any assumptions about how you spend your time alone. I'm sure you need a break. I hope that will help things."

"Thank you so much, Carmella," I said, and gave her a quick embrace. "Jessie and I really appreciate that."

For the next two months, that's how our life went on. I still felt like a third wheel sometimes, and Jessie and I eventually left them on their own so we could go out to dinner or take in a movie. We had done that when it was just David we were leaving home, but we felt a greater responsibility now that Izzy was there, too.

chapter thirty-nine:
aaron

AFTER A PARTICULARLY hard day at the office, I got home and found in the mail a flyer from the OMRDD (Office of Mental Retardation and Developmental Disabilities). After reading it, I believed that someone had answered my prayers. I called Jessie immediately and told her about the flyer.

"Jessie, I think we have a solution. OMRDD is holding a meeting about how you can make your own house into a group home with social services staffing it. You have to donate the house to an agency with a community residence program, and your kid is guaranteed placement there for life. It's being held next week. Maybe we can do that. David and Izzy would be able to stay in our house. Would you come to the meeting with me? I need your input, and you can explain the big words to me." I tried to make a joke out of the request.

"Definitely, and I think you should ask the Romanos to come. It would be better if they heard all the information firsthand, and they'll be able to ask their own questions. Are you sure you want to give up your house?"

"For this? Absotively. I'll find a house nearby. One that we could make our own."

"That sounds lovely. You can shack up with me in my flat until then."

I agreed, and the next day we made plans to attend the meeting with the Romanos. They were surprisingly agreeable, too. With three bedrooms upstairs and one downstairs, our house might be a good choice to transform into a group home. Now we could see what the government agency had to say. We agreed not to mention it to David and Izzy until we had more information.

• • •

The OMRDD meeting was great. They said that transforming my home to a group home was completely possible. The Romanos and I were still smarting from the kids running off to elope, but that was history we couldn't change. We'd all be close to David and Izzy, and they'd get the supervision they needed from nonrelatives. We figured it would be easier for them to adhere to rules that were set for the whole house, not just for them. In just the past two months we had butted heads on several things. David felt as a married man, he could do as he pleased no matter what my objection. I immediately began working on finding individuals for the house.

Hunter signed on that night. He and his mother came right over to the house as soon as we told her about it.

"I can't tell you how good it makes me feel that Hunter will be living with friends and will be well taken care of. The kids in group homes are so much more independent than the ones that live with their parents. I've known it for years, and now you've given me a great option," she said, before hugging me so hard, I couldn't breathe.

We had hoped Hunter would have a friend that he would share his room with, and Izzy would find a woman who could take Carolyn's room—and it actually worked out. David and Izzy both knew Callie, who was twenty-three, from work, and they asked her if she was interested in moving into the house.

Callie was all for it, but she told Izzy she wasn't sure what her parents would say. Izzy got her phone number, and I called her parents. Before I could even finish my speech, they said thanks, but they were not interested.

"We're very happy having Callie at home with us, and so is she. We're not interested in moving her into a group home. I know some people are very happy with that arrangement, but it's not for us. Thanks for thinking of Callie; we do appreciate the offer. Good luck," she said, and she hung up quickly.

Next Izzy and David asked another girl they knew from work, and Wendy's parents reacted exactly the opposite of Callie's.

"Wow, that is a wonderful offer," Wendy's mother said. "Wendy mentioned it to me when she got home, but I didn't know what to think, if it was real or something in the future, or what. We think it would be great for her. Would you mind if we came to see the house before making up our minds?"

I told them to come right over, and they were there in less than twenty minutes. Jessie gave them a tour of the house. "There are three bedrooms and bathrooms upstairs, and one downstairs. Wendy would have her own bedroom and bathroom, here," she showed them. "It's not very big but it suited David's sister when she was growing up. The room is already decorated for a girl, but of course, Wendy can do whatever she wants with it."

"It's perfect," her mom, Dorothy, said. "When will you know if OMRDD will approve it and provide the supports?"

Jessie explained that OMRDD had told me that as long as all the residents were high-functioning. In this case, that meant either having a job in the private sector like David and Izzy and Wendy, or functioning well in a volunteer program, as Hunter did with Meals on Wheels. the house could be run with a resident manager or couple, with only the need for added support on their days off. Each resident had to have a job or program he or she attended regularly. If Wendy was on board, we just needed a roommate for Hunter.

We asked a few other guys from David's high school class, but their parents either weren't interested or were in the process of making other arrangements. It looked like we might be short a resident, and then Hunter asked another member of his Meals on Wheels group. He gave Devon's phone number to me, and I made the call to his parents. Devon's father sounded as if he had just won the lottery.

"Our son is a little older than Hunter. He's 26, and he's been on the waiting list for five years. Last time we asked, they said, maybe another three or four years. We are definitely willing to pay a share of a home where he will be guaranteed a place for the rest of his life. Thank you, you've answered our prayers. My wife is standing here, and I think she's going to burst, will you talk to her, too?"

"Oh, my goodness, I can't tell you what this means to us. My husband and I had Devon late in life—probably why he has Down's—and even though he helps out a lot here—I promise he will do his part at the house—we are both nearing seventy and want to make sure he has a comfortable, secure, family situation of his own. He's our only child, we've been praying for a chance to get him to the top of the list, and now you say he can join this house because we're donating it to the social service agency. And Aaron, may I call you Aaron? I really appreciate your pricing of the shares. You know you could get more on the open market, but this is just so kind of you." She finally took a breath, and I invited her and her husband and Devon to see where he would be living, before they made a final decision.

"Of course," she said. "But I can't believe it's so close to us. We'll be able to see him all the time, oh, thank you, thank you."

They came over within the half hour, and Devon's mom could not stop complimenting the house. Everything was perfect, the room, the furniture, the kitchen, the yard, even the cats.

"Will the cats be staying? Devon loves cats. What are their names?"

"Stan and Ollie," said David. "And Aaron said we can keep them."

"Jessie, this has got to be a minor miracle," I said that night in bed.

"Not really, there are so many individuals who are living with parents who want to see them somewhat on their own, and this house is just right. Your parents just never wanted to let go. Now we've got to get the legal stuff done, and we have to hope the agency will work quickly."

"I never thought my parents were doing David a disservice wanting to keep him home with them, but just look at him with Izzy. He's so happy and has so much more confidence, I wish they could see him now," I said.

"I believe they can," Jessie answered, snuggling into me.

• • •

I called the agency first thing the next morning, and they said they would need about a month to get the staff together. Meanwhile, they wanted to make sure the house met their standards. In short order, the agency approved the house without any conditions and said they had a married couple in mind for the house managers. I thought that would be perfect.

It felt like forever before all the papers were signed, monies transferred, and agency approval was given. I also personally pledged to donate 10,000 dollars a year to defray operating costs; with our inheritance it would not be a burden. And in about four weeks, I started moving my stuff out to stay with Jessie, and the new residents of the house and the management were all moving their stuff in. By then, the house looked radically different, with all the mementos and photographs everyone brought. They were making it their home. We bought Izzy and David all new bedding and donated Mom and Dad's plus all the other linens and blankets to Goodwill, so that the rooms no longer looked like LeShay rooms. I kept my parents' old comforter—the one they had used before the Jackson Pollack version.

One day, with the house to ourselves, Jessie and I finally went through my parents' things. We donated my parents' and Carolyn's clothes, keeping some special clothes of Dad's that had memories attached for David and me. I would later go through the jewelry from Mom and Carolyn with David, and he would give some special pieces to Izzy. I'd already selected a necklace that I wanted to give to Jessie. It was a golden locket, and I planned to replace the photos there with one of myself. I also wanted to give some of Mom's jewelry to a few of her close friends. I knew each would be an emotional visit, but Mom's friends were a special support group, and each woman gave her an open ear and the encouragement and strength to cope with whatever the problem of the moment would be. I pocketed Dad's wedding band when Jessie wasn't looking. We packed up much of the family photos and souvenirs of our travels. I put some special things in the master bedroom David and Izzy would share, and the rest went into storage for now. It was rough, but the house had to lose its ties to the LeShays so that it could become a home for David, Izzy, Hunter, Devon, and Wendy, and the resident managers, Carol and Rob Masterson.

When the Romanos and I met with the Mastersons, they told us their philosophy on running such a house after fifteen years and some of the ways they would bring everyone together to be a family. They were leaving another group home whose residents now had either passed away or needed to be in a nursing facility.

"I'm the head chef, but everybody helps cook," Carol said. "We'll all have chores to do, and everyone is responsible for their own rooms. They are treated as the adults that they are, not as children. As we get to know each other, we'll plan outings and activities that everyone enjoys for weekends and some evenings, too. That's not to say that we will always travel as a group. It's actually becoming frowned upon—the agency would rather smaller groups or pairs travel together; they feel it fits in better with the community. The residents will choose when they want to participate, and Rob or I will stay home with those who don't want to join the group. We'll also determine each individual's abilities for travel, public transportation, shopping, and the like. It's a kind of an initial testing period. But regardless of what anyone else says, we want to see all their abilities for ourselves before we agree on independence issues. We will certainly respect David and Izzy's right to privacy as a married couple, and the agency has counselors who are available to them as they settle into their own marital relationship. Of course, family is always welcome to visit. We'll be inviting you for special events and occasions, but please, you are all free to come as often as you like, as long as your family member is agreeable."

Rob let Carol do the talking, but he nodded a lot, and then added, "I'm a handy guy, and sometimes I'll help the residents with projects they may want to do. Carol usually calls the shots, but I have my role here, too."

"He's being modest as usual. We both serve as parent figures for the group, and we expect to get along well together. You've put together a good mix of young adults," she said.

The new residents' parents even paid to have the whole house painted inside, and they wouldn't let me contribute to the cost. They were so grateful for this "godsend," as the moms called it. It was like a *House Hunters* renovation, but just aesthetically. No walls needed to be torn down or kitchens and baths gutted. I took a picture of the measuring wall on the family room doorway that had our height measurements on it, and then I watched as they painted over it with a bright yellow.

We left the bedroom furniture and living room couches there, but one item of furniture they replaced was the dining room set. They bought a huge, farm-style table to seat twelve with an indestructible, rugged top, so there was always room for guests, and my mother's formal dining room went to a thrift shop. They bought a rustic china cabinet to match and filled it with unbreakable dinnerware, and I had to admit, it was much better suited to this active group than the formal set my mother had inherited from my grandmother. I took a few special serving pieces, my favorite soup bowl, the sterling silver cutlery service for twelve, and the good china my mother had always used on holidays for when I had a family of my own.

David and I donated our share of the house to the agency, and Izzy's parents insisted on paying their share, too. In the end, I had enough money to use as a down payment for a new home of my own without even going into our inheritance. I wanted my house to be for Jessie, too, and things between us were looking like that was a strong possibility. Still, we hadn't formally broached that subject. For now, I figured that I could stay with her in her flat, put a few things in a small storage unit, and then look for the perfect house.

On September 3, 2005, the Sunday of Labor Day weekend, the house was finally ready. I had moved all my things out, and the residents had moved in just about everything they needed. We had a ribbon-cutting ceremony, and the *Westbury Times* took a picture. I flashed back to the photo the papers had printed of my family after the accident. Here was my new family. I felt very good about all we had accomplished, especially for David, but that asterisk would always be present in my life. *What if it had never happened?*

All the parents and the immediate neighbors were invited to a barbecue to introduce the new residents. The Stillmans came to the barbecue, and Father Charles, and Helen, and neighbors from both sides of the street. Max, Shelby, and Zoey came, too, and also Rashi and Adrianna. I kept myself busy flipping burgers, and Jessie was queen of the buns. I was happy, but there was a lump in my chest as I closed this chapter of my life. It almost felt as if I was erasing my family. I knew I would be torn inside, so I'd discussed how I should handle it with Dr. Shannon. I just kept flipping those burgers, and if my eyes teared, I'd blame it on the smoke. Meanwhile, David was grinning from ear to ear.

After we had cut the cake and everyone was enjoying the overly sweet chocolate fudge cake with whipped cream frosting, Jim Stillman took me aside.

"Aaron, I've been wrestling with myself whether or not I should show you this, but I decided I had no choice. Before you read it, I want to tell you there is nothing to worry about. I did some investigation of my own. It's just the one crank who sent this letter out, and he has no legal recourse. I don't want to spoil this at all for you, but just take it as what it is, something from a bigoted, ignorant, and lonely man. I know for a fact he got no response, but you should know about it."

I swallowed hard and held out my hand. "Let me see it, Jim."

The letter was short and to the point. "To all concerned neighbors: The LeShay home is being converted to a house for the retarded. There will be a bunch of retarded adults there with token supervision, and they will be freely moving about our community just a few blocks from our elementary school. There will be a meeting at my home this Monday."

I didn't recognize the name of the man who wrote the letter.

"I parked outside his house that night for over an hour, Aaron. Nobody came. I then went in and spoke to the guy. He was a son of a bitch but mostly, just a bitter, lonely guy trying to stir up some trouble, hoping to get some attention. I left there confident that he would not be heard from again. With no one supporting him, he came close to admitting he might have overreacted."

"Thanks, Jim. That was very good of you to do. That guy could have been a nut with a gun. You took a risk confronting him."

"I'm telling you, by the time we spoke, he had seen he had no one to back him up. He even admitted some of his neighbors had told him to mind his own business. I told him his fears were misplaced and talked to him for a while, explaining why his protests were inappropriate. I almost think he was glad to get anyone to take him seriously."

"Well, we have a security system in place. I'll share this with Carol and Rob, and we'll have to hope you put an end to it. It's upsetting, but it doesn't surprise me. People fear anyone who is different. This guy is an ass, but he's not the first to show his prejudice."

The party began to taper off at about nine, until I was the only nonresident left. Jessie had done more than her share of work in the kitchen and went ahead of me back to her flat. David and I sat on the front steps like we did when we were kids.

"Well, David, you've got it all now, brother. You and Izzy will take care of each other, I'm sure, and Carol and Rob are super, but don't you ever hesitate to come to me for any reason, or just to call and say hello. I'm going to miss you, even though I'm just a few miles away."

"But you'll come here all the time, right?"

"Yes, but you have your own life here now, and I don't want to intrude on it."

"Aaron, you could never 'trude. I love you." He hugged me, causing me to tear up again.

I wiped my eyes. "Boy, that smoke did a number on me," I said. "Listen, no matter what, we'll always be Batman and Robin, deal?"

"Deal!"

"And I'm going to buy a house right around here soon, I promise."

"Are you going to marry Jessie?"

"I want to. But unlike you, I don't rush into things." I tried not to smile.

"I think you will!" David said. "So don't wait too long, brother. Being married is fun!"

"Okay, David, I won't wait too long. I'm going to go and let you get back to your wife."

We hugged each other tightly once more. I was the one to break the embrace.

"Goodnight, David. Be good," I said and walked to my car without turning back for a look at the home that was no longer mine. On the way home, I drove past the address of the lone agitator. His house was a block away. I had never known him growing up, and Jim told me his name was Mr. Gordon. He lived in a small Cape Cod; there was one light on in the front room. I imagined he lived alone and was probably sitting up watching TV. Even in the dark, the streetlamp let me see that the house was in need of repair. The cement driveway was badly cracked, and the shrubs surrounding the house were uneven and had more dead branches than live ones. I believed Jim was right and that we wouldn't hear from him again.

But two weeks later, Carol had a better idea. As the leaves started piling up on the ground, she saw the reluctant neighbor working hard to keep his yard clear. His shoulders were rounded, and his head had just a wisp of white hair left. After quickly holding a house meeting, they all decided to ask Mr. Gordon if he would like their help.

Mr. Gordon tried to insist he was fine, but Rob and Carol had a way with people. In just two hours, there were twelve bags of brown leaves neatly stacked at the foot of Mr. Gordon's driveway. Once they were all busy, Carol ran back to the house and quickly cooked up a batch of slice and bake chocolate chip cookies. She handed Mr. Gordon a cookie still warm and his eyes lit up like a kid's; she had won over the lonely man with some cookies and a chance for him to get to know his new neighbors, who always liked to help him out. At the first snow, David, Izzy, and Hunter got there early. When Mr. Gordon woke up he knew immediately who had shoveled his walk.

chapter forty:
jessie

IT WAS AMAZING how quickly that group became a family. They loved their home and their new rooms. David and Izzy had moved upstairs to the master bedroom, so it was a change for them, too. Carol and Rob had the guest room and bath on the main floor. About three weeks before Halloween, some of the parents came over to help put up decorations. There was a long-time unofficial competition on that block to see who would do the best design for the holiday.

Carmella and I were together cutting out paper pumpkin streamers when she asked me if I would give her a completely honest opinion on something.

"Of course I would, Carmella. What's worrying you?"

"It's not a worry, really. It's just that Louie and I would truly like Izzy to be married in the church. We would feel better about the whole thing. Do you think I'm being silly, or that she and David would object to it?"

"Object? I think that's the sweetest thing," I said. "Were you planning a big reception?"

"Oh, no, we'd want a wedding ceremony in the church with only close friends and family, maybe about twenty-five people, and then I'd have everyone back to the house for lunch and wedding cake."

"Sounds absolutely perfect, you go, girl! I'm sure the kids will love it."

And I was right. When Izzy came over to us, Carmella asked her if she would like to be married again in the church and have her own wedding dress altered to fit her, she said, "Oh, Mama, I'd love that! Thank you so much. When can we do it?"

"I don't know, let's look at a calendar. I think a Saturday afternoon would be best, don't you?" she asked her daughter, just like any mother of the bride. We all poured over the calendar.

"With all the holidays coming up, do you think we should wait until after January?" Carmella asked her.

"Oh, no, Mama. That's too long. Look, here's Saturday, right there." She pointed to an empty box.

"I see, December 10th. That sounds wonderful, Isabella, shall we go ask David?"

"Yes! He's out hanging up spiders."

David was thrilled with the idea, and he decided he and Aaron should rent tuxes so Aaron could be his best man.

Aaron was attaching a skeleton to the garage door, and the three of them ran over to tell him the news, while I watched from the front porch.

"I think that will be fantastic," Aaron said. "We'll have to call Father Charles right away and ask him if that date is good."

"I'll do that right now," Carmella said. Shrugging a little in embarrassment, she explained, "I have him on speed dial."

After about two minutes she was off the phone and shouting, "It's a go!" They told everyone in the house their news and made them promise not to make any other plans for December tenth.

About a half an hour later, after finishing the pumpkin streamers, I went to look for Aaron. He was done hanging the skeleton, and I couldn't find him outside anywhere. I called out his name a few times in the house, and finally I heard a faint answer from the family room, "I'm in here, Jessie."

"So, what do you think about the church wedding?" I asked him.

"It's, it's really sweet," he said, but he was clearly in distress.

"What is it, Hon?" I asked.

"It's nothing, just life. I know everything's working out well now, and I'm happy for that; I just can't help thinking of what brought everything to this point. I never could have imagined my life like this. It's like that saying, 'Man plans, God laughs.' Well, he must be hysterical at all that's changed in my plans. I'm sorry, Jess, I can't help getting depressed sometimes, even when things are okay, like they are now."

He was sitting on the couch, with a magazine he had been pretending to look through on his lap. He looked so vulnerable and so caring. I thought about how much I loved him. What were we waiting for? Almost without giving it thought I got down on one knee before him. "Would you like to make it a double wedding?" I asked.

At first, he didn't speak; he simply stared at me. I got up and sat with him on the couch. "I mean it. I couldn't ask for better coffee, or for a better man. Aaron, will you marry me?"

Aaron still didn't say anything. He just took me in his arms and gave me the best kiss I had ever had. "Jessie, you are the most wonderful woman in the world. I am so honored and happy that you would ask me to be your husband. Yes, yes, a million times yes."

We kissed again and again, and finally, when we came up for air, I asked, "So what do you think about a double wedding—the twin thing and all. Do you think they'll go for it?"

"Absotively, m'lady. There's not a bridezilla bone in Izzy's body. I'm sure she and David will go for it; let's go ask them."

"For real, Aaron?" David asked when Aaron and I told them our idea. "That is the best!"

Izzy threw her arms around me. "Jessie, we be brides together; I'm so happy."

And that settled it. Louie and Carmella were pleased, too, and I asked if there was room for a few more, as I needed my folks and three brothers to be there.

"The more the merrier," said Louie.

"It's three in the morning there now, I'll have to wait a bit before I call them, but I'm sure they'll be buying their plane tickets as soon as I call them."

"This doesn't give us much time," said Aaron. "It's a good thing I started without you."

"Started what?" I asked.

Aaron took a folder out of his knapsack and showed me

listings of homes in the neighborhood. "I really like this one. It's two blocks north of here, and I think you'll like it too."

"Wow, you got me," I said. "How did you manage to keep this from me?"

"Hmmpf, you want me to give away my secrets before we're even married, not a chance, woman."

The upshot of it all was like a fairy tale come true. The next day, Aaron showed me the house, and he was right. It was a sprawling brick ranch home that had four bedrooms, with a great sunroom on the back that opened onto a deck, and a big, open kitchen, dining, and living area with a cathedral ceiling and skylights. It had a great backyard, and when I saw that it was fenced in, I made up my mind that when the excitement died down, it would be perfect for a new puppy. We put an offer on it that night, which was quickly accepted, and since the couple was very motivated to sell, we got a promise that we could close on it before Thanksgiving.

"Now my folks will have a place to stay when they come in for the wedding," I said.

"Um, are they coming with us on our honeymoon?" Aaron asked.

"You silly bloke, we can go on a honeymoon the next week, after they've gone home, okay?"

"Okay, okay, whatever you say."

"So you think we can take a honeymoon with buying the house and everything?" I asked. Aaron thought about it for a while. "You'll probably want to go down under for New Year's again. Why don't we plan on stopping in Hawaii on our way back for a few days? We have to have some honeymoon, right? And it will be great to break up our trip that way."

"Hmm, sounds like a plan to me. But just for five days max. And I'll do the booking. If I left it up to you, we'd end up in the Presidential suite of the most expensive hotel on Hawaii."

"Are we having our first fight about money, dear?" Aaron asked.

"No fight. Just let me make the arrangements, and all will be aces!"

"Whatever you say."

Aaron did some excessive spending anyway and two days

later came home with a two-carat emerald-cut diamond set in a platinum band with tiny diamonds on either side. I noted it was much bigger than the one he had given Becca.

"This is really too much," I said, quickly slipping it on my finger. "It's the most beautiful ring I've ever seen. You needn't have been so extravagant." I examined my hand from every angle and admired how it looked, mentally checking my calendar for the first opportunity to go for a manicure. "Although I have to admit I'm glad you did. But from now on... we have to be more careful with money."

"I promise, Jessie, but I couldn't give you anything but the best."

"I do love you, you silly bloke."

"And I you. Thank you for making me the luckiest man on the Earth."

"Hey, even I know you stole that line from Lou Gehrig."

chapter forty-one:
aaron

IT WAS SUDDENLY two days before the wedding. Our men friends insisted on throwing David and me a bachelor's party, even though David protested, "I'm already married." I insisted we have it on the eighth, because I didn't want to walk down the aisle with a hangover. We met the guys at Max and Shelby's house, while Shelby and a bunch of other women friends threw a bachelorette party for Jessie and Izzy. If it was just Jessie, they might have gone to a male strip club, but instead, they decided to indulge in chocolate, wine, and music, and they reserved a private room at the Melting Pot for fondue and wine and brought music and a CD player that they danced to once they had enough wine. Women are sometimes much more practical.

Max went the beer and a shot route, and soon we were playing different variations of drinking games. I switched David's drinks with root beer and wine cooler, since there was no way he could handle booze. Zoey was spending the night with her grandparents, so we were free to make asses of ourselves. We put a cable channel that was playing a Seinfeld marathon. We made a drinking game out of it, and we had to take a drink every time someone said "Jerry" or another character ate his food. Didja ever notice that Elaine ate even more than Kramer? Then we set up the ping pong table for beer pong, but by then we could hardly set the cups straight. Even the root beer and wine coolers did a number on David, Hunter, and Devon, and soon we had reached the sloshy, sentimental part of the evening, right about midnight.

Max started it off with a toast about how he had the privilege of knowing David and me all our lives. "They really are Batman and Robin," he said. "I know plenty of people who are strangers to their own brothers, but not these two. I love you guys, and I'll always be there when you want to switch it up to The Three Musketeers."

A slightly inebriated David extolled my virtues. "Aaron saved me at the lowest. He's helped me be a regular guy with a wife and everything. I love you, Aaron, and I love Jessie, too."

Punch and Jessie's brothers and their wives had arrived that day from Australia, London, and Oslo. They should have been wiped out by their flights, but they weren't ones to miss a good party. Punch and his sons gave us an incredibly drunken version of *Waltzing Matilda,* swearing that if we could unlock the hidden messages in that song, we'd have all life's fortunes laid at our doors.

Soon, we were so relaxed that I heard snores coming from my friends. By the time Shelby and her party came back, they dragged us one by one into their cars and drove us home. I was staying with David, and Izzy with her parents, so that the grooms and brides would spend the day before the wedding apart. David and I slept through the morning, not rising until the noon sun was no longer directly overhead. At about 1:30 I hit the shower. David and I stayed in our old room, which now belonged to Hunter and Devon. That might have made me sad, but I was too busy concentrating on not dropping the soap, slipping on it, and breaking my leg. Hey, I told myself, at least I'd have my own private physical therapist.

Carol had broken her policy and reopened the kitchen to make David and me her special blueberry and cheese crepes with bacon. We made our appointment to pick up our tuxes, and then we decided to go to the movies and see *The Chronicles of Narnia.* It had been one of our favorite books as kids, and our parents had read it to us at least five times. We indulged ourselves with over-buttered popcorn, slushies, and some Sno-Caps to round it off. After the movie, David wanted pizza. I was a little worried we'd get sick from all that junk, but hey, a man only has one last night of freedom, so we went for it. I was sure our brides were eating delicately so as not to risk any new bulge appearing through their wedding dresses.

Jessie and her family were staying at our new home, which we had dubbed "The Fortress," because it was solid brick. We had been having extensive renovations done throughout the weeks the wedding was being planned. Inside, it was fantastic. Outside, it looked like it would withstand any attack, and we felt safe there.

• • •

The ceremony was set for noon, and by eleven David and I were sitting on his bed, dressed in our tuxes and trying not to wrinkle them. We killed time by playing a guessing game about superheroes. We would see how many hints it took for David to guess the superhero I was thinking of. It was an old childhood game we used to do when we had trouble falling asleep at night. When the game was finished, we faced each other and straightened our matching bow ties. David opened his arms for a big hug, and I stayed in his arms, feeling such love for my brother.

"David, this feels so right," I said. "Although you scared the hell out of me with your elopement, you did what was right for you. You and Izzy are a perfect couple, and you deserve to be together. I hope Jessie and I are as happy as you two. Thanks again for sharing your wedding day with us."

"We love you Aaron. This will be the best wedding in the world," he said.

We locked up the house and headed for the church. Our brides were already there, sequestered in the bridal room, ostensibly putting on those last-minute touches they always needed. Grooms all look alike, so David and I each patted our hair into shape and waited at the entrance to greet our guests. David held the rings that Jessie and I would exchange, and I held a new set of rings for David and Izzy. There was no groom's side or bride's side; everyone was there for both of us, even the guys from my office knew David, just from all the talking I did about him. The fifty guests arrived on time, and when they were seated, the organist played an intro to the *Wedding March.*

David and I walked down the church aisle together. When we got to the altar, we shook hands, then clasped each other in a hug and stepped apart to make room for our brides. Izzy did indeed look like a princess. Louie was dressed in his best suit with a red tie to match ours, and he ever so slowly walked the beaming Izzy down the aisle. Carmella's wedding dress had been tailored perfectly to fit Izzy, and in the years that had passed, it had turned from a bright white to a creamy ivory. She kissed her father, then stepped up to David and took his hand.

Jessie came next. She was a vision in a flowing white silk dress with long sleeves with lace insets and a deep neckline of lace and sequins. That handkerchief hemline turned out to be an uneven bottom with points, which gave her an ethereal look. She held onto her father's arm, which made Jessie seem smaller and daintier than usual. Her "I can do anything" persona had been replaced with an "I am a bride in love" one, and she literally took my breath away. I heard murmured ahhs of approval as they made their way down the aisle, Jessie trying to keep Punch's jaunty step to a slower stride so that she could savor the moment.

We knelt together in front of Father Charles as he performed a slightly abbreviated wedding Mass. I can honestly say that when my brother and I turned to our brides for our first wedded kisses, clichéd or not, there wasn't a dry eye in the church, including the four newlyweds, and even the priest.

Our walk back down the aisle was more like a prance; we were laughing and giggling all the way. We were just so happy and relieved to have that formal part of the ceremony behind us. Now we all looked forward to a fabulous spread at Carmella and Louie's.

Punch had surprised us with a white Rolls Royce limousine waiting to take the four of us to Carmella's.

"Once around the park, my good fellow," David said.

The limousine took us on a route that included driving through Eisenhower Park. We passed the duck pond, which was thawing, but still inhabited by ducks and seagulls. There were a few stalwart golfers on the greens, and they stopped their putting and driving to wave at us as we passed. It was a mild day for December, so there were some parents pushing little bundled up toddlers on the swings, and they stopped in mid-swing to stare at the glamorous car with the two newlywed couples standing up through the sun roof and waving to anyone who could see us. We even took a ride past Waldbaum's. David used my cell phone to alert the manager we were passing by, and as many staff members as possible crowded just outside the entrance to wave us on and wish us good luck.

We were just about to make our way to Carmella's when I asked the others if we could stop by the cemetery for a moment. They agreed, and the driver took us to the Holy Rood cemetery right across the street. We all got out, and Izzy and Jessie laid their bouquets on my parents' and sister's graves.

"We hope you are watching this from Heaven," I said. "David and I were just married in a double ceremony at the church. All you taught us has kept us strong. We think of you every day and wanted to visit you before we go to Izzy's house for a wedding luncheon."

"I miss you all," David said.

"You would be very proud of your sons," Jessie said.

"Amen," Izzy added.

"We wish you were here," I said.

Nothing left to be said, we piled back into the limo and went straight to Izzy's house, where all our guests were waiting impatiently for us to arrive so they could dig into the incredible buffet Carmella had prepared.

Carmella had been careful to avoid messy dishes, lest some of Izzy and David's friends had trouble with them. She had pushed furniture against the walls and rented several tables so that we could eat without having to balance everything while standing. The cacophony of voices very quickly dissipated as the sound of knives and forks against plates was about the only thing heard. Even Izzy's little brothers were too busy eating to make noise or run around.

Louie had built a fire in the fireplace, and Max took many posed and candid photos for us. Zoey showed up in a lot of them, as she followed her dad around.

Louie and Punch even took turns making toasts. Louie went first.

"I never expected to be throwing a wedding for my beautiful Isabella. Her mother and I always thought we'd have her to ourselves forever. But that stubborn young groom of hers, David, swept her off her feet, and we now see a new Isabella– Izzy, a woman who knows so much more than we had dreamed possible. And through their determination and love for one another, they have made their own dreams come true. May God bless them and grant them a long and happy life together."

"Amen," the guests raised their glasses, clinked them together.

Punch was up next. "When my Jessica left for the States five years ago, I didn't really expect to have her home with me and her mom again. She's always been an adventuress and wanted to see the world. We wish her and Aaron a lifetime of happiness, surprises, trips to Australia, and one day we hope they will make us grandparents. Jessie, we approve of your choice. Aaron is one of a kind. Aaron, you treat my girl right, or you'll have Punch to answer to. We love you both and could not be happier to be here and share in your joy today."

Another round of amen's and glasses clinking went around the room. In a few hours, after the wedding cake was gone, guests began to leave. Louie had surprised Carmella by hiring a serving and cleaning staff (the thought would never have crossed her mind), and we were left to put up our feet and reflect on what a wonderful day it had been.

"Mom, you are the greatest," said Izzy. "Thanks for everything."

We all draped Carmella in compliments, who modestly insisted, "It was nothing."

Then Louie changed the mood to laughter by claiming, "That's true, it was nothing for Carmella; the truth is I did everything."

chapter forty-two:
aaron

WE MISSED WATCHING the ball go down on Dave Clark's New Year's Eve show because we were right in the middle of changing a diaper. Well, Jessie was doing the changing, and I stood over her making faces at Lauralynn, so that she would tolerate the indignity of it all. We heard the countdown from the hall, stopped for a quick kiss, wished each other "Happy 2008," and returned to our task. Finally, our baby back bundled up, we sleepily made our way back to the bedroom, where we tucked two-month-old Lauralynn into her bassinet beside us and watched the crowd at Times Square go crazy with their hats and noisemakers. Gazing at my two girls, I felt my heart would burst with joy. I had never been so happy, besides my wedding day—not even then.

"You'd love to be there, wouldn't you?" Jessie said to her.

"Hey, I'm twenty-five, and at this moment I feel way too young to do anything like that," I said. "And don't put any ideas in her head. I am NEVER letting her near Times Square on New Years."

Jessie took four months maternity leave, and then, because she begged us to let her, Carmella became our nanny for Lauralynn when Jessie went back to work.

"Give me that baby," Carmella would say the minute she walked in the house. Then she'd proceed to exclaim over

Lauralynn's beauty and precocity, talking directly to her all the while. "Did my precious girl miss Grandma Carmella? We are going to have fun today. I brought you a new book, and soon you'll be reading it to me, Lauralynn." Sometimes it was hard to give Carmella information she needed to know because she couldn't take her eyes off the baby.

We insisted on paying Carmella, but the way she cared for our daughter and quietly put our house in order, cleaning everything to a brilliant shine, she was worth much more than she would allow us to give her. She also spoiled us by cooking our dinner several times a week and keeping it warm on the stove. We couldn't have dreamed of a better situation. LL, as we sometimes called her, was an extremely easy baby, with a very sweet disposition and a smile that kept me permanently twisted around her little finger.

We made a habit of taking her out in the stroller on Saturday mornings and stopping at David's house, where the residents all gathered around if she was asleep to admire her, or took turns holding her when she was awake. Everywhere we took her, she was showered with love, just as she deserved to be.

As soon as she could sit up sturdily, she had a lot of fun playing with our twin Bichon Frises that Jessie had insisted upon adopting about two months after we moved into our Fortress. They are small, fluffy white dogs, and they don't shed. They love running around together in the backyard, and when baby Lauralynn was agreeable, they would jump on her and lick her on the face. I think "yick," was her first word and "doggie" was her second. We named the pups Wizard and Ozzie. It was hard to tell them apart, but Wizard had a black spot on his left hind leg, and he was definitely the alpha dog who called all the shots.

Those first two years with Lauralynn were probably the best of our lives. I knew that other people thought they had extraordinary babies. Yet, I believed in my heart that she was far superior to any child I had ever met or ever would. I had never been so fascinated and so in love with any other human being. And I had never been so tolerant. What I normally would have considered to be odorous stenches of sloppy secretions and sour vomit, I just took as the normal smells of healthy babies and didn't let it make me sick to my stomach. The sight of snot running down into bowls of oatmeal did not at all gross me out. And ear-splitting squeals in the middle of the night were just our sweetie calling for comfort and sustenance from her beloved parents. I now experienced unconditional love. Of course I love Jessie with all my heart, but we made Lauralynn. She's a part of the two of us, and all of the members of our families.

That's why I couldn't quite get on board with the idea of having a second child when Lauralynn turned two. She filled my heart completely; I didn't feel the need for another child.

Ever the practical one, Jessie pointed out that she wasn't getting any younger, and she wanted the kids to be close in age. I wanted to wait another year or two to conceive, so that Lauralynn would be older, potty-trained, and in pre-school or kindergarten. But Jessie got stubborn.

"Aaron, we decided to have two children."

"But you're still young, and don't you want some more time to dote on LL?"

"I'll still dote on her; babies sleep most of their first year anyway. And I'll take another four months maternity when the baby is born."

"Sleep? Well, maybe during the day, but I don't recall getting much sleep at night," I said.

"Well, I'm the one that has to carry the baby, so I think my decision should hold more weight than yours. I'm trashing my pills. If you want to make love to me, then you'll just have to take your chances."

Of course, I didn't want to approach this second miracle feeling reluctant, so I soon agreed that I was in, and with all the gusto of the first time.

Fortunately, we were very talented in the reproductive area of our lives. Douglas "Punch" Jonathan LeShay was born two months before Lauralynn's third birthday, on September 17, 2010, a whopping nine pounder with red hair and Jessie's green eyes. I was relieved to see that my heart could expand again to love this little guy as much as I loved his sister and mother.

With a boy and a girl in each kid's bedroom, and the fourth bedroom set up as an office/guest room, we had reached capacity in our comfy Fortress and also had fears of tempting fate. The fit was just right. We felt incredibly blessed to have two healthy children. We agreed if we were sure we were through baby making when I turned thirty in three more years, then I would have a vasectomy.

The expression I've heard the mothers say is, "One is like one, and two is like ten." I get it now. Juggling two kids on totally different schedules is what makes most mothers appear to be magicians. Just leaving the house was a major operation of the troops. An outing around the block required a double stroller, double-sized diaper bag filled with juice boxes, diapers, wipes, pull-ups, emergency formula bottles, a change of clothes for each kid, books, rattles, and other distractions, plus all the things Jessie carried in her purse for herself.

Lauralynn had been potty-trained before Douglas arrived, but she had undergone a little regression and could no longer be counted on, so she was back in pull-ups. Jessie had to hang the bag from the stroller after both kids had been buckled in, or it would tip over. If she used the shoulder strap for the bag for any amount of time, Jessie might need a trip to the chiropractor. The past year of putting Lauralynn to bed after dinner and having some time to relax had all gone out the window, and Jessie and I spent our evenings jiggling, rocking, singing, and cajoling Douglas to settle down, usually to no avail. By the time we laid down for a few hours before we'd get up for the next feeding, we were wrecked.

To make matters worse, while Lauralynn was usually able to sleep through the baby's wailing in the evening, the wee hour cries for feeding came from the bedroom next to hers. He woke her up, too, and the occupancy of our bed doubled, sometimes even tripled if the dogs realized we were all together. We often fell asleep like that after the feeding: parents, children, and dogs, and I feared we were setting bad habits that would be hard to break. We weren't the kind of parents who believed in home schooling and the family bed. We agreed we wanted our kids to grow up confident and independent. But we were just too damn tired to follow through during the first three months of Douglas's life.

"I go back to work in one month," Jessie said in a rare moment of total breakdown. "We've got to get Douglas on a schedule, or it won't be fair to Carmella."

"Well, at least with Louie cutting down his hours at his office to part-time, she'll have his help," I said.

"Yeah, I can just imagine Louie's help. One whimper, and he'll turn the baby back to Carmella."

"Well, what do you want me to do about it? You were the one who insisted we have the kids so close together!"

"That's not fair!" Jessie said.

"Maybe it is, and maybe it isn't, but this is what you wanted, and I agreed. You're the mother superior. You make the decisions here. Just tell me what I can do to help, and I'll do it."

"So you're leaving this problem all up to me?"

"I wouldn't put it exactly that way. But you know how to handle these things far better than I do, so, I repeat, just tell me what to do, and I'll do it."

Just then, Douglas starting crying, demanding his mid-morning feeding. I changed him and brought him to Jessie, who had moved to the rocking chair into our room. I decided that would be a good time for me to read the Sunday paper, so that's what I did, taking it into the family room. Jessie scowled as I left, flipping on some soft music for them. I usually stayed with her for the feedings, but I just had to have a little time to myself that day. Of course, easier said than done, and a few minutes later, Lauralynn plopped down on my lap and wanted to read the paper with me. Cute, but not much reading accomplished.

After twenty minutes of reading with my daughter, the doorbell rang. The Sunday paper would just have to wait. Uncle David and Aunt Izzy were there to play with the kids.

"Good morning everyone," David said.

"We brought you bagels," Izzy said. "I put in the kitchen, okay."

"Sure, Izzy," I told her. But Lauralynn jumped up from the paper and hugged her legs, and Izzy dropped the brown bag on the coffee table and got down on her knees and started tickling and chasing Lauralynn around the room on all fours.

"Where is my nephew?" David asked.

"Here he is," Jessie said. She was wearing her red, milk-stained bathrobe, and I could see she had just finished a tumultuous nursing session with Douglas. Instead of calmly suckling as his sister did, Douglas viewed each nursing session as a time to practice his boxing, and he would fling his tiny fists into the air, often pummeling whatever part of his mom he could reach. He would never be a poster child for La Leche League.

"Can I hold him?" David asked. Knowing the drill, David moved to the couch and I sat next to him, just to make sure Douglas was safe in case David was distracted. One time, David was holding Lauralynn and Wizard jumped on him, startling him so much he would have dropped the baby if Jessie had not caught her as he jerked his hands up reacting to the little dog's yipping.

Jessie placed our son in David's lap, checked to see if I was being attentive, and then announced, "I'm taking a shower now; I'll be in there awhile." She looked at me, telegraphing the message that the kids were in my hands now, and to make sure David and Izzy didn't get too wild with Lauralynn.

I helped David get a good hold on Douglas and optimistically grabbed the *New York Times Magazine* section before sitting back on the couch. I'll just read the letters section, I told myself, but halfway into the second letter, Lauralynn was standing next to me on the couch, throwing her arms around me, her face wet with instant tears.

"I bumped my head," she cried, "Aunt Izzy tripped me."

I looked at Izzy sitting on the floor and watched her break down into tears at being blamed for LL's bump.

"I didn't. It was a accident. Sorry, baby. Sorry, Aaron," she sniffled and grabbed at the tissue box on the table. "It wasn't me, baby, it was table. Bad table," she said, pretending to hit at the table.

David practically threw Douglas onto my lap to get to Izzy so he could console her. I wish someone had taken a video then, because Douglas started wailing at being abruptly dismissed, and that set Lauralynn to crying harder as she was not going to relinquish my attention to her boo-boo. A quick placement of a bagel in her hands calmed Lauralynn down, and then I was able to get up and give Douglas a binky and rock him in my arms.

David and a red-eyed Izzy decided to cut their stay short. Izzy was mortified that they had made the kids cry. In the bathroom

I heard the shower go on, and I was pretty sure Jessie had heard the commotion and opted out of it.

"Thanks for the bagels," I shouted after them as they exited without the usual long goodbye and kisses and hugs.

It was a very bumpy time for Jessie and me after Douglas was born. Jessie felt I wasn't shouldering my share of the work with the kids, and I felt she shouldn't have been so naïve about how much more work a second child would be while Lauralynn was so young. And no matter what anyone says, or how carefully you divide the tasks, the onus is always on the mother. She's the mother, and she knows best. The truth is, we were spoiled because Lauralynn had been such a dream baby. She had rarely cried for more than a few minutes and was so easy to soothe. We were able to recognize her needs just by her body language and expressions. We hadn't bargained on having a red-haired terror like Douglas, who had earned his nickname, Little Punch. I swear there is something about redheads that goes along with ornery dispositions, and later, the tendency to get into mischief.

Sadly, shortly after Douglas's first birthday, Carmella suffered a mild stroke, which left her significantly weakened on one side and with very slow speech. Her speech pattern was ironically close to her daughter's now. So after some frantic scrambling to find a replacement for her, we hired a private nanny for Douglas and Lauralynn, who was now in preschool. Our new nanny, Magda, was good, but she was no Carmella. I think Douglas tired her out, and by the time Lauralynn got off the bus from pre-kindergarten, she tended to allow the two of them to zone out in front of the TV. Although LL liked to play with Little Punch, she often took advantage of her superiority, as oldest children are wont to do, with the end result being our son throwing a tantrum that no one but Lauralynn thought was amusing.

Raising young children is hard, but it's also hard to resist. Once Douglas was past the terrible twos and the tantrum threes, he became a fantastic four, and Jessie and I became tempted to have another baby.

"What do you say, Aaron, will three be our lucky number?" Jessie said.

But I didn't have the courage to go through with it.

"Jessie, we both have Down syndrome in our family. It's usually a birth defect, but sometimes it's genetic. Let's be happy with our healthy son and daughter."

A little reluctantly, she agreed. Our family was complete.

epilogue

DAVID AND AARON celebrated their fiftieth birthdays July 10, 2033. Their blonde curls were liberally mixed with gray ones now, and crow's feet framed their eyes. Jessie and Izzy, too, had been touched by the passage of time, but each was still beautiful to her husband.

It was David's turn to have the party at his house. David and Izzy and some of the others had been in the house for more than half their lives now. Hunter had succumbed to pneumonia just prior to his fortieth birthday; and another young man had moved into the house in his place. Carmella and Louie were now together in an Assisted Living Residence nearby, but they were there to celebrate, as were their grown sons Anthony and Joseph and their families. Carol and Rob had retired after fifteen years, and they had been replaced with another married couple, Samuel and James.

Around the time of their thirty-fifth birthday, Aaron had come up with a plan for honoring his parents and sister and in the process had found a new career with a purpose he cared about. He and Jessie worked together to set up a nonprofit foundation that would truly make a difference to children. Before starting anything, Aaron told David and Izzy their idea.

"Can Izzy and me help?" David asked.

"It won't be for another year until we're ready to open, but yes, you can donate some of your trust money for our start-up fund, and there will be work for you both at the Foundation office. Just keep at your jobs for now, but you can look forward to working to help children when we get started," Aaron said.

"The LeShay Foundation for Children," said Izzy. "I like how that sounds. And it has all our names on it!"

"How you think of it, Ari?" David asked.

"Well, Jessie and I were talking about taking the kids on a really long vacation, maybe even around the world. It occurred to me that while seeing the world is a wonderful gift, just being together would be the best part of the trip. I thought about how so many children don't have parents like Lauralynn and Douglas do, and how lucky *we* were to have our parents when we were children. That's when it came to me that I could do this in honor of Mom, Dad, and Carolyn in a lasting way. It would also be a new career for me, an escape from the world of finance I've never liked. This Foundation, if run correctly, can help children without parents for many, many years, even when all of us are gone. I thought it would be a fitting tribute to our family."

"I like how you think," said David. "I'm proud of you."

• • •

Once the Foundation was up and running, Jessie went back to physical therapy and was active as a member of the Advisory Board. She also helped Aaron to write the mission statement:

The LeShay Foundation for Children will help any child who is parentless and requires resources and guidance to continue to take his or her life on a path toward happiness, good health, and personal fulfillment.

It provided mentoring services, scholarships, free summer programs, and supervised housing for teens that were either aging out or incompatible with the government foster care system they were in. It worked with schools and caseworkers to find the children that it could help. The Foundation gave grants to schools and other organizations to provide counseling and peer groups for children and helped groups such as Big Brothers/Big Sisters to fund their services as well.

Aaron's favorite part of being Operating Director was to meet with children and social work teams and come up with a way to help a child who felt like a misfit or a hopeless case. Sometimes he would tell them his own story, especially when the child was a teenager and believed he or she could manage on his os her own without help. Aaron made a conscious decision to keep the Foundation small enough to keep the personal touch and big enough to assist many children. The Foundation also had a separate advisory board to help families raising special needs children. Aaron hadn't only replaced work in his life; he had found a calling.

When the time came, Aaron shed no tears at the ribbon-cutting ceremony that was held at the newly furnished office of The LeShay Foundation for Children. It started with just Aaron, Jessie, six other employees, and David and Izzy. They had a solid growth plan in place for the years to come. Down the road, as Lauralynn and Douglas chose careers, there would always be a place for them as well, if they wanted. Over time, the Foundation had found its niche in the childrens' services community, and the staff grew each year.

Just in time for the Foundation's ten-year anniversary, Aaron met a set of ten-year-old brother-sister twins who had lost their parents a year earlier in an auto accident. They were hit head-on by a drunk driver. The twins were living with their grandmother, but her health had recently taken a sharp downward turn. She was diagnosed with pancreatic cancer, and she had only a few months to live.

When he told Jessie about the case, she met them and had the same reaction as Aaron: let's adopt them ourselves. Their grandmother was overjoyed that she could see them in a good home before she died, and Aaron and Jessie were thrilled to have Katie and Corey join their family. They built an addition to their Fortress, and there was now room for the large family they had always wanted.

Still, it was a bittersweet birthday. The things Aaron noticed David "slipping" at in the office were undoubtedly signs of early-onset Alzheimer's, the dilemma that living longer with Down syndrome had first made apparent in the 1990s. In the 1950s, individuals with Down syndrome didn't usually live past their thirties. Back then, doctors tended to treat them with a kind of benign neglect, especially newborns. Now, although they generally receive proper medical care from birth and onward, around the time they hit the age of fifty, many develop Alzheimer's. The neurologist had put David on a medication that was supposed to slow the process, but the difference was minimal. Izzy had finally convinced him to get a hearing aid, as his deficit had worsened. At least his hearing was something they could actually help him with.

David appeared at the picnic table with an empty bowl from the kitchen, intending to have filled it with nacho chips. He put it down and noticed it was empty.

"Now what was I up to?" he said.

"You were going to fill that bowl with nacho chips; they're in the kitchen," Aaron said. David dramatically hit himself in the head and started back toward the kitchen without the bowl.

"I'll get them, Uncle David," said Katie. "C'mon, Corey, we'll get two bowls."

The house's miniature poodles, Coffee and Cocoa, who had been adopted after the passing of Ollie and Stan, chased after the twins; stopping to gobble up food on the ground.

David's Alzheimer's saddened Aaron, but he took comfort in knowing that David would be well cared for the rest of his life and that Izzy would always be able to remain with her family. He wondered: Are you still a twin when your twin is gone? He consoled himself knowing that David had far surpassed any expectations people had for him when he was born.

I only wish my parents could see him now, Aaron thought. *Jessie says they can. I like to think she's right.*

author's note

The following essay is reprinted with the gracious consent of its author, Emily Perl Kingsley. I first read it when I was just a kid, and it touched my heart. I've known a lot of people who have made that trip to Holland, and they embraced the tulips and laughed at the windmills. Thank you, Emily.

Welcome To Holland

by Emily Perl Kingsley

I am often asked to describe the experience of raising a child with a disability - to try to help people who have not shared that unique experience to understand it, to imagine how it would feel. It's like this...

When you're going to have a baby, it's like planning a fabulous vacation trip - to Italy. You buy a bunch of guide books and make your wonderful plans. The Coliseum. The Michelangelo David. The gondolas in Venice. You may learn some handy phrases in Italian. It's all very exciting.

After months of eager anticipation, the day finally arrives. You pack your bags and off you go. Several hours later, the plane lands. The flight attendant comes in and says, "Welcome to Holland."

"Holland?!?" you say. "What do you mean Holland?? I signed up for Italy! I'm supposed to be in Italy. All my life I've dreamed of going to Italy."

But there's been a change in the flight plan. They've landed in Holland, and there you must stay.

The important thing is that they haven't taken you to a horrible, disgusting, filthy place, full of pestilence, famine and disease. It's just a different place.

So you must go out and buy new guide books. And you must learn a whole new language. And you will meet a whole new group of people you would never have met.

It's just a <u>different</u> place. It's slower-paced than Italy, less flashy than Italy. But after you've been there for a while and you catch your breath, you look around. ... and you begin to notice that Holland has windmills...and Holland has tulips. Holland even has Rembrandts.

But everyone you know is busy coming and going from Italy... and they're all bragging about what a wonderful time they had there. And for the rest of your life, you will say, "Yes, that's where I was supposed to go. That's what I had planned."

And the pain of that will never, ever, ever, ever go away... because the loss of that dream is a very very significant loss.

But...if you spend your life mourning the fact that you didn't get to Italy, you may never be free to enjoy the very special, the very lovely things...about Holland.

CPSIA information can be obtained at www.ICGtesting.com
Printed in the USA
BVOW02s1641080915

416170BV00002B/7/P